Starlight Cottage

K.T. DADY

Starlight Cottage
K.T. Dady

Copyright © 2021 K.T. Dady

All rights reserved.
No part of this book may be reproduced or used in any manner whatsoever without the express written permission of the author, except for the use of brief quotations in a book review.

This is a work of fiction. Names, characters, places, and incidents are the product of the author's imagination or, if real, are used fictitiously.

Cover design by K.T. Dady.
Cover photography: Canva.

Look up at the stars and dream.

1

Jake

Jake Reynolds sprinted into the lobby of River Heights, shook out his black umbrella, and headed straight to the lift.

The building manager quickly stood up and brushed his hands down his blue shirt, knocking his name badge sideways in the process. He cleared his throat and put on his best smile. 'Mr Reynolds, I have a…'

'Not now, Stan.' Jake was slightly breathless as he waved one hand above his head.

The lift opened immediately and Jake stepped inside. As the door hummed to a close, he took a slow, deep breath and stared forward at his reflection in the mirrored door.

Christ, Jake, you look like crap.

He raked a hand through his neatly-trimmed mop of short dark hair and stretched his eyelids, then blinked tightly, trying to bring them back to life. It was no good. His bright azure-blue eyes were dry and bloodshot from lack of sleep and too much whisky. He lowered his head as he waited for the lift to arrive at his floor.

The door pinged open, and he walked straight into a woman and her dog. Her rather smelly, damp dog.

He struggled to get around them without touching the animal or the woman who he was shuffling left to right with.

Come on, will you just pick a side.

She gently guided her golden retriever out of his way whilst quietly apologising.

He didn't respond and made his way over to his front door as she entered the lift. He stopped suddenly and turned back to face her, as a thought had crossed his mind.

What are you doing on my floor?

He knew there was only one apartment taking up the top level of the building, as it belonged to him. 'Excuse me, did you just come from my apartment?'

She lowered her head, blatantly avoiding eye contact. 'No. I got off on the wrong floor. I was just waiting for the lift to return.'

His brow furrowed at her dowdy appearance. He figured she was telling the truth. After all, the only other person in his apartment was his younger brother, Josh, and there was no way someone who looked like her would be connected to him. The women who latched on to his brother did not look shabby, and they definitely didn't hang around with smelly dogs.

Josh's voice rang out as soon as the front door opened. 'Did you remember the parcel downstairs?'

Jake's shoulders drooped. He quickly closed the door and balanced his damp umbrella against the wall, then turned back to the woman and dog.

'Hold the lift.'

He managed to place his hand into the closing lift door, triggering the safety mechanism that automatically slid the door back open.

Don't think I didn't see you quickly press the button to close the door on me.

He took a deep, silent breath to steady his annoyance as he stepped inside. He glared at her bowed head and took a wide step over to the other side of the lift whilst twitching his leg away from the sniffing animal.

Get off me.

The woman's voice was barely a whisper as she gently cupped her hands around the dog's neck and moved him towards her. 'Stop it, Max.'

Jake looked into the mirror to get a better look at her face, but she still had her head tilted down. Her damp, long, dark hair looked in need of a good wash. Its greasy, thin strands were tied up in a scruffy knot at the back of her head. He slowly rolled his eyes over her oversized grey sweatshirt and baggy dark jeans that were hiding her obvious slim frame, and he had the sudden urge to iron her soggy clothes.

Those clothes need drastic help. She needs drastic help. I'm not sure who smells more, her or the dog. Maybe it's a combination of them both. I wouldn't mind putting her in my shower right now. Ha! I'm having thoughts about a strange smelly woman in my shower. Don't laugh. Whatever you do, don't you laugh. This is not the time to crack up.

His eyes manoeuvred down to her white trainers.

At least they look clean.

One of the laces needed tying, and it was starting to irritate him. He quickly removed his eyes away from the irritation before it got the better of him. He glanced over at the orange plastic bag that she had scrunched tightly under her arm and focused on that instead.

I wonder what she has in there.

She suddenly moved her head up a touch and stared absentmindedly over at the panel of buttons.

Jake caught her ice-blue eyes and in-need-of-the-beach pale face.

Late twenties, maybe? She actually has a sweetness about her face, but she lacks, what's the appropriate word... presentation.

He glared down at her dog as it nuzzled into the side of his leg. His eyes narrowed at the sight of long golden strands that had clearly absorbed a lot of rain water. A thin blob of saliva hung loosely from its soggy mouth.

A collarless pedigree in need of a soapy bath and dental hygienist. Get off. Go snuffle somewhere else.

He tried to wiggle his leg without showing any sort of frustration.

The woman smiled sweetly into the mirror. 'I think he likes you.'

Jake didn't smile back. His nose twitched at the damp dog messing with his brown trousers. He lowered his hand and attempted to push the dog's face away from his leg without using too much force. He unclenched his teeth, because he knew that if he didn't relax his jaw the next thing out of his mouth wouldn't sound so polite. 'If you wouldn't mind.'

Get your smelly dog off me. He's probably covered in germs.

She sheepishly lowered her head to her dog. 'Sorry.'

He caught the submissive look in her eyes before she turned away.

Hmm! Compelling. Distracting, almost. Don't even think about it. Concentrate. I haven't got time for this. She does have very pretty eyes.

'Shouldn't he be on a lead?'

The woman pulled the dog closer to her, and Jake watched her snuggle her dirty hair into the animal's damp fur. He tried not to let his face express the disgust he felt towards the lack of hygiene.

Good God, you don't actually care, do you?

The lift pinged open and everyone inside headed out into the light-grey-and-white toned interior of the lobby.

The perfect room for acoustics smelled brand new and looked ready for a moving-in team to get to work. Its large space welcomed only a long, laminated, dark desk with one door behind it and another door to its right. A matted-silver lift was along the righthand wall, and not so much as a fake potted plant added to the décor.

The ten-minute downpour of rain had stopped beating against the glass-fronted building, allowing a last flood of early-evening light to roll all the way to the back of the entrance. The effect gave the marble-looking flooring a slippery appearance.

All occupants of the lift headed straight towards the newly-titled building manager, Stan, who before that title was simply called a receptionist, even though he preferred concierge.

Mrs Rogers, from the second floor, had got everyone in the building to sign an agreement to rename Stan's job description because he did so much more for the residents than sit behind a desk all day buzzing people in and out. He had become quite the right-hand man around the place. So, in her opinion, he needed a new title and a slight pay rise, or anything that discouraged him from taking early retirement.

Stan's dark eyes widened at the trio heading his way. His dark, weather-worn face screamed a thousand hard luck stories, and his thickset smile was as warm as the setting sun on a summer evening. He removed his aching spine from the comfort of a spongy back support on his wide office chair and stood to greet them.

Jake went to speak to the man but stopped when he noticed that the woman and dog were standing by his side. He took a slight side step away from them, but it was no good. Max had found his leg again and was wiping his nose along a pair of rather expensive trousers.

He used his hand to gesture to the woman to speak first.

Hurry up, so that I can get this dog away from me.

Stan's eyes nervously flittered between the pair.

'Mr Reynolds,' he questioned.

Jake glanced down at the woman's wedding finger. 'Please see to Miss…' He waited for either of them to fill in the blank.

She spoke first. 'Anna. My name is Anna.'

Hmm, a soft and sweet tone with a hint of nerves. Look at the way she's looking at me. She won't be able to hold my stare for too long. The Reynolds eyes will weaken that glare she's giving me.

'Anna is one of the cleaners here,' said Stan quickly.

Is she now?

Jake went to say something to her, but she shied away. He knew she would, and it filled him with a smug satisfaction. He turned back to Stan. 'Do I have a parcel, Stan?'

Stan seemed half asleep. 'Hmm?'

Jake widened his eyes at the man. 'A parcel. For me. Somewhere back there.'

Stan didn't look as though he wanted to move. 'Oh, yeah, right. A parcel. One sec.'

What's up with him today?

Jake watched him disappear into the back room, and then he rolled his eyes back over to Anna. She didn't look in the mood for a chat, which was okay. He wasn't in the mood either, but he was picking up on a weird atmosphere, and it was bothering him, but not as much as Max's nose stuck on his leg. He felt his temper bubble.

'Would you get your dog away from me.' The jolt in his tone caused him to still. He took a calming breath and loosened his jaw and softened his face. 'Please.'

Anna bent over and wrapped her arms around Max's neck and gently moved him away.

'Sorry,' she muttered.

'Stop saying sorry, and just hold on to him instead.'

He noticed a sharpness in her eyes as she looked up at him. 'Don't you like dogs?'

Jake felt slightly awkward. He didn't want to come across as an animal hater, but he also didn't want to be dominated by her snappy tone. 'Not attached to my leg. No.'

Shut up, Jake. You're taking your bad mood out on the poor woman. If you carry on, she'll probably cry. She actually has a teary look in her eyes. Leave her alone. Get a grip.

Stan returned with a brown box. 'Here you go, Mr Reynolds.'

Jake took the parcel, avoiding Anna completely. 'Thank you.' He swiftly turned back towards the lift.

'Mr Reynolds,' said Stan quickly. 'Seeing how you're the only one in the building without a cleaner, I was wondering if you might consider hiring Anna. She's looking for more work.'

Jake turned just in time to see the look Anna gave Stan. It was quite clear she wanted him to shut up. He slowly rolled his eyes between them. 'Sorry, I don't need a cleaner.'

Even one who has started to intrigue me.

He narrowed his eyes as the lift door closed, wondering why Stan and Anna looked so shifty. He caught his face in the mirror and sighed deeply at himself whilst shaking his weary head. He felt tired, and it showed.

2

Anna

'Stan, I can't believe you just asked him that.'

Stan cleared away a clingy piece of phlegm attached to the back of his throat. His voice was sore-throat rough as he said, 'Hey, a job's a job, and you need all the help you can get right now.'

She stopped leaning on his desk and straightened up. 'But his cleaner? He was bloody horrible and a right smarmy git.'

But those eyes. Those bright blue, intense eyes. My throat actually closed up when he looked at me. Who has that effect on people? I was like a tongue-tied idiot every time he spoke to me.

Stan shrugged his big lumpy shoulders and sat down in his green chair. 'I panicked. I saw you come out of the lift with him, and I didn't know what to say, and then it made sense.'

Anna's eyes widened. Her heart was still racing slightly as she rubbed away the goosebumps on her arms. 'He saw me outside his front door. I told him I got off on the wrong floor.'

Stan nodded. 'That's good. I think we're safe. He'll just think you work in one of the apartments now. Just don't use his floor anymore for the lift. Use the floor below. Mrs Silk lives on that floor, and she is a big animal lover, so it would make sense for her to let you bring Max to work with you. He'll think you clean her apartment. You'll have to look out for Jake Reynolds before coming and going, that's all.'

Oh, what a mess. What a great big bloody mess.

Tears were weighing heavily in her eyes. 'I'm sorry, Stan. I nearly blew it for both of us.'

He sat forward and wagged his index finger at her. 'You stop that now, Anna. It's all going to be all right. You'll be sorted in a few months. Until then, just keep your head down around here. These people don't understand people like us. They don't have our problems. That playboy will have forgotten about you as soon as he stepped inside his big plush apartment to count all his money.'

Anna muffled a laugh. 'Playboy?'

Stan scrunched his nose. 'You saw him. All good looks and more money than sense.'

She remembered exactly how good he looked, and she thought there was something endearing about the anti-dog man. Something bordering on enigmatic. A coldness filled with warmth. A hidden Jekyll and Hyde complex that gave glimpses of its secret. She saw it all sitting deeply within his piercing azure-blue eyes.

As a bookworm, Anna Cooper would often look at strangers and try to uncover their inner character. The moment Jake Reynolds stepped into the lift with her, she had envisioned a tall, elegant, historic gentleman. A throwback from a pallid era. An older-looking Edward Cullen. A modern-day Mr Darcy. A well-mannered Heathcliff. There would be light and shade as he moved effortlessly from page to page in a story filled with mystery, fantasy, and romance. She placed him around thirty-five in looks, but gave his personality more maturity, brought forward by years of Dickensian torment and harsh lessons.

He smelled so nice. Fresh, with a hint of something creamy. I wonder what it would feel like to snuggle into his chest. *Oh, don't think of him like that. He was a rude man, and there's nothing snuggly about that.*

'Max wouldn't leave him alone. Talk about embarrassing. I didn't know what to say, and then he got all moody.'

'Don't worry about him.'

'I worry more about you. You could lose your job.'

Stan waved his hand up in the air. 'Let me worry about that. You just get back there and wash your hair.' He nodded over to his back room.

She smiled softly. 'Thanks, Stan. I just got soaked running around after Max in the rain. He bloody well just ran out in it. I know he thought it was funny, but I didn't. I look like one big drip. Gawd knows what that posh man thought of me in the lift. Not that I care, but still.'

Okay, so maybe I did care a bit. How can I not? Look at me. What a wreck. He was standing there with his nice clothes and tidy hair, smelling lush and looking sexy. I just know he looked down his nose at me. Okay, snap out of that. Just because he looked down at me doesn't mean I have to do the same. There's nothing wrong with me.

'Anyway, Stan, the leisure centre should be back open next week, thank God. I really miss having a shower.'

'That's good news, but you know you can use the sink in the staff toilet anytime.' He patted Max on the head as he approached. 'You wait here with me, boy.'

Anna made her way out the back, feeling cold and deflated. She pulled out a plastic measuring jug, a blue hand towel, and a bottle of cheap apple shampoo from her plastic carrier bag and glanced glumly down at the small white basin that perched close to the toilet that made Stan's staff bathroom.

This is my life. I actually want to cry. Come on, Anna, stop that. This is just temporary. Be grateful. I have a sink, hot water, and shampoo. That's a lot more than some.

She picked up the jug and turned on the tap and awkwardly washed her hair. Afterwards, she plugged in her small hairdryer and quickly dried her hair without making too much fuss.

Max gave her a big tail wag when she reappeared from the toilet.

'You need a bath too, Max.' She glanced over at Stan. 'I'll take him to the parlour next week.'

Stan lowered his coffee cup, glaring at its stained rim. 'Don't waste money on things like that, Anna. You need to save every penny. Not that I'm trying to tell you what to do. Dogs aren't that fussy about their coats, that's all.'

She ruffled Max's ears affectionately. 'I can't leave him looking all shabby. It's only fair. I don't mind spending some money on my best boy, do I, Max?'

Stan frowned at Anna's hair flopping over Max's head. 'Well, okay, but just get your hair off him. You've just washed it.'

She giggled as she straightened up. 'You know, Stan, I've never had parents, but if I did, I'd want my dad to be just like you.'

Stan tried not to smile. 'Aww, go on, away with ya.'

She leaned over and kissed him on the cheek. 'And don't think I don't know about that stash of doggy biscuits under your desk.'

Stan grumbled. 'He likes them.'

Anna called Max towards the lift and waited patiently for him to slouch his way over to her. 'See you in the morning, Stan.'

Stan smiled their way. 'Have a good night, and remember, this will all be over soon.'

I hope so.

'I'm back in at seven, Anna. Come down then. I'll have a bacon roll with your name on it.'

'Thanks, Stan. Look forward to it.'

She waved over at him as the lift door closed, and she made sure she didn't press the button for the top floor. The last thing she wanted to do was to run into moody Jake Reynolds again. He couldn't find out about her. No one at River Heights could.

The lift door opened and Anna and Max stepped out. She looked around and then made her way over to the stairwell to walk up to the next level.

She listened at the top floor door before opening it, and then she put her finger to her lips, telling Max to shush. She was so glad the floor had carpet, as Max couldn't tiptoe, and he was far too heavy to carry.

Making her way across the small landing to the door that led up to the roof, she prayed that Jake Reynolds stayed in his apartment. She quickly punched in the code, and the roof door clicked open. She hurried Max up the stairs that were on the other side and quietly closed the door behind her.

The large grey rooftop of River Heights looked like one giant slab of boring concrete. There were a few raised blocks dotted around and hardly anything else, except for the makeshift home behind the second block.

Anna sighed deeply at the teal-blue tent before her. 'Home sweet home, Max.'

Max settled down on his comfy grey bed that was in the middle of the three-part tent.

She followed him inside, turning left to the compartment she had turned into a bathroom. She removed the jug and shampoo from her bag and placed them down onto a small wooden shoe rack, which she used as a shelf. Opposite was a portable camping toilet, a small plastic bowl, a bottle of water, and a bar of pink soap.

Max already had his eyes closed, happily oblivious to his homeless status.

'Wish I could fall asleep that fast,' she mumbled, stepping over him.

She leant over to another shoe rack in the middle section of the tent and picked up a portable stove and a blue tin kettle and took them outside to a green-and-white picnic table. She shook the kettle to see if there was any water inside. There was, so she put it on the stove and lit the burner. She went back inside to a plastic storage box and pulled off its white lid to pick up a Pot Noodle and a fork from inside. She took them outside to the table and then went over to the edge of the rooftop whilst waiting for the water in the kettle to boil.

Up in the sky, ghostly clouds appeared as darkness snapped into place as though the curtains had been suddenly closed.

The muffled sound of the narrow street below went partially unnoticed. She had become immune to the lively noise of London a long time ago. People seemed to like walking along any stretch of pavement by the River Thames at any hour, so the area was never really quiet.

The visualisation of happy couples holding hands and workers going home to their warm beds, central heating, and families lingered only for a second. She couldn't afford to compare their lives with her own. She didn't have much to protect herself, but she could at least control her thoughts. Her heart would only ache relentlessly if she allowed her current situation to completely take over her mind.

A cold, gentle breeze blew across the roof, reaching the gap between her sweatshirt and neck, bringing with it a faint waft of rain-meets-pollution, which settled into her damp nostrils.

She cuffed her nose on her sleeve as her eyes fixed on the gloomy Thames below. She wondered what secrets it held. What it might say if it could talk. The tales it would tell. Pea soup fog and thick ice. Fire and disease. How the stench and noise of the busy working waterway gave little breathing room to its dark liquid. Did it long for those days? It was quite empty now. Almost dead, with a forgotten purpose. Just how she was feeling.

She walked back over to her plastic table and sat down on the damp seat, wondering what kind of character Charles Dickens would have made her.

Weak? Strong? Desolate? Maybe one with a happy ending.

She sighed deeply, looking down at her food.

Her bones were already numb, but not from the November temperature. It was from the lonely feeling of isolation.

Happy 30th birthday to me.

3

Jake

'Josh, stop shouting at me. No one is expecting anything from you.' Jake ran his fingers through his hair in annoyance. He steadied his breathing and tried once more to calm his little brother. 'I'm going to sort this.'

Josh curled his hands around the crystal whisky glass resting on his brother's kitchen table. He glared down at the shiny white surface gleaming up at him. He could almost see the reflection of his bright blue eyes.

'I just don't want to be a pen-pusher,' he mumbled.

Jake sat opposite him and refilled his own glass from the tall bottle sitting between them. 'I don't either, but I'll do it because it has to be done. We own the family business now. We're all that's left.'

Josh swigged his drink. His eyes fell glumly into the glass. 'Don't remind me.'

Jake quietly watched his brother. He knew he was grieving the recent loss of their grandfather. He was too. It had only been a week since the funeral, and now Josh was the only family he had left. His thoughts turned to his grandmother, and how Josh went off the rails when she died three years before. Josh wasn't the only one to sink so low at that time.

Edith Reynolds was the rock of the family. All three men left behind had struggled so much after her death.

Jake assumed his brother was thinking about their parents, who had died when they were kids. Josh had relied heavily upon their grandparents from that moment on. John and Edith had been the ones who had raised them. Josh was thirty-two, but he still needed the level of guidance, care, and stability that their grandparents had given them. He knew that Josh was feeling lost, as he felt that way too.

'It's going to be okay, Josh.'

Josh rolled his eyes over to meet with the face that looked so much like him. 'It's never going to be the same again, Jake.'

Jake sank inside at his brother's broken voice. He hated seeing him so sad.

'I think you've had enough to drink now, Josh.'

Josh lowered his head and tightly pinched the bridge of his nose. 'Don't tell me what to do. You're drinking.'

Knowing of the potentially explosive situation he was in with his brother, he didn't argue, instead he tried to lighten the mood. 'I bet Gramps gave you some advice before he died. I know he gave me some. What did he tell you?'

The corners of Josh's mouth curled at the memory. 'He told me to grow up, find a wife, and settle down.'

Jake breathed out a laugh. 'Well, he's not wrong.'

'Really? Find a wife? What is this, the 1950s?'

Jake flashed his perfect teeth. 'Maybe not the wife part, but you should think about settling somewhere. You're thirty-two, and you have no fixed abode.'

'I use this address. Don't need anywhere else.'

'Josh, I'm fine with you staying here whenever you're in town, but that's the problem. That's what Gramps meant. You never stay in one spot for long. You waste money renting places here, there, and everywhere. Why not find a place you can call home?'

Josh glanced around at his sterile surroundings and scoffed to himself. 'Do you call this operating room a home?'

Jake frowned at the comment towards his clean and tidy ways.

His plush apartment looked unlived in and lacked anything colourful. Its shiny sleek lines and black-and-grey open plan kitchen made the contemporary style home an unlikely match for any family who owned fridge magnets and animal ornaments. The long, wide corridor that led to many other rooms would have been perfect for roller skating or, at the very least, a sock slide, but the top floor of River Heights had Jake Reynolds as its owner, so it was never going to see any socks sliding across its floor unless it was an accident.

Josh frowned with amusement. 'Jake, maybe you should do something about this place.'

'What's wrong with my place, Josh?'

Josh shrugged. He knew he was treading on thin ice. 'It's not healthy being so... clean.' His words lingered in the air for a minute. 'And this minimalistic look. I mean, what's the point?'

Jake got up from the table and headed for the kitchen, taking both whisky glasses with him. 'That makes no sense.'

'Does to me.'

'You like colour. You like art. That's your thing. We're not all the same.'

'Clearly,' Josh mumbled.

The large, shiny black fridge creaked, gaining Jake's attention. 'I'm going to make us some dinner. Chickpea burger okay with you?'

Josh shrugged. 'Sure, but tell me what Gramps said to you when he knew he was dying.' He then mumbled to himself, 'I bet it was stop being so fussy.'

'I heard that.'

Josh peered over at him. 'Well, what did he say to you?'

Jake turned and leant his back against the large stainless-steel sink. He laughed to himself as a vision of his grandfather came into his mind.

John Reynolds had a hard, rough face, with piercing blue eyes that both his grandsons had inherited. He was tall, thickset, and had always been told that he had a touch of John Wayne about him.

Jake remembered vividly what his grandfather had told him. 'He said I was to stop focusing on myself and start helping others, look after you, and take care of the business.'

Josh laughed. 'Basically, he pointed out how selfish you can be.'

Jake's shoulders drooped. 'I'm not selfish.'

'You are. Even Gran used to say that you needed to think of others more.'

'Gran always said that I had a lovely heart, thank you very much.'

'Gran said that to me too.'

Jake looked glumly down at the shiny white floor of his kitchen. His heart ached, and it was all he could do to stop tears forming in his eyes. 'God, I miss that woman.'

Josh started to pick at his fingernail. He had nothing to add to his brother's statement.

Jake raised his head sharply. 'Hey, how about you come to Pepper Bay with me? Gramps wanted his ashes sprinkled in the same place we did Gran's. We can get on with that sooner rather than later. We can spend Christmas there. Come back in the spring.'

The legs of Josh's chair screeched across the floor as he abruptly stood up. 'You know what, forget dinner, I'm not staying.'

I shouldn't have mentioned Pepper Bay.

Jake watched his brother head for the door as though the building were on fire. 'Where are you going?'

Josh shook his head as he left, his voice trailing behind him. 'Don't know. New York, maybe.'

Jake took a moment to think, as a feeling of helplessness rushed over him.

I can't let him leave. He's not in a good way. He needs help.

He headed towards the door, but Josh had already got into the lift and was on his way down. He impatiently pressed the button a few times, hoping it would hurry up and return.

Come on. Come on. Stupid thing.

He quickly stepped inside as soon as the lift arrived. It seemed to take ages to hit the ground floor.

'Everything okay, Mr Reynolds?' asked Stan. 'Your brother practically ran out of the building.'

Jake looked out of the large glass doors. Josh was nowhere in sight. He took a deep breath and turned back to the lift. Keeping his eyes on the floor, he acknowledged the question. 'Everything's fine, Stan.'

Stan barely heard him, his voice was so quiet.

The lift pinged open and Jake stepped back inside.

I'm not selfish. You're selfish, Josh. Always running away and leaving me to deal with everything. I do help others. Don't judge me on my past. When was the last time I did something for someone? Don't count Josh... erm.

He suddenly threw out his arm to stop the lift from closing and looked over at Stan, who had gone back to reading his book.

'Hey, Stan, about that girl, Anna.'

Stan raised his eyebrows. 'What about her?'

'Tell her she can have the cleaning job at my apartment. She can start tomorrow. Nine sharp. Is that okay?'

The corners of Stan's mouth began to rise. 'That's perfect. Thanks, Mr Reynolds.'

Don't thank me. Thank my grandparents.

Jake lowered his eyes as the lift door closed, then glanced at himself in the mirror before returning his eyes to the floor.

Walking back into his apartment, he looked around at the emptiness. Everything suddenly felt extra quiet. He sighed deeply, knowing there wasn't anything to clean, and went over to the window to stare down at the River Thames. It looked as glum as him. He slowly raised his eyes to the dark sky.

'She can mop the floors or something. I'm sure she can find something around here to clean. Happy with that, Gramps?'

4

Anna

Anna knocked on Jake Reynolds' door at 9 a.m. She was slightly peeved she had to be there but knew that the extra money would help her to move out of her homeless situation a lot faster. She stared blankly at the solid, light-wood lump of a door that divided her from the grumpy man who smelled nice and looked way more handsome than anyone should.

This should be fun.

A sudden urge to run away filled her whole body except her feet. She glanced down at them and wondered why they didn't feel obliged to join the mood.

It was too late to do anything, as Jake opened the door widely, forcing her to surrender to her day.

She quickly looked up and plastered on a fake smile. 'Morning. I'm Anna Cooper. You're expecting me.'

'Jake Reynolds, how…' His voice caught in his throat as his eyes immediately rolled down towards Max. 'Oh, I didn't know you were bringing your dog.'

Anna swallowed hard. She didn't want to lose her cleaning job before it had even started, but Max came first. She tried to find her voice in amongst the jittery feeling in her stomach and the slight whirl in her head. 'He goes everywhere with me.'

Jake nodded slowly. It was clear he was pondering over the idea whether or not to allow the dog entrance.

Anna waited patiently. She bit her bottom lip and tried hard not to fidget her feet.

If he doesn't hurry up and make up his mind, I'm leaving.

Max was sitting quietly at her side with his best smile washed across his gentle face.

'Okay,' Jake mumbled, appearing to talk more to himself. He moved to one side of the door. 'Come in.'

Anna reluctantly crossed the threshold.

Bloody hell, look at this place. It goes on forever.

Her eyes darted everywhere.

There's nothing to clean, and he doesn't have a cleaner. He must be like some sort of Mrs Hinch.

Anna knew that she wouldn't complain if she had such a place to live in, but she felt the apartment wasn't very homely. She stretched her eyebrows slightly to stop herself from frowning at the lack of warmth surrounding her. She immediately wanted to place a potted plant somewhere or add a painting to one of the plain white walls. She felt the place needed something, or perhaps just someone who cared.

This isn't a home. It's a showroom, and to think I live just above it. All this time, I had no idea what was below me. It would be so nice to have a home. Somewhere that's mine. Somewhere safe and warm. Okay, don't cry. Now is not the time. Now is the time to earn some more money to get another step closer to my forever home, or any home. I'm glad the heating is on in here.

Jake closed the door and went to stand beside his kitchen table. She glanced at the opened laptop sitting on top of the shiny white surface and watched whilst he placed his phone down beside a notepad and pen that were also there.

The intensity in his eyes hit her as soon as they looked up and locked into her stare. She felt as though a spotlight had just appeared and he was about to interrogate her for a crime she did commit.

She lowered her eyes to hide her guilt, but she didn't know what her feeling of guilt was for.

For staring at him? For secretly inhaling his scent? For wondering what kind of protagonist he would be? Blimey, he's so handsome. So much more than yesterday.

His arm stretched out to his side. 'Let me show you to the cleaning cupboard.'

Anna waited for him to turn and then managed to finally gulp down the ball of saliva that was wedged in her throat. She followed him over to a large white door, desperately trying to ignore the fact that her trainers were making a squeaky noise on his polished floor. The sound was echoing in her ears, and she just wanted the ground to open up and swallow her, or at least just take her embarrassing footwear. She quickly narrowed her eyes when she realised they had widened far too dramatically for a broom cupboard door opening.

The small room had an array of white shelves stacked neatly with grey metal containers, each labelled with a room name.

Wow! Talk about organised. Looks nice though. Wish I had a cleaning cupboard, or just a cupboard in general would be good. For God's sake, I'm actually standing here missing cupboards right now. I'm starting to wonder about myself. I do miss certain things though. I miss Henry Hoover's smiley face. Has he got a Henry? What is that? Looks like a baton. It's definitely not a Dyson. Is it even a vacuum cleaner?

Jake cleared his throat slightly. 'If you could please make sure you put everything back in its place when you're done, that would be great.'

'Sure,' she replied.

His eyes rolled down to look at the dog.

Anna followed his stare. 'Go and lie down, Max.'

Max happily trotted off to find a comfortable space.

Good luck finding a cushion.

Anna reached up to grab the bathroom box. She thought it would be a good place to start, and also somewhere away from the tall, good-looking man who smelled nice and seemed to easily drain oxygen from her brain.

The container was on the top shelf, and she immediately realised her five-foot-four height needed tiptoes. Before she knew what was happening, Jake was leaning over her, reaching up an arm to pull down the box. She could feel his chest pressed almost to her hair. So close, she could lean back slightly and just rest there, but that would be weird. A touch of static hair stuck to his top as he moved back and gently placed the box into her hands.

A rich cologne, hinting at wealth, drifted over from the fibres of his overpriced casual clothes as he moved his hand to her hair and tamed it back into place with one slow stroke. He then quickly jolted his hand away as though he had just burned himself.

'Thank you,' she said, feeling the blood in her cheeks stir from his unexpected touch.

He gave her a slight nod. 'I'll leave you to it. I'll just be at the table, if you need anything.'

'Are you working?'

Don't ask him questions. What are you doing, Anna?

'Yes.'

'I'll try to keep the noise down as best I can.' She quickly turned away.

I have to get out of here. I need to be away from this man. I can't believe he stroked my hair. Oh, ruddy hell, I have to get a grip. I almost melted. I'm so stupid. What am I doing? Concentrate. Right. Work.

She stopped walking. 'Where's the bathroom?'

Jake frowned with curiosity. 'I thought all the apartments here had the same layout.'

Oh crap! Do they?

Anna had to think fast. 'Some people like to change things around.'

'Oh, okay. Well, mine's just down there, third on the right, and I have another one in my bedroom, second on the left. In fact, just look around. It's best if you familiarise yourself with everything. There shouldn't be too much mess, as I live here alone.'

Anna tried to steady her galloping heart.

That was close.

'Okay.' She hoped her voice didn't sound as shaky as she felt.

She watched him sit in front of his laptop and went to say something when Max curled up by his feet under the table and fell asleep. Jake had ignored him, so she did too. She quickly made for the bathroom.

Large, light-grey, ribbed tiles made the walls, and plain shiny ones made the floor. There was a large round bath in one corner and a walk-in shower along the opposite wall. A tall black cabinet stood next to the doorway, and a square toilet and sink alongside that.

'Needs a window in here,' she mumbled.

She lowered the cleaning products to the floor whilst wondering what exactly needed sprucing up. The whole room looked brand new, untouched, and much better suited to a home-styling magazine for single men.

Bachelor pad for the super-rich, mid-thirties, lonely hearts club band. Blimey, this place looks lonely.

She walked over to the bath and ran her hand along the edge. 'What I wouldn't give to jump into you right now. Just ten minutes to warm my aching bones.' She shook her head at herself for talking to a bath.

The shower cubicle looked inviting. There was enough room in there for at least four people, and the large square showerhead gave the impression it was ready to treat its occupants to a tropical waterfall.

I can imagine the models who have had that luxury. I bet he only dates models. Diamonds and caviar. Flash cars and weekends in Dubai. How the other half live. I wonder what that feels like. Never having to add up while shopping for food. Travel whenever you want. Always having somewhere to live.

Anna sat on the edge of the bath and sighed. She remembered the rickety shower in her old house. The home she had shared with her ex-boyfriend, Rob.

Home! That's a laugh. He made sure I never felt like it was my home.

Her thoughts turned to the pastel-blue shower cubicles at the leisure centre. The showers there were much better than Rob's. Although, she did have to pay to use the swimming pool facilities.

Maybe one day I'll actually learn how to swim. Maybe one day I'll get to have a shower again without having to wear a swimming costume.

'Let's clean the already sparkling clean shower,' she told the room.

No doubt, I'll make it looked smeared. Maybe I should use a duster. It looks polished. I could sit on the loo and run the tap and pretend I've cleaned the room. Oh, I can't do that. He's going to pay me. I'm going to have to clean it. A spray and wipe. That should be okay.

She stood and glanced down at her trainers and wondered if she should take them off. She decided it would be more hygienic if she removed her shoes and socks. She was sure Jake Reynolds wouldn't appreciate footwear in his shower.

'I bet he doesn't even use this room,' she mumbled.

She picked up the mandarin-fragrance bathroom spray, entered the cubicle, and looked straight up at the showerhead, as she noticed it had lit up with tiny blue lights all around the rim.

What's that?

Suddenly, freezing cold water sprayed out of it, along with powerful jets that shot out from tiny nozzles built into the tiled wall.

'Argh!'

5

Jake

Jake jumped when he heard a scream. His head shot up, along with Max's, both of them staring down the passageway that led to the bathroom.
What the bloody hell was that?
He sprinted through his apartment and quickly swung open the bathroom door to see that Anna was standing outside the shower, dripping wet and shivering.
Oh my God, look at her.
He bit in his lip, trying not to laugh at the wet slump before him. He quickly opened the cabinet and pulled down a large grey towel from the top of a neat pile.
'Bloody thing just came on by itself,' she said, catching her breath. 'And it was freezing cold.'
A laugh escaped his lips, and he turned to see she was less than impressed. He moved towards her and wrapped the soft towel around her shoulders and started to rub along her arms. 'I guess the shower was switched on to automatic.'
He felt her shudder at his touch and snatch herself away from him.
'I can manage.'
'Sorry,' he said softly, backing away.
Anna lowered her head and took a calming breath that didn't relax her chattering teeth. 'Thank you.'
He was finding it extremely difficult not to smile. 'Let me get one for your hair.' He quickly turned back to the

cabinet to get a hand towel and, without thinking, draped it on her head, then stepped back.

She pulled the towel from her hair and rubbed the tip of her ponytail whilst he shifted slightly in his footing. 'I have a dressing gown you could wear while your clothes are in the dryer.' He waited for her to respond.

Her eyes rolled up slowly to meet his, and he found himself feeling awkward, which made him feel even more awkward because feeling awkward was a whole new feeling for him. He always oozed confidence and was never lost for words.

'Thank you,' she said. 'I guess it would help.'

He nodded and remained staring at her.

Anna arched an eyebrow. 'Where will I find it?'

He jolted out of his trance-like state. 'Oh, yes, erm. Wait there. I'll get it. You take your clothes off.' He rushed out of the room, shaking his head at himself and swearing under his breath.

You take your clothes off! What am I saying? I've got to stop laughing as well. It was so funny. She doesn't even realise how adorable she looks soaking wet. So different to how she looked in the lift. She's now taking her clothes off in my bathroom. Jake, do not think about that woman naked. Concentrate.

A navy dressing gown was hanging on a hook behind his bedroom door. He raced back to the bathroom with it and then stopped with his hand dithering over the door handle, wondering if she had actually stripped off. He pushed the door slightly and wiggled the dressing gown through the crack, relaxing a little when Anna removed it from his hand.

He put his mouth close to the door. 'I'm sorry I didn't warn you about the shower.' He was thinking about what else he could say when she opened the door, making him jump back. She was wrapped in his soft fleece robe, staring at him. He was staring back, and his piercing eyes started to crease in the corners.

It sure as hell looks better on you. Look away, Jake. Look away now.

He rolled his eyes down to the wet grey tracksuit sprawled over her arm.

'Where's the dryer?' she asked.

He took a moment to process her words, as he was looking at her long dark hair. It was out of its scrunchie and hanging loosely down onto his dressing gown, wafting a faint apple scent his way as she stepped closer.

'Dryer?' she asked, moving the damp clothes towards him.

'This way.' He waved her to follow, stopping just short of the kitchen to open a door.

Anna entered the utility room and placed her clothes in the dryer.

'Here, let me,' he said, taking control of the digital display panel on the front of the sleek black machine. He turned to see her watching her tracksuit flipping around in the dryer. There was a hint of sadness in her eyes, and it made him feel as though he should be doing more to help her. 'If you go to my room, there is a hairdryer you can use.'

She smiled, and he felt the corners of his mouth rise.

'I'll make you a cup of tea to help warm you up,' he added.

Although, there are other ways. What? Where the hell did that come from? Behave yourself. What's a matter with you?

'Thank you.' Her voice was soft and sweet as it trailed over her shoulder.

That awkward feeling was back again as she squeezed past him to exit the room and her arm brushed against his.

Why do I suddenly want to hold her? Get a grip, Jake.

He went to the kitchen, switched the kettle on, and then glanced down at Max, who seemed to be following him.

Max had his tongue hanging out to one side of his happy mouth.

'Yeah, you can laugh, but you're going in that shower next, stinky.'

Max made a slight gurgling noise.

Jake raised his eyebrows at him. 'Oh, you reckon, do you? Trust me, you're having a bath, mate.'

Max lowered himself to the floor and covered his nose with one paw.

Jake frowned in amusement. 'What? It's not that bad. Have you seen the size of that bath? It can fit all three of us in, and I'll have you know that my shampoo is made from natural ingredients. You'll love it. In fact…' He quickly marched off to his bedroom.

Anna jumped when she saw him in the doorway.

'Anna, I was wondering. While you're wet anyway, and… well, the dog smells. Would it be okay if we bathed him? We could use my shampoo. It's for sensitive skin and hasn't been tested on…' He shot Max a glance before mouthing the word, 'Animals.'

Anna's laugh was muffled as though she didn't really want to laugh at all. 'I'm not sure what to say.'

Oh God, please say yes. He stinks.

Jake shrugged casually. 'It will make his coat nice and shiny.'

'Then he'll match everything else around here,' she said, then quickly looked back at the sleek hairdryer she was holding.

He smiled warmly, choosing to ignore the flash of embarrassment he just witnessed in her eyes. 'Yeah, I guess he will. Will you let me bath him?'

She nodded. 'Okay. He does need a bath. I was going to take him to the groomer next week once I got paid, but Stan told me not to waste…'

He wondered why she had stopped talking, and an uncomfortable silence loomed for a few seconds.

Say something.

He looked at Max. 'I'll get a towel and the shampoo. You get the dog.'

Max gave a slight growl and ran off.

'Hey!' called out Jake.

Anna giggled. 'You run the bath. I'll fetch him.'

Jake headed for the bathroom and turned on the bath taps. He bent to rest upon his knees and swirled the water around with one hand.

Oh, Jake, what are you doing?

He got up to get a towel and a bottle of almond milk shampoo from the cabinet and then went back to check on the water. He poured a small amount of the shampoo into the bath and rested on his knees again, inhaling the fresh, creamy smell.

A scraping noise came from the doorway as Max's nose slid inside. His two front paws were stretched out, acting as brakes.

Oh my God, that is so funny.

Anna was wrapped over Max's back. She looked breathless and dishevelled. Her half-dried hair was sticking to her mouth like cooked spaghetti.

Jake couldn't help but let out a quiet laugh.

'Almost there,' she said.

'Should I help? Will he bite me?' he asked, nervously waving a hand forward.

'He won't bite you, so if you think you can lift him, go ahead.'

Oh, please! Of course I can lift him. If I can't, then I need to have a serious word with my personal trainer.

Jake got up and curled his hands around Max's smelly body and lifted him up.

Bloody hell, he is heavy.

'Wait,' she cried. She ran towards the bath, rolled up the sleeve of the dressing gown, and plunged her whole arm into the water.

Jake stood there, holding Max, trying not to struggle with the growing weight.

They should introduce dog-lifting down the gym.

'Okay,' said Anna. 'The water's okay. You can put him in now.'

Jake was glad to place Max in the bath.

Max had lost his smile.

Anna pointed at the small shower attachment connected to the bath taps. 'Is that safe to use?'

He breathed out a laugh. 'Yes, that's safe.'

She smiled and removed the showerhead and started to spray Max's back.

'He does pong a bit,' she admitted.

Jake nodded as he tipped some of his expensive shampoo onto the dog. 'I've never bathed a dog before.'

Anna smiled softly at Max and leant over to kiss him on the nose. 'You hear that, boy. This man is a learner, so you behave yourself.'

I'm not a learner at everything. Stick around. You might find out. Oh, shut up, Reynolds. What are you going on about? I actually think I've lost the plot today.

Max made a sound like a huff, and Jake flinched as spray from the dog's nose hit him in the face. 'Oh my God. I can't believe he just did that.'

Anna giggled, lowered the shower, and placed her hands upon Max's back and started to gently massage the shampoo into his fur. 'I'm so sorry. Max is just showing his frustration at being held captive in the bath. He's not normally this rude. Let's hurry and get him sorted. Here, place your hands like this.'

Watching her movements, he joined in, making sure he kept to his own side of the dog, because if his fingers accidently entwined with hers it was quite possible he wouldn't let go. It was also quite possible he would pull her hand over towards him so that her body would have to follow, and it was quite possible that the action would leave her sitting on his lap.

He concentrated on his task to distract himself from her and her apple hair. 'It's actually quite relaxing. I could do with a massage myself.'

She giggled. 'Is that a hint?'

A slow smile built on his face, as he struggled to hold it back. He kept his eyes on the dog. 'No, it wasn't a hint.'

Anna grabbed one of Max's paws to wash around his claws. 'I've never had one myself.'

Jake found himself grinning. 'Is that a hint, Miss Cooper? Would you like to go next?' He watched her blush, and it amused him.

You really are quite cute. You have kind eyes and a gentle smile and...

'You smell like apples.' As soon as he had blurted out the words, he wished he hadn't, and he desperately hoped he wasn't the one now blushing.

She glanced sideways at him. 'I have apple shampoo, but all I can smell is yours.'

'It's almond milk.'

Why am I talking about shampoo? Oh, why am I talking at all if all I can say is stupid things. What is wrong with me today?

'Do his feet your side,' she said, nodding down at Max's paws. 'Then we can rinse him off.'

Jake did as he was instructed, then leant back whilst Anna rinsed away the foam.

'Pull the plug out, Jake, and then we can dry him while he's still in the bath.'

He pulled the plug whilst thinking about how much he liked the sound of his name when it rolled off her tongue. He slowly glanced over at her mouth, wondering what it would feel like to kiss her.

Max started to shake.

'Quick, get the towel,' she said, grabbing it from the floor.

Jake got a face full of wet dog before she got a chance to throw the towel over Max.

She giggled. 'You always have to be quick at that point.'

'I'll remember that for next time.'

Next time? Why am I talking about having a repeat performance?

'He won't need another bath now till spring, hopefully,' said Anna.

Jake joined in with the towel rubbing, and Max was enjoying every minute.

'Okay, you can lift him out now,' she said, leaning back to sit upon the floor.

He grabbed the towel-wrapped retriever and carefully placed him on the tiles.

'Stand back,' she said, grinning widely as she pulled the towel off Max's back.

'What for?' Jake then covered his face with his arm as Max shook his fur.

Oh, gross!

Max had the happiest of looks on his face as he raced out of the bathroom and off down the passageway.

Jake looked down at his black tee-shirt and dark jeans. 'Oh my God, I'm covered in hairs.' Without thinking, he quickly whipped off his top. 'Now I need a wash.'

He glanced down at the state of his bath and threw his tee-shirt down to his side. He turned to face Anna and noticed her eyes were on his well-defined abs. He quickly folded his arms, and she looked away.

Mr Awkward was back.

Stop acting weird.

'At least I have something to clean now,' she said, nodding at the bath.

Jake stood and lowered his arms in an attempt to look relaxed. 'Yeah, I guess you do.' He bent over and picked up the damp towel. 'I'll put this in the washing machine and make us that tea.'

'Thank you, Jake,' he heard her say as he walked away, and he felt a strange jittery feeling hit his stomach.

6

Anna

Anna felt more relaxed the moment Jake walked away to put on a top. She sat at his table, waiting for her tea, whilst he went into his bedroom to get changed. When he came back wearing a navy tracksuit, she thought he looked even better than he did before. She was still surprised that he had bathed her dog. She was also worried about her clothes in the dryer, praying they didn't shrink. She didn't have many clothes, as she knew she would have no room for them where she was going after Rob had evicted her from his house. When she finally did go back for the rest, he had already thrown them away.

'How do you like your tea?' asked Jake, pouring the boiling water into two beige mugs.

'Just milk, please.'

He looked over his shoulder at her and gave her a warm smile, and Anna felt a flutter hit her straight in the stomach.

Go away, stupid feeling. You're not welcome. It's those flipping eyes of his. They're doing my head in. I can't look at him.

She frowned to herself and looked over to see where Max had got to. He was lying in a sunspot that was beaming in through the window, and she knew he would need a walk soon.

Jake placed her tea down in front of her upon a red coaster that he was carrying in his other hand, and her eyes focused on his manicured fingers as she waited for him to sit down opposite her.

'Do we need to dry him with the hairdryer?' he asked, looking over at Max.

She shook her head. 'He'll be okay. It's nice and warm in here. I'll give him a brush later.' She watched him look down at the table and close his laptop. 'I'm stopping you from working.'

'It's okay, Anna. I can't really concentrate anyway.'

Because of me? Do you find me distracting? Of course he doesn't. I'm not shower-model material. Calm down. Stop being daft, and don't look at his eyes, whatever you do.

It wasn't easy. She tried so hard not to look, but she did and caught a small amount of sadness in them as they rolled her way. The look disappeared within a second. 'Is everything okay, Jake?' She watched him quietly nod and sip his tea.

I need to leave. I'm supposed to be the cleaner. This wasn't how I expected my morning to go. I'm sitting in his bloody dressing gown. God, it smells so good. Wish I could have a bath, put on my PJs, curl up under his arm and watch telly. How nice would that be? In another life, maybe. Nice things don't happen to me. Men like Jake Reynolds don't happen to me.

Anna fought back the disappointment building. 'I should clean that mess in the bathroom.'

He shifted his weight in his chair. 'Drink your tea first.' His voice was firm like a parent. 'It can wait five minutes.'

She wasn't sure if he actually wanted her company or if he really did need a distraction from whatever was bothering him. She knew it wasn't Max any longer. Not now he smelled like almond milk shampoo.

There's definitely something on his mind. It's none of my business. Don't get too involved.

'So, what do you do?' she asked, nodding at his laptop.

Jake flipped over his phone to see if he had any messages or missed calls. He placed it back down on the table. 'I now run my grandfather's business.' He was still looking down at the table.

'Has he retired?'

His brow furrowed slightly as he swallowed hard.

'He died recently,' he said quietly.

She could clearly see that it wasn't an easy thing to say, and now she wanted so badly to reach over the table and hold his hand. It was so close, but she couldn't touch him. 'I'm so sorry, Jake.'

He rolled his eyes up and gave her a quick empty smile. 'It's okay.'

Good one, Anna.

There was a short silence between them, which was broken by Max having a stretch on the floor.

Anna felt the need to say something. 'What business do you have?'

'We own the coffee shops, Café Diths.'

Bloody hell! They're everywhere.

'Oh, that's nice. So, your grandfather started that?'

He nodded and smiled a smile that didn't quite reach his eyes. 'Yeah. He got the idea from Gran.'

Anna hugged her tea. 'Well, we women always have the best ideas.'

Jake's eyes filled with amusement. 'Oh, is that right?'

She avoided eye contact as she felt her stomach flip, wondering if he could tell.

He started to stroke the cuff on his sweatshirt. It was obvious his mind had drifted. 'My gran had a tea shop on the Isle of Wight, Edith's Tearoom, in a quaint little place called Pepper Bay.'

Anna felt her heart warm. She snuggled further into the cosiness of the fresh scent embedded in his robe. 'Sounds lovely.'

He smiled over at her. 'It is. We still own the shop. Gran never had the heart to sell the place. She'd owned it since she was twenty-one. She grew up in Pepper Bay. Her home was called Starlight Cottage. Still is. Josh and I still own that too. We're all that's left of our family now. Josh is my younger brother.'

'Where are your parents?'

Jake stopped smiling. 'They died in a car accident when we were kids. Our grandparents raised us since Josh was ten and I was thirteen. We didn't have any other grandparents, as my mum was an orphan.'

I know how that feels, and now I want to hug you.

Anna had been raised in and out of care homes and never quite found her forever family. She had never lived anywhere that felt like home. She knew that was the reason she had latched on to Rob so quickly.

She had ignored all the red flags that came with him and tried so hard to create a loving, happy home. Somewhere she could belong, with someone who wanted her.

Her dreams of a family had died way before they even started. She knew within the first day of meeting him that he wasn't right for her, but he was the only one to have noticed her, and there were so many times throughout her life where she had gone unnoticed.

He had physically pushed her on their third date, but still she had let it go, with thoughts of how she could fix the situation so that it was as perfect as she was pretending it to be.

He had pretty much told her how everything that was wrong with their relationship was her fault, and she had spent a long time believing his spiteful words.

Every day since the end of her relationship with Rob, she had silently thanked the sky. She knew that she would never play make-believe again nor would she lower her standards to accommodate someone else.

'Anyway,' added Jake. 'Gramps met Gran in Pepper Bay. He was on holiday, walked into her tea shop, they fell in love, and that was that. He had big dreams that spread way further than the Isle of Wight. Gran loved him, so she moved here to London with him, but they agreed to never sell her family home or shop. They would take us there every summer and sometimes at Christmas.'

'When was the last time you went there?'

'Last year, when Gramps found out he was dying. He wanted to go there one last time. He always said that every time he walked into her tea shop, he could see her standing behind the counter, with a big smile washed across her beautiful face just like the first day he saw her all those years ago. So he wanted to see that one last time.'

Anna felt tears fill her eyes.

Don't cry. Don't cry.

Jake shifted in his chair, looking slightly uncomfortable. He gulped his tea and turned to look over at Max.

She swallowed the lump in her throat before asking, 'Will you keep Starlight Cottage and the tea shop now?'

He nodded slowly. 'Rather keep them than any of the coffee shops we have around the world.'

Oh, he can be quite sweet.

'Pepper Bay means a lot to you.'

He looked her way and smiled warmly, and Anna felt that flutter in her stomach return.

'I don't really talk about Pepper Bay with anyone other than Josh. Don't know why I'm telling you. You don't want to hear about my life.'

Anna didn't want him feeling awkward talking to her. She didn't mind if he revealed anything about the things in his life. He was only human, but she understood that he might not want to talk to a stranger about certain things. Although, in some weird way, she didn't feel much like she was sitting with a stranger.

'It's just life, isn't it? There's nothing wrong with talking about your life,' she said. 'We all have one. The rough, the smooth. We've all got a backstory, a now story, and, hopefully, more of a story to come. Besides, everyone knows it's always easier to talk to a stranger.'

Jake glanced into his cup. 'Funny, Anna, you don't feel like a stranger.'

Anna tried to keep a straight face. 'Might have something to do with me wearing your nightclothes.'

He sat up. His shoulders looked strong as his posture aligned, and a sharpness entered his eyes as they stared at her mouth. 'Will you be able to work here tomorrow as well?'

I wish I could. I wish I could come here every day, and I really wish I could wear your dressing gown every day. You have no idea how warm my body feels right now.

'I can't tomorrow. I can on Thursday.'

His face hardened. 'Why can't you come tomorrow?'

'I have another job.'

Anna watched his shoulders relax as he placed both his hands down onto his lap. She wondered what he was thinking.

'Cleaning the other apartments here?' he asked.

She shook her head. 'No. I work in a bookshop just up the road. Actually, I own it. Well, twenty percent. My ex owns the rest. I get to work there two days a week. Tuesday and Wednesday.'

His jaw seemed clenched. 'Your ex?'

Anna's body suddenly felt lead-heavy. She hated thinking about him, let alone talking about him. She couldn't wait for the day when he was completely in her past. 'Rob. He won't buy me out, and I can't afford to buy him out. I can't afford to just walk away either. Not yet. So, I put in my two days a week.'

She watched his eyes studying her. He was sitting still and giving her his full attention, looking as though he were concentrating on an exam question, not wanting to get it wrong.

'How's that working out for you?' he asked.

It's a total nightmare. I love the bookshop, but I wish I was free of Rob.

She raised one shoulder to her cheek as she twiddled with the handle on her cup. 'It's okay.'

He was still watching her.

She was happy for him to talk about his life, but she wasn't ready to talk to him about all of hers. She knew, after what she had said to him about talking, it made her a hypocrite, but she couldn't risk letting him know the truth about her situation.

The phone started to vibrate on the table, and Anna used that as an excuse to quickly get up. 'You get that. I'll clean the bathroom.'

She could feel his eyes boring into the back of her as she rushed off.

7

Jake

Jake looked glumly out of his car window at the cold and dreary grey November morning. He glanced down at his phone and shook his head and then put it to his face. 'Josh, it's me. I'm on my way to see Mike. It's our first Café Diths meeting. I know I said I'd take over, but it would be nice if you at least showed up. Call me back, and you'd better not be in New York.'

I shouldn't have said that. He needs to be wherever he feels safe right now. I'll call him back.

'We're here, sir,' said the chauffeur.

Jake ran his finger down his dusty-pink tie and sighed deeply before getting out of the car. He looked up at the tall, blue-glass building, having little desire to go inside, but duty called. He raised his phone to his ear. 'Josh, I just want to know that you are all right. Call me back, please.' He took a deep breath and entered the premises.

Walking through the colourful lobby, Jake smiled to himself as thoughts of his grandfather's footprints filled the area.

Each day, John Reynolds would walk the same route that led to his office on the tenth floor.

Jake failed to have his grandfather's enthusiasm. It wasn't his dream. It wasn't his job. He had never worked a day in his life. He didn't have to.

John made sure no one in his family had to work. He would have liked his grandsons to join him in the office once in a while, he even sent Jake to university to gain a business degree, and he'd allowed Josh to do a degree in art, but nothing changed for the Reynolds boys.

Edith would spoil them, allowing them to spend money all over the place without knowing how to earn some.

John would try to put his foot down, force the boys to grow up and take life seriously, but he always gave in to his wife in the end. He knew he was fighting a losing battle. He just wished that someday the boys would settle down and give something back to the world.

'They have good hearts,' Edith would say.

'I wish they would use them,' John would reply.

Jake entered the boardroom, and a part of his soul died. There was no sign of Josh, not that he thought there would be. He knew full well Josh was in New York. He just wished his brother was with him so that he could keep a close eye on him.

Time to step up, Reynolds.

Mike walked over with his hand stretched out. 'Jake, glad you made it, mate. Come on, sit over here.' He plonked Jake down in a tall, cream, leather chair at the end of a long mahogany table that had other tall leather chairs, each one a different colour. 'This was where your grandad sat.'

Jake could already feel his grandfather's disappointment surrounding him.

Mike introduced the other five members of John's work team, who were sitting around the table staring at Jake. There were three women and two men. Two of the women looked younger than him.

Lance looks like a throwback from a 1950s boy band. Arthur has a more refined appearance and an obvious acquired taste for animal brooches, judging by the fox and the duck upon his lapel. Regina, well, what can I say, tall, blonde, and leggy sums her up. I'm guessing Shay is a Madonna-in-the-80s fan, and Caroline has Uma Thurman written all over her.

The somewhat eclectic group before him was not what he had expected to find working as board members for his grandfather. He felt slightly out of place amongst them, not to mention overdressed in his navy, fine-pinstriped suit.

It was clear that Mike was in charge. He didn't sit down, he did all of the talking, and oozed charisma, knowledge, and a whole other language that only his work colleagues appeared to understand.

Even though Jake had a business degree under his belt, it had been a long time since he actually studied anything to do with business, so he felt well and truly out of the loop.

He watched the short, stumpy, middle-aged man control the room with ease and could see why his grandfather had put Mike in charge. At least Mike looked happy about being there. He seemed to like talking statistics, strategies, and finances, and also about anything linked to the East End of London, as he seemed to be very proud of his roots.

John Reynolds took business very seriously. He loved every minute working with, for, or on his company. He had chosen his team wisely, making sure he picked people with the same level of passion as him, along with loyalty.

Jake was quickly getting the idea that his grandfather cared little for appearance, age, gender, or postcodes, and he was also discovering just how intelligent, resourceful, and motivated John's team were.

The Café Diths team made him feel welcome. They spoke highly of his grandfather, and they made sure that he knew what was what about the company. A few teary-eyes made an appearance as John Wayne jokes were made and memories were spoken of.

Jake felt more and more relaxed as the meeting went on, especially when he realised all he had to do was take over his grandfather's role, which pretty much consisted of having the final say and signing documents every so often. Everything else was done for him.

'Your grandfather's business is safe in our hands, Jake,' said Mike. 'We're family here, and we've been working this way for many years, mate. You don't have any worries with us. Nothing's getting naused up around here just because John is gone.'

Jake smiled and nodded. 'I know, Mike, and thank you. Thank you all. My grandfather never had a bad word to say about any of you. He loved his team very much, which is why he left you each two percent of the business.'

A flurry of whispers passed between the group.

Mike laughed to himself. 'He bloody well never said anything about that to us.'

'He once told me that he would make sure we were all right if anything happened to him,' said Shay, her husky voice projected across the room. 'Told me he had to make sure I never ran out of purple lipstick.'

Caroline pointed at her. 'Obviously, she hasn't.'

'I remember when you wore it once,' said Shay, grinning at her.

'I had to try.'

'Even I tried it,' said Lance. 'Clashed with my eyes.'

Arthur chuckled. 'Everything clashes with your eyes, Lancey, except red.'

Lance widened his dark eyes. 'Red? What am I, the devil?'

'Ooh, I love bright red lipstick,' said Shay.

'I simply refuse to wear bright red lipstick,' said Lance. 'You can't make me.'

Regina twiddled her long blonde curls. 'I prefer coral.'

Mike turned back to Jake. 'That's enough about lipsticks. We need to know what's going to happen next.'

Jake was staring at Shay's purple lips. 'My grandfather's solicitor will be here after lunch to talk things through with you.'

Mike finally sat down. 'Blimey! I don't know what to say.'

'Between you all, you now own twelve percent of Café Diths,' said Jake. 'Hopefully, this won't change things too much.'

Everyone shook their heads.

Arthur smiled warmly. His wiry grey beard had a slight bounce. 'We have a saying around here. If it's not broken, don't try fixing it.' His voice was deep and warm like a Santa at the shopping mall.

Jake grinned to himself. 'Yeah, Gramps said that a lot.'

Mike stood up. 'Well, we were having a champagne lunch in honour of John, but now we can also celebrate and honour John's generosity. Will you be joining us, Jake?'

'Sure, love to.'

Mike told everyone to head for the bar, and Jake wasn't quite sure if that meant leaving the building.

Mike patted him on the back. 'Come on, you haven't seen this room yet.'

The corners of Jake's mouth curled as he was led over to the other side of the office floor to an open space filled with soft colourful seating, a pool table, a bar, and a large TV that had a video game being played on it by two men in their early twenties.

'What is this place?'

'We've had this for a while. Your grandfather's idea. It helps everyone relax. We call it the Fun Room.'

Jake nodded over at the beach-hut bar. 'Looks like fun.'

'We just need a barbeque, but health and safety won't allow it.'

Jake pretended to look shocked. 'No, really? Can't think why.'

Mike headed for the bar. 'It's okay. There's a little bistro around the back of the building. They make pukka burgers and ribs. The delivery will be here soon.' He stepped behind the bar and bent down to a small fridge. 'Beer, Jake, or champagne?'

'Beer's fine.' He took the bottle that was wiggled his way and turned to look around at the room that his grandfather had created to help stop his workers from carrying too much stress.

This is a great idea, Gramps. Definitely something Josh would have thought of as well.

Mike leant over the bar. 'So, anything new happening in your life, Jake? You know, your old gramps always dreamed you and Josh would give him some great-grandkids one day.'

Anna entered his mind. It wasn't a shock. He had thought about her all night. 'Gramps always said that family was important.'

Mike swigged his beer and nodded. 'He was right. I'd be lost without my wife and kids.'

'How did you know your wife was the one?'

Mike grinned widely and a twinkle hit his eyes. 'I don't know. It's hard to explain. I just know that the moment I met her, I didn't want to leave her. We stayed talking till two in the morning, and that was from lunchtime. We ended up outside the beigel shop down Brick Lane. She had tuna mayo, and I had salt beef. We had a nice cup of Rosie and sat at the bus stop. Proper taters it was that night, but I didn't care. I didn't want to be anywhere else.'

Jake didn't quite understand everything that Mike had said, but he did identify the dreamy look in Mike's eyes. He smiled to himself. 'My grandfather said he knew straight away when he met my gran.'

'Yeah, he told me that story. Pepper Bay, right? He walked in her tea shop, saw that big beautiful smile she had, and fell in love on the spot.'

Jake drank some beer whilst smiling at his grandparents' love story.

Mike slid a bowl of crisps across the bar towards him. 'My daughter reckons that love at first sight doesn't exist, that it's lust at first sight, because you can't love someone you don't know, but I'm not so sure.' He shrugged. 'I don't know what to call the moment I met my Leigh. All I know is, my brain turned to mush, and I was putty in her hands.'

Jake breathed out a laugh. Once again, his thoughts turned to Anna. He tried to force the thought out of his head. 'You got any gin back there, Mike?'

8

Anna

One of Anna's favourite smells was books. She simply loved working in her bookshop. She even enjoyed sleeping on the floor amongst them for the few weeks that she did before Rob found out and put a stop to it. If it weren't for Stan's camping idea, she wouldn't know where she would be.

Rob had never been kind to Anna throughout their five-year relationship. He had left her with emotional scars, nowhere to live, and twenty percent of a bookshop that she wasn't allowed to sleep in.

At least she got Max out of the break up. He was all she would have fought for anyway, but it turned out she didn't have to. Rob's new girlfriend was allergic to dogs, so Rob didn't try to fight Anna for the dog he never liked. He would have, just to be horrible, if it weren't for Izzy.

Anna hated Rob. She wished so hard for her future to arrive so that she was no longer living out her nightmare. In her future, she had a home, a job, and no more connections to Rob. She wanted to walk away from the bookshop, but it was the only income she had.

She sat on the floor, stacking a bottom shelf with fishing books, thinking about her new job at Jake's. Her hand clutched a yellow duster that made her think about how little there was to clean in the posh apartment. She smiled down at the cloth and wondered if there would be a man for her in her future too. Not that she was looking for one, but

Jake Reynolds had stirred something inside of her, and now she felt awake to the possibility.

Anna Reynolds. Proud owner of a penthouse overlooking the River Thames. Warm, cosy, loved, and eating bespoke chocolates every day. I'll add some colour to the walls, dog toys to the floor, and bliss to the bedroom. Bliss?

She giggled to herself.

I need to get a grip before I start doodling Anna Cooper 4 Jake Reynolds in my notebook. Oh my God, I remember doing that in school. Not much changes, really. No matter how old you are, you turn into a right goofy idiot as soon as you like someone. Look at me. I've already tried on his last name for size. Oh well, there's no harm in daydreaming a little.

Although Rob had put her right off men, she still believed in love and that heroes did exist.

Books had taught her that adventures were possible, and if a female lead was strong enough on the inside, anything was doable. She had read the words of male poets from bygone days, revealing to the world how much they were filled with love. They proved to her that there were men capable of the purest form of affection. She believed in the happily ever after and often dreamed of having one of her own.

She had more important things to worry about now, like finding somewhere to live. She was happy on her own, looking after herself. She had a plan, she had a goal, and she had Max.

Stan said that all she had to do was save enough money to put down a deposit on a flat, with some more money to cover the rent for the first couple of months, then she could apply for a full-time job somewhere and tell Rob to go get stuffed. He swore a lot during that conversation.

Anna had worked alongside Stan's wife, Marsha, for two years before Marsha died. Stan was the only friend she had left. She gave thanks for his friendship every morning and every night.

What do you think of my new job, Marsha? That Jake Reynolds is a bit of all right, isn't he? I think there's a lot more to him than meets the eye. I guess that's the same for all of us, really. How funny was he bathing Max. I wish you were still here, Marsha. I'd like to know your opinion about him. It was weird being around him. He's so far out of my league, but he felt familiar, somehow. I don't know. Anyway, I'm getting on all right up on the roof. Stan's great, but you already know that.

Stan had offered Anna use of his bedsit whilst she sorted herself out, but she flat-out refused to be a burden on him and his tiny home. After a long discussion about her living arrangements, they agreed to disagree, and that's when Stan had come up with the roof idea. He had once read about a homeless man camping on a rooftop, so he thought that if she was living at River Heights at least he could keep an eye on her. Plus, he knew just how secure the building was, and he couldn't think of another way to keep the stubborn woman safe.

Anna gazed over her shoulder at Max, who was snuggled down behind her, and stroked his head.

Max's happy eyes beamed her way.

'Not too much longer now, Max, and we'll be free.'

Max nuzzled his nose into the side of her leg.

On hearing the shop door open, she quickly straightened the books on the shelf and got up to greet her customer.

Much to both her and Max's disappointment, Rob was loitering over by the counter. The air felt instantly loaded, blocking her sinuses and bruising her head behind her eyes.

Oh great! What does he want?

She often struggled to find her voice around Rob and always had to think about which tone wouldn't rattle him. Afraid to poke the bear. Even though she was no longer with him, she still had the habit of being careful around him.

'It's Wednesday. What are you doing here today, Rob?'

'I own this shop. I can come in whenever I like.'

She ignored his snap and looked up at his spiky blonde hair.

Your new hairdo looks stupid. You look stupid. I really hate you. Go away. Go on. Ruddy well sod right off.

Rob saw Max sprawled out down one of the aisles. 'I don't like him in here. He'll put the customers off.' His squeaky voice hurt Anna's ears.

Oh, get lost, and take that nasty pepper aftershave with you.

She walked behind the counter to place the cloth down upon a shelf below the till. 'They love him. He always gets fussed.'

Rob's button nose snarled over towards the dog. 'He smells.'

'He only had a bath two days ago.'

Rob shot her a sharp glare. 'Are you trying to pick a fight with me, Anna?'

What?

Seething resentment was rising towards her brain, where she was sure it would one day erupt. She didn't want to bicker with him. She just wanted him to leave her alone, preferably forever.

'Why are you here, Rob?'

'I was passing. Thought I'd check you haven't done anything stupid to the place.'

The only stupid thing I've ever done was getting involved with you, you evil piece of...

'When have I ever done anything stupid to the shop?'

His fake-tanned face glowed to the back of the shop. 'You put up stupid bunting once.'

It wasn't stupid. The material was vintage, and it got many compliments.

He turned back to her. 'Izzy thinks this shop needs modernising. It's too stuffy, and it smells like books. She's going to bring some essential oils to burn tomorrow.'

Anna frowned. 'We have children that come in here, babies in prams. Some of those oils aren't good for them to breathe in.'

Rob started to pace along the front of the counter like a lioness on the prowl. 'Oh, what do you know about essential oils? They're all the same, just different smells, and it's better than this dusty smell lurking in here.' He pointed over at Max. 'Plus, it'll get rid of his smell, and if you tell me the oils are dangerous to animals, then he can go. You're only against the idea of having a nice fragrance in here because Izzy suggested it. You're so jealous, Anna. Really! Grow up.'

Anna felt at a loss for words. She never was good at arguing with Rob. Half the time he never made sense. He would only confuse her and often leave before she had time to respond, if he wasn't already yelling at the top of his voice about more stuff that didn't make sense or was completely irrelevant to the issue. She sighed deeply, trying to hide her shaky breathing.

Rob seemed finished with his rant. He headed for the door.

Don't say it. Don't say it.

'Why don't you and Izzy buy me out?' she asked quietly.

He stopped and looked over his shoulder, revealing hatred in his orange face. 'Why should we? If you don't like being here, just leave. You're lucky we allow you to work here two days a week.'

Anna fell flat. She had no more words. She didn't want the conversation to continue and just wished he would leave. She hated seeing him, hearing his voice, and being spoken down to. Ever since she met him all he had done was chip away at her, so she struggled with her confidence around him. She had little confidence, low self-worth, and a whole heap of psychological scars. He hadn't abused her physically often, but the emotional abuse had been full on, and she still hadn't fully healed from her time with him. Sometimes, she wondered if she ever would.

Rob twisted his mouth into a smirk. 'Got nothing to say?'

'It was just a suggestion,' she said, lowering her eyes towards the till.

'Just try thinking before you speak, eh, Anna.' He swung the door open whilst huffing. 'I'm not made of money.'

She took a slow and steady breath as Rob finally left.

It was as though someone had walked through the shop saging and using feng shui, because suddenly the air felt fresh and clear again. The heavy weight pressing down on her throat disappeared, and her brain settled down and relaxed. She could breathe. She didn't have to overthink. She was free.

Max got up and waddled over to rest his head upon her thigh, and she affectionately ruffled his face.

'He's the one who smells,' she mumbled, picking up the shop's phone, which she knew she wasn't allowed to use for personal calls. 'Hi, Stan. How's it going over at River Heights?'

'You okay, Anna? You don't normally call from work.'

She pinched the bridge of her nose and closed her eyes for a second. 'Just fancied a chat.'

Stan's voice dropped a key. 'He's been in again, hasn't he? The plague of all plagues. Cyrus The Virus. Dementor of the Year…'

'Yes, but I'm okay, Stan. Let's talk about something else. I just want to clear away the last remnants of him.'

'Okay. That's good. Well, let's see now. What's been happening around here. Well, Mrs Silk has bought another puppy, so her dog walker will be pleased. That's four she has now. Mrs Rogers bought me a giant bar of Dairy Milk. So, look forward to sharing some of that with you later on. Jake Reynolds keeps looking at me like he's going to say something every time he comes and goes, but he never does. I don't know what's up with him. You're due back at his place tomorrow morning.'

I know.

9

Jake

It was Thursday, just before nine in the morning, and Jake was standing behind his front door listening out for the lift door to open. He had no idea if Anna really would return to clean his already clean apartment after the strange day they had shared on Monday.

I don't think she's coming. Why would she come back? My shower attacked her. She had to strip off and wear my dressing gown, and then I pretty much insulted her dog by pointing out how much he smelled. No, she's definitely not coming back. I hope she does come back. She has to come back. Please, come back, Anna. Why am I stressing so much over this?

His eyes were wide and his mouth slightly open as though that would enhance his hearing. He glanced over at the kitchen sink. The crockery waiting to be washed up had been annoying him all night and all morning, but he wanted to leave Anna something to do, if she did show. His eyes flickered over to the dishwasher.

Breathe, Jake.

He thought he heard a door close, and it definitely didn't sound like the lift. He jumped back when a thud hit his front door. He counted to five using his fingers and then opened the door widely.

Anna smiled warmly, and Max ran straight inside.

Jake's eyes followed the dog.

'Morning,' she sang out.

He closed the door as she entered. 'Yes, good morning, Anna.' He could see Max sniffing the floor. 'Has he been to the toilet yet?'

She glanced over her shoulder. 'Yes, he's probably just smelling you.'

He waited until she turned to the kitchen, then warily sniffed his armpit. 'Do I smell?'

Anna turned quickly and smiled. 'You smell lovely.'

They both froze into a state of awkwardness.

She quickly added, 'Max is checking out your scent.'

He silently watched her head straight for the sink. Not knowing what to say next, he opted for some small talk. 'Did you walk up the stairs?'

'We used the lift.' Her soft voice carried over her shoulder.

I know that you didn't. Why are you lying?

He frowned with curiosity, then looked over at his laptop on the table. 'I'm just going to get on with some work.'

The water from the kitchen tap filled the silence between them for a moment.

Max trotted over as soon as Jake sat down, flopping his head upon Jake's lap. Jake raised his hands and stared down at the dog, who seemed quite content to be there. He tentatively lowered one hand and patted Max on the head.

'Hello,' he mumbled. He then looked over at Anna. 'The bed needs making as well, just so you know, when you're done, that is. I'm sure you'll see for yourself, anyway…'

Stop talking.

He stared towards the screen on his laptop to see the files Mike had sent him. He needed to distract himself from the woman at his sink, the dog on his lap, and the unmade bed in his bedroom, which had been another thing bugging him all morning.

He tried to work, but it was no good. The minutes on the clock had ticked by, and all he had done was stare blankly at his dulled screen. He just couldn't concentrate, even when Anna was in his bedroom. Especially with Anna in his bedroom, touching his bed, his sheets, his pillow.

I should go and talk to her. No, I shouldn't. I should let her get on with her work. I have work to do too. What could I talk about? The weather, dogs, what about Christmas? Everyone talks about Christmas as it approaches. It'll be here next month. Oh God, it's going to be Christmas soon. I don't want to talk about it. I don't want to think about it. I'll probably be on my own this year. Oh God, don't cry. Get a grip. I should go to Pepper Bay. Spend Christmas there, even if I am on my own, at least I'll feel better there. I wonder what Anna is doing for Christmas. She might be in my bedroom right now thinking about it too. I wonder what it feels like to live with a woman. If she was my partner, that would be her room as well, and her bed. I would be sharing that bed with her every night.

Jake had never woken up with a woman in his bed before. He never invited any of his dates over to his home. He preferred to go to theirs and leave before morning. He didn't like complications or women hanging off his arm, thinking he belonged to them.

He never felt attached to anyone other than his family. He sometimes wondered if he actually had the ability to feel more towards a woman other than a moment of lust. The women in his rich circle always seemed happy enough to get a night of lust from him, not so happy when they couldn't get their hands on his wallet.

At times, he felt unlovable, or a golden ticket to someone else's dreams. He assumed that all women would only ever want the status symbol and not the man.

The boring conversations he had endured about materialistic matters had been washed away by copious amounts of whisky or gin. He never felt a comfortable fit in amongst his privileged friends.

He'd had a recurring dream one year about someone pointing at him and shouting *fraud* and *fake* from across a crowded nightclub. He would wake covered in sweat and hung over.

The woman in his home felt like a breath of fresh air. She obviously didn't care too much about clothes, judging by her relaxed appearance, and she made him feel awkward but comfortable, which intrigued him. She hung out with a building manager and a dog, and she seemed happy enough.

Anna was in his bedroom, and not for the first time. He thought about her standing in that room just three days before, wearing his dressing gown and drying her hair as though she lived there. It hadn't bothered him in the slightest. Even the faint smell of apple that he had inhaled that night when he put on his dressing gown had made him smile.

If Josh ever borrowed his clothes, he would make sure he washed them straight away, but he hadn't wanted to put the dressing gown into the washing machine. He didn't want to lose her scent. It had kept him company all night as though she were sitting by his side. He knew it was a strange feeling to have, somewhere up there with drunk logic, but he just left it alone. He had been intrigued that his mind played over Monday's scenario and brought questions simmering well into his night. He wasn't as settled during the two days she wasn't around. He had stopped himself from finding out where her bookshop was and popping in on the off chance.

Jake took a deep breath and looked down at Max's big head putting fur on his black trousers.

I knew I shouldn't have put these on.

Max snuggled closer to Jake's hip, and Jake smiled and patted his head.

'You know, I actually bought something for you. Not sure if you'll be interested but...'

Max lifted his head and followed him over to a kitchen drawer, wagging his tail as a small cuddly toy came into view.

Jake rolled his eyes towards the Kermit the Frog toy he was holding. 'This was all I could find at short notice. I know it's not a diamond collar, and believe me, I've seen dogs wearing them, but I thought perhaps you could snuggle with it, or chew it. I really don't mind. It's yours. You have complete control.' He handed over the toy. 'His name is Kermit.'

Max sniffed Kermit, nudged the toy with his nose, and then gently opened his mouth and took it away.

Jake smiled, feeling pretty pleased with himself. He watched Max look for a comfy position and could see that there wasn't one on his hard floors. There weren't any sun spots either, and there wouldn't be anytime soon, not now it had started to rain.

He needs a bed.

Max snuggled down with Kermit, and Jake squatted to stroke the dog's golden coat.

'It's much nicer to have someone to snuggle with than have diamonds, eh, boy?' he whispered.

Max immediately fell asleep, much to Jake's surprise.

Anna walked towards him, making him jump slightly. She noticed Max's new friend. 'Oh, you've bought him a toy. Thank you so much. Looks like he loves it.' She glanced over at the window to see the rain.

Jake stood up and noticed her shoulders slump.

She looks like she needs a hug. Why do I suddenly want to offer one? I'm not a hugger. I don't want to hug. I would hug her, if she asked for one. Do you want a hug, Anna? Do you want to ask me for one? You can. I won't mind. Oh God, it's all I can do to stop myself from hugging her. I need to do something with my arms before they grab her without my permission. Behind my back. Yes, that's perfect. Now, say something to make her stay.

He jolted, making a sudden decision. 'Would you like a cup of tea?'

She shook her head. 'No, thank you. I'm going to give the spare rooms a dust.'

'Wait.'

She glanced back at him.

I don't know what to say. Oh crap! Why did I say wait? What is wrong with me?

'I just wanted to check if everything was all right.'

Yes, perfect. I managed some words.

'Yes, all sorted. Almost finished.'

'I meant with you.'

I shouldn't pry.

Her head lowered a touch. 'I'm fine.'

Fine, the small word that holds the biggest lie. You don't look fine at all. You look sad. I know it has nothing to do with me. I've been on my best behaviour.

Anna walked away, so he went back to his laptop. His face now as dreary as the rain.

I wish she would talk to me.

10

Anna

Anna had finished her job at Jake's, then enjoyed the sandwich he had made her for lunch, even though she had no idea what the filling was. Something vegan, maybe. Looked pink. Had a pasty texture. She had felt too embarrassed to ask. He seemed excited by whatever it was. Maybe he had invented it and she was his first taster, or maybe it was just a posh paste in a jar from Fortnum & Mason or somewhere else she didn't shop.

She had told him she would see him again on Monday, thinking that Monday and Thursday could be her work days at his, but he had wanted her to come back the next day and over the weekend. She needed the money, but there was nothing for her to clean, so it felt silly for her to come each day that she wasn't at the bookshop.

Jake had been quite determined about the situation. He offered more money for the weekend shift and almost sounded as if he were pleading at one point.

She was worried that he might be feeling lonely, so she agreed to come on Saturday as well. She didn't have much else to do with her life, and she knew what lonely felt like. At least she would have another person to talk to. Plus, his apartment was warm, and her bones ached so much. She wished she could work for him every day but knew she couldn't because she was supposed to be pretending to work for Mrs Silk on the floor below him. She had a secret to keep. A secret that now felt heavy and unwanted.

She left the building, hating all the lies. It felt wrong and went against her character. There was something weirdly comforting about being around Jake, even though he made her stomach flutter and heart pick up an extra beat. She found herself wanting to spend more time with him. She just knew that she had to be careful, for her sake and Stan's.

Max had worn himself silly on his long walk along the South Bank, and he had made loads of new friends along the way. He especially liked the ones who took the time to tickle his tummy.

Anna was just pleased the rain had held off long enough for their walk. Her head had cleared, and she had stopped analysing the look in Jake's eyes when she had left him sitting at the table. She hadn't been sure how to read him. Was it just her imagination? His unspoken words told her that he needed her to stay, but her logic dismissed that theory. Why would someone like him need her? Why would anyone need her? There wasn't anything she could bring to his life. He had it all. She had stared at him whilst he pitched his extended job offer, but her mind had been elsewhere.

You're so perfect. You're the top table with the raffle prizes. I'm the white elephant stall, filled with useless junk that people just browse over, smile sympathetically at, and walk away from. You don't need me around you constantly. I bet you have loads of people in your life. I bet you attract everyone. You're the window display toy that everyone wants. I'd like to be like you. I'm not even on the shop floor. I'm out the back, down the stairs, in the basement, over in the corner, squashed into the rejects box. You don't know how lucky you are being you. You're not one of the broken toys.

Anna had rebooted herself on her walk and happily made her way back to her rooftop home to enjoy a few chapters of her book whilst Max took a long nap. She ended up joining him for a couple of hours.

* * *

Anna had been invited downstairs to have her dinner with Stan. They were eating noodles out of takeaway cartons that he had ordered and had delivered to River Heights. They didn't normally eat at the reception desk, but the building had been so quiet, Stan assumed everyone was home for the evening, so they wouldn't be disturbed. They sat in the lobby chatting about global warming, which was one of Stan's favourite subjects. Max was sprawled on the floor by the side of the desk, with Kermit at his side.

Outside was cold and dark. The porch lights gave the only warm glow to the grey pavement.

Anna was happy and warm sitting on the small wooden stool that Stan had brought in especially for her. Her stomach was almost full, and the dampness had left her bones alone for a while.

Jake entered the building.

Oh crap!

He stopped in his tracks when he saw them and did a double take at Anna. Her head was just peeping over the top of the desk.

She had a long noodle hanging out of her mouth that she quickly slurped up whilst smiling awkwardly. 'Hello.'

Stan lowered his food, knowing it wasn't a good look for him to be eating out front.

Jake gave a slight nod. 'Hello.'

Max trotted over to greet him, with Kermit hanging out of his mouth.

Jake leaned over to stroke his head before making his way to the lift. He glanced once more over at the reception desk. 'Smells nice.'

Anna felt her cheeks redden.

Max clambered inside the lift, making Jake laugh. 'Sorry, mate.' He gently nudged him out. 'You stay here with Anna.'

She turned to Stan as the lift closed, taking Jake up to his apartment.

Stan slumped backwards in his chair. 'I thought he was going to say something about the food.'

She grinned. 'He did. He said it smelled nice.'

'Yeah,' said Stan, looking worried. 'We should eat out the back from now on.' He reached below his counter and pulled out a can of air freshener and sprayed the air in front of him.

Anna pulled her food away and coughed.

He put the can away and stood up to stretch. 'Anyway, it's knocking-off time, Anna. You can finish that upstairs, and I'll see you in the morning.'

She also stretched as she stood, then made her way over to the lift. 'Okay, but stop bringing me breakfast every morning. Save your money, Stan.'

He waved her comment away. 'Please, kid, it's just a roll or pastry, half the time.'

There was no point saying anything else. Stan could be just as stubborn as her, and he was way too kind for his own good.

The lift finally came back down from Jake's floor, and Stan pointed over at her. 'Remember, get off…'

'The floor below. I know.'

Max entered the lift first.

'Have a good night, Anna.'

'Night, Stan.'

Max looked up at her and the food.

'You've had your dinner, greedy guts. You can have a night-time snack as soon as we get home.'

Home, that's a laugh. Oh well. It is what it is. For now. Oh, back to the cold.

Max rubbed his head against her leg, and she smiled down at him, glad of the distraction. 'What do you fancy, a beef chew or a chicken biscuit?'

The door opened on Mrs Silk's floor, and Anna could hear the old lady's TV blaring. She quickly hurried Max over to the stairwell to make the climb upwards. When they reached the top floor, she listened at the stairwell door before opening it.

All clear.

As she passed by Jake's front door, she wondered what it would be like to be tucked up in his huge bed for the night. How those soft pillows might feel under her head, and how warm and cosy she would feel snuggled beneath the hypoallergenic duvet he had. She knew he would be sleeping right below her tent, because she had worked out the floorplan whilst she was in his bedroom. It had made her laugh to herself. All that time she had no idea who was right beneath her. Even his bed faced the same way as hers.

Some people don't realise how lucky they are to have a bed, a bedroom, a door they can lock.

There was only a camp bed and sleeping bag waiting for her. She took a breath and smiled to herself.

I'm lucky too. Some people aren't as lucky as me. At least I have a tent and the safety of the roof, and for that, I am grateful.

Max sniffed the threshold and then suddenly pawed Jake's door.

Oh flipping heck!

'No, Max,' she whispered, pulling him away whilst spilling some of her noodles on the floor.

She quickly opened the rooftop door, hurried him inside, and quietly closed the door.

Max ran up the stairs, ready for his snack.

Anna froze as she heard Jake's door open. She daren't move up the stairs in case he heard her footsteps. She glanced up, hoping Max didn't come back down.

11

Jake

Jake had been loitering behind his front door, debating whether or not to go back downstairs to talk to Anna. He was agitated about the fact that he was feeling agitated. All he wanted to do was have his planned night, which consisted of him putting on his pyjamas, making a cup of Horlicks, like his grandmother used to do for him, and watching a movie whilst pretending he wasn't sitting alone in an apartment that he felt little attachment to. He didn't want to keep thinking about Anna, but she wouldn't get out of his head. The urge to go downstairs and speak to her was overpowering his night.

He was desperately trying to think of an excuse to go down to her when he heard a scratching noise that seemed to come from the bottom of his door.

What was that?

Taking a step forward, he paused when he heard a door close. His brow tightened as he leaned towards the framework. There weren't any other noises, so he slowly opened his front door.

The small stretch of landing outside was empty.

He walked over to the lift and listened. It wasn't running, so he checked out the stairwell. There weren't any footsteps heading down the stairs.

He raked his hand through his hair as he headed back to his apartment. He stood in his doorway and looked once more at the lift.

I'm hearing things.

He was about to close his door when he suddenly noticed a small splodge of noodles on the grey carpet.

How did that get there? Stan was eating noodles with Anna in the lobby a minute ago.

Walking into his kitchen for a wet wipe, he wondered if Stan had been outside his door for some reason.

He went back outside and quickly cleaned up the mess on the floor. Whilst still in a squat, he glanced over at the door that led to the rooftop.

Maybe Stan was doing some sort of maintenance up there.

He went back inside and closed his door. Something didn't feel right, and whatever it was, it was bugging him.

He threw the wet wipe in the bin and stared over at his front door. Stan often walked around the building doing whatever his job had him do next, but Jake knew that Stan wouldn't walk around eating noodles.

He glanced over at the digital clock on the kitchen side.

He was just eating his dinner, and he wouldn't be doing any work now anyway. It's home time.

Too many questions were simmering in his mind. He had little choice. He was going downstairs to talk to Stan because he couldn't have the mystery of the noodles bug him all night.

The lift seemed to take forever, which only irritated Jake some more. Something wasn't sitting right with him, and he had to figure out what it was.

Finally!

He entered the lift and just as the door was about to close he swore he heard a dog bark. His arm immediately stretched out, forcing the lift door to open. He walked over to the rooftop door and rattled it.

It was locked.

He looked at the panel of buttons to its side. He punched in 1 2 3 4.

The door remained locked.

'Hmm!'

Jake made his way back into the lift and pressed G. As soon as it landed on the ground floor, he went straight over to Stan's desk to see that the building manager had already left for the night. A faint smell of stale food combined with a weak-smelling potpourri lurked in the air, causing him to scrunch his nose. He walked around to the back and checked the staff room door.

It was locked.

He glanced over to the shelf that sat under the counter. He couldn't see much. A can of forest pine air freshener, a box of tissues, a bag of dog biscuits, and yesterday's newspaper.

Sitting down in Stan's chair, Jake rubbed the growing stubble on his chin and huffed. He grabbed the air freshener and gave the lobby a quick spritz. As he put it back, he noticed a drawer. He stared at it for a second.

There's no way that's unlocked.

He gave it a tug, and it opened.

'Bad move, Stan.'

He rummaged through the paperwork and bits and bobs of stationary inside. There wasn't much there of interest. Deflated, he pulled his hand out, catching it on a piece of paper that was stuck to the roof of the drawer.

Jake leaned forward, tilted his head, and carefully peeled off the lime-green sticky note whilst grinning at the four digits written on it in fine black ink.

He placed everything back into its unorganised state and got in the lift.

4681. 4681. 4681.

The lift arrived at his floor, and he went straight to the rooftop door and punched in the numbers.

'4681,' he mumbled.

The door clicked open.

Oh bloody hell, it opened.

'Now what?'

He listened before opening the door fully. He couldn't hear anything, so he peeped around the hefty door to see the set of grey steps leading upwards. Slowly, he made his way up the stairs to the closed door at the top. Placing his hand on the panel, he gave it a gentle shove and felt his heart skip a beat as the door opened.

What are you doing, Jake? And why are you so bloody nervous? Get a grip.

He took a breath and stepped out into the darkness of the rooftop, and the cold air immediately hit his nostrils, causing him to sniff.

The rain had held off, but the ground was still wet. The sound of late-shift workers heading home down in the street below was mixed with the smell of damp night-time air.

Jake wished he had brought a coat and a torch. He quickly patted his pocket for his phone, but he dropped his shoulders when he remembered that he had left it on the table. He took a step forward into the dark November night. All he could see was an empty rooftop.

This is stupid.

Suddenly, a flicker of light caught his eye. It was coming from the far end of the roof, behind one of the big blocks that he could barely make out.

He tried his hardest to keep quiet as he tentatively made his way towards the light. His heart was in his throat, and he was struggling with trying to breathe normally.

Out of the darkness, a hefty weight suddenly hit him straight in the thighs.

'Oof!'

What the…

He almost had a heart attack and quickly composed himself when he saw it was just Max, but his heart hadn't got the memo and was still galloping off towards the moon.

Anna's pale face appeared around the corner of the block. Her ghostly appearance caused a second wave of adrenaline to rush through him. Her eyes were filled with just as much fear.

'Jake?'

'Anna?'

What the hell are you doing on the roof?

She took a step forward, and he could see her better. The dull light was glowing behind her back.

'What are you doing here, Jake?'

He heard the wobble in her tone and could see the worry in her expression.

'Sorry,' he managed through a shaky exhale. 'I didn't mean to startle you. Max scared me half to death.'

Max ran behind Anna, moving Jake's eyes that way.

Anna half-glanced over her shoulder and then looked back at Jake.

He stepped forward and stopped moving when he saw her step back.

Shit! Is she scared of me?

He raised his palms towards her. 'Anna, it's okay. I just want to know what you're doing up here. Is Stan with you?'

She shook her head, and he lowered his arms. Concern washed across his face. 'Anna, what's going on?' He watched her lower her head slightly and, even in the darkness, he could see her face flush. She wrapped her arms around herself as a waft of wind caused her to shiver. He immediately took off his grey cardigan and waved it over at her. 'Anna, you're cold. Here.'

She didn't take it. Instead, she turned away and disappeared into the light behind the block.

Jake hesitated before following her. Cautiously looking around, his bright eyes widened as he came face to face with the campsite.

Christ! She's living here.

Anna gestured towards the picnic table outside the tent. 'I would offer you a seat, but it's still a bit wet.' She pointed inside the opened flap in the middle of the tent. 'You can sit on the cushion in there, if you like.'

He felt his heart sink at her home and her broken voice. He rolled back the tears he felt appear in his eyes before stepping fully into the dim light of her battery-operated lantern.

12

Anna

Oh God, I want to die.
    Anna entered the tent and sat next to Max and waited to see if Jake would join them.
    He bowed his head to enter and lowered himself to the cushion on the ground opposite her.
    She watched his eyes darting around her home. She had to say something. 'It's just temporary.'
    Jake's throat gave away his hard swallow. 'How did you end up here?'
    Anna felt lightheaded. She wanted to cry, so she tensed her brow in an attempt to stop that from happening. 'My ex threw me out when he moved his new girlfriend in. It was his house, so there wasn't much I could do. He wouldn't let me sleep in our bookshop, so Stan came up with this idea. It's just till I save enough money for a flat. A deposit.' She cleared the dryness from the back of her throat, as there was hardly any moisture left in her mouth.
    Jake's chest lifted and fell slowly as he adjusted his body slightly and looked down at Max. 'How long have you been here?'
    'Just a few weeks. I was staying at the shop before. Well, as I just said, Rob found out and kicked me out of there too.'
    Jake's lips tightened. 'He sounds lovely.'
    She attempted a smile, but it was weak, and glanced over at her tin kettle. 'Would you like some tea?'
    Oh, Anna, shut up!

Jake followed her eyes and gave a slight shake of the head.

She shivered again, and this time she had little choice. He wrapped his cardigan around her shoulders before she had a chance to say no.

'Thank you. I do have a coat,' she said quietly, glancing over her shoulder at the bedroom section of the tent.

Jake's face softened. His eyes were filled with compassion as he gave her a gentle smile, making her heart warm. She snuggled further into the fresh smell of his light-grey cashmere cardigan.

'Have you eaten?' he asked.

'Yes. Stan bought me noodles.'

He nodded. 'Ah, yes, the noodles.'

She looked down at Max. 'He's just had a chicken biscuit. For a snack, not dinner. He's had dinner. I make sure he eats.'

Jake arched an eyebrow in amusement. 'Good to know.'

'Jake, I... I don't know what to say to you.' She paused. 'Please don't tell anyone. I'll have to leave, and I've nowhere to go just yet, and Stan will lose his job, and he doesn't deserve that. He was just trying to help me, and...'

His hand was suddenly resting on hers, silencing her immediately. 'It's all right, Anna. I'm not going to tell anyone.'

The light touch filled her stomach with a hundred butterflies, but her head was trying to focus on more important matters. 'Really?'

He nodded. 'Really.' His voice was soft and low.

She felt his fingers gently close around her hand, making it clear he wasn't about to let go of her. She didn't mind. She liked his hand holding hers. It was warm and soft and caring.

His firm tone surfaced. 'But you can't stay up here, Anna.'

Her body slumped. She felt so lost and alone, and now he was going to make her leave. 'Please, Jake, let me stay.'

'Anna, it's November. You can't spend winter up here. You'll freeze.'

She shook her head. 'Not true. People survive in the cold in tents all the time.'

He let go of her hand and sat back. 'I'll take your word for it, for now. Can't say I've ever been camping, so I'm not sure how warm it can be.'

Anna stared over at his hand. She missed it already. She snuggled hers beneath her legs and turned her attention to Max.

'It can be quite cosy,' she said softly.

Oh, who am I trying to convince?

Jake raised his eyebrows. 'Yeah, maybe now, but what about if it snows?'

She looked dreamily up at the sky outside of the tent and smiled.

Jake was not smiling at all. 'There's nothing pretty about snow when you're stuck in it, Anna.'

Her blue eyes rolled over to him. 'You have to admit, it is a little bit nice up here.' She pointed outside. 'You can see all the stars. Look.'

He looked up at the dark sky where three stars were playing peek-a-boo with a broken cloud. 'The stars up here once saved my life, Anna. I know what it feels like to be afraid and alone. To feel as though life has abandoned you altogether. I know how lost you must feel.'

She could almost feel the pain she could see in his sad eyes. 'How did the stars save your life?'

He looked outside, clearly avoiding her eyes. He nodded at the wall opposite them. 'The door downstairs was open. I came up here and climbed up on that wall. I didn't really know what I was doing. I felt so numb. It was a few days after I had returned here from my grandmother's funeral. I was so alone, even though I wasn't. I still had my brother and grandfather, but they didn't seem to count. Standing on that wall made everything simple. All I had to do was take one step and I would never feel again.'

Without thinking, she reached over and held his hand, wanting to do so much more. He needed to feel cared for, and she wanted to hold him until he did. 'Not many talk about suicide so openly.'

'I was one of those people once, but now I know that we have to speak openly about it. If we don't, the stigma remains, and what good is that to anyone.'

'I do get rundown sometimes, but I've never been suicidal. I try hard every day to think of anything positive so that I don't dwell on what's happened in my life. It's so easy to dwell. I'm currently in healing mode. That's what I call it.'

He nodded slowly. 'Healing mode sounds good. I got some therapy and that really helped me. I still have my ups and downs, like anyone, but I've never wanted to take my own life again. It was just that one time.'

Anna felt deflated as he slipped his hand away from her hold.

'I looked up to the stars, and I heard her voice. I didn't know if it was just my imagination or she was actually talking to me, but my gran spoke, and I listened.'

'What did she say?'

The corners of his mouth curled upwards. 'Well, she wasn't impressed. Basically, she told me to get down and that I was needed here. She said I had to help people. I guessed she meant my brother. She told me to sort my life out. To stop being so flaky and start being a responsible adult.'

Anna couldn't help smiling warmly at him. 'I like your gran. Sounds like a straight talker.'

He raised his brow as his smile widened. 'She was.'

She watched his eyes peer back up at the sky.

'My Gran's childhood home in Pepper Bay is just up a hill heading towards a clifftop, and when night falls, you can see a million stars.' He glanced over at her. 'I guess that's why someone decided to call it Starlight Cottage. That's why the stars up here that night helped save me. I stopped and just stared at them for a while before I heard my gran.'

Anna tried to imagine the house on the hill. 'Starlight Cottage sounds like somewhere special.'

He nodded. 'Yeah, it is.'

'I'd like to live somewhere like that one day. A cottage in the sky. How magical.'

Jake's facial expression effortlessly moved from warm to serious. 'Why don't you?'

What?

She frowned at the sparkle in his eyes.

'No one's living there, Anna. You could stay there until you find your feet.'

Is he serious?

She almost laughed. 'Are you serious?'

Jake nodded. 'It's perfect. I could take you there right now. There's heating, electricity. It's been renovated over the years, so it has a lot of mod cons. Not your average cottage on the Isle of Wight.'

'You want me to move to the Isle of Wight?'

He appeared to reel in his excitement. He lowered his voice and softened his body language. 'Pepper Bay is beautiful, Anna. I think you'll love it there.'

I think I would too, but flipping heck, the Isle of Wight!

She removed her hands from beneath her legs and started to twiddle her fingers. 'It's just... well, I've never done anything on a whim before, and... well, what would I do there?'

He looked deep in thought as she leaned closer to him. 'What about my shop, Jake?'

He scoffed. 'Tell him he can stuff it. I've got a good mind to buy the whole street just so I can kick him out. See how he likes it. I'll...'

She placed her hand on his knee, and he stopped talking immediately. 'Don't let Rob wind you up as well. I have enough of Stan hating on him.'

Oh, ruddy heck, I'm touching his leg. Hold his hand not his leg.

She swiftly pulled her hand away, and Jake leaned forward. 'Look, Anna, obviously, you're independent, but you don't need that measly twenty percent of that shop.'

Yeah, okay, Daddy Warbucks. Not everyone is as rich as you.

'It might be measly to you, but that's all I have.'

He held a hopeful smile. 'Please, Anna. I'm not trying to offend you. I just want to help.'

Avoiding meeting his eyes, she quietly said, 'I know. Your offer sounds like a dream come true, but if I move away, I'll have no income, so how will I save for my own place?' She looked up through her lashes to see his mouth twist to one side. His leg bounced for a few seconds before he went back to sitting still with no readable expression.

'What if I found you a job in Pepper Bay?'

Really?
'Doing what?'
Jake shrugged. 'Not sure yet, but we can go and see what's available.'
You've clearly never job hunted before.
She muffled a laugh. 'You make it sound so simple.'
His bright eyes looked deadly serious as he adjusted his position to stretch out his long legs. 'It is simple. I can fly you there right now. You can stay a few days, check out the area, see what's what, and if you don't like it, I'll bring you back here. I need to go there myself anyway.'
Anna felt her mouth lift. 'Fly me there?'
He smiled. 'Yeah, it's a lot quicker.'
She started to stroke Max.
'Max can come too,' he added.
Say yes, Anna. Do something crazy.
'I don't know,' she mumbled.
Jake leaned forward to join in with the stroking of Max. His hand brushed against hers, and she was sure that he did that on purpose. He stopped moving his fingers. 'I think you do know, Anna.'
She daren't look at him for fear of falling into his dreamy eyes. She knew she was already smitten. All she had thought about since meeting him was his almond milk shampoo smell, captivating eyes, and what his lips would feel like pressed against hers. 'I'm tempted.'
'Be brave, Anna.' His soft but dominant voice seemed to float right through her.
She raised her eyes to see that his were waiting for her. Her heartbeat accelerated. 'Well, my next shift in the bookshop isn't till Tuesday, so if…'
'You want to leave now?'

She shook her head. 'I need to tell Stan. Could we go in the morning instead?'

Jake smiled. He seemed satisfied. 'Sure, we can do that.'

Anna felt her heart lift. Her head was whirling from her decision, and she was struggling to believe the words that were coming out of her mouth. Everything inside her was telling her to take the chance. It was crazy and wild, and so not like her, but Jake's confidence was seeping into her, breathing new air into her lungs. She really could go. She really could try something new and exciting. She wiggled her hand towards the rooftop. 'You go home now, and I'll see you in the morning. I think an early night is due for the both of us.'

Jake breathed out a huff of a laugh. 'Yeah, right! If you think for one moment that I'm going to leave you up here alone, you've got another thing coming.'

Anna raised her eyebrows at his gallant manner. 'I live here, Jake. I'm okay.'

'Sorry, Anna, but either you pack up your things and stay downstairs with me tonight, or I'm sleeping right here.' He slapped his hand down on the floor, making Max jump.

She stared blankly at him.

Is that right?

Jake cleared his throat and swallowed hard. 'I mean, I have spare bedrooms. All with locks too. Much warmer and safer than up here.'

She watched his eyes idly wander around her tent.

'Your choice,' he whispered.

13

Jake

'Oh my God, how do people find camping fun? My back aches, my knees feel cramped, and I still feel cold,' said Jake, getting out of a dark, chauffeur-driven car. 'I can honestly say that I have never in my life been so thankful for my shower this morning.'

Anna giggled as her feet touched the runway of the small airfield they had arrived at. 'No one made you sleep in my tent.'

Jake raised his brow in amusement. 'I beg to differ.'

Anna went to speak but stopped when a man started waving over to them from a nearby helicopter.

'That's Frank. He's our pilot for today,' said Jake, sounding quite casual about the fact. He glanced sideways at her and smiled to himself.

Are you impressed, Anna? Of course you are.

Her eyes were wide, and her body stiff. 'Are we going in that?'

'Normally, I'd fly myself, but my helicopter is too small for the three of us.' He saw her mouth drop open a touch. He smiled and nudged her arm. 'Come on.'

Frank secured Max into a harness whilst Anna nervously watched.

'Your turn,' said Jake, guiding her into the helicopter. He felt her body tighten as he strapped her in. 'It's okay. We won't be in here for long. About half an hour.'

Anna's eyes were on Frank, who was sitting up front.

Jake doublechecked her seatbelt before fastening his own. He handed her a headset and watched in surprise as she immediately placed it over Max's ears.

Max had no qualms about wearing it. He sat up straight, peering out of the window.

You actually look quite cool, Max.

He tried to hide his grin as he handed her another pair. His hands hovered around her head as she adjusted it. Once he was satisfied that she had it on correctly, he lowered his arms.

Anna gave him a big smile before turning to hold on to Max as the helicopter started up and made its way into the hazy sky. Jake tightened his grip on her hand as it suddenly shot his way, and she didn't let go until they landed on the Isle of Wight.

A wide stretch of barely green grass topped the clifftop of Pepper Bay, and a worn, beaten track led down the hillside, away from the dark swirls of the sea below.

Anna looked around them. 'Are we allowed to park here?'

Jake grinned.

She tried to take her small amount of luggage from him, but he held on to her cabin case tightly, along with his own.

He watched her eyes light up as she stared out to sea whilst the helicopter blades faded into the distance, replaced by the cry of seagulls hovering up above.

Immediately, a warmth filled Jake from head to toe as the salty air landed on his lips. All of his best memories were in Pepper Bay, Starlight Cottage, and Edith's Tearoom. He felt so pleased to be back.

A grey stone cottage with a brown slate roof perched in the near distance. Its renovated add-ons either side elongated the once small house built for a family of four.

Home.

Anna gasped in awe. 'If only I was a writer. The stories I could write about this clifftop alone.' She glanced down at Max, who was running around in circles on the grass. 'Something magical. Horses, carriages, windswept cloaks.'

Jake smiled to himself. 'This way.' He nodded downhill. 'That's Starlight Cottage.' He watched her eyes almost sparkle.

'I wasn't expecting it to be so big.'

Jake stopped on the pathway to take in the view of his grandmother's childhood home.

Hey, Gran.

'How many bedrooms does it have?' asked Anna, taking a step down the path.

Jake followed her down. 'Six. The part in the middle is the original cottage. It has three, but after Gran's parents died, Gramps had the place renovated to make more money on the sale. The two sides were added, and there's an extension around the back, plus a cabin, a double garage, and an indoor swimming pool that has a sliding roof.'

'Wow! It's absolutely stunning.'

'Yeah. Once it was ready to sell, Gran refused. She just couldn't do it, so it's stayed with us. We used to come here every summer, growing up. I think I might have already mentioned that.'

A crack in the clouds allowed a small amount of winter sun to wash over the large stone walls of the cottage.

'If I lived here, I'd never move,' said Anna, picking up speed.

'You've not seen inside yet.'

She glanced over her shoulder and gave him a dreamy look. 'I don't need to. I'd happily pitch my tent right here on the side of this pathway.'

Jake nodded.

I believe you.

'Well, I'm glad you like it.'

Max ran ahead and stopped at the gate. His tongue was flopped out, and he was panting through a smiley mouth.

Jake approached and unlatched the pale-blue, rustic gate.

Anna read aloud the embedded name on the top plank. 'Starlight Cottage.' She smiled warmly up at him. 'That's an adorable sign.'

He smiled back and led the way down the pathway made of stepping stones.

Anna looked along the grassy verge as she followed him.

Flowers, once in bloom, lined the edges, waiting to be cut back, uprooted, cared for.

She stared at the square frosted window sitting in the top end of the light-oak front door.

Jake smiled as he opened the door. 'Welcome to my home.' He held one arm open towards her.

She stepped inside. 'Don't you call London home?'

He found his face close to the back of her head as he closed the door and swiftly turned to the small hallway. He didn't realise she had stopped there. He quickly tapped a code into his phone that disarmed the security alarm as the faint scent of apple shampoo made his heart flutter. He swallowed hard and cleared his throat as he manoeuvred around her.

'This is the only place that has ever felt like home,' he said quietly.

'I can see why,' she mumbled.

Cool air filled the bright hallway as though someone had left the door open all day.

The oak country kitchen, through an archway to their left, gave a sense of warmth and cosiness, from its lemon gingham window dressing to its large cream range cooker. The brown stone floor was lined with only one beige rug that sat below a white butler sink, which was deeply rooted within an oak worktop. A cream Welsh dresser, filled with Wedgewood crockery and Waterford Crystal, lined the wall behind a six-seater solid oak table. Modern spotlights were embedded into the perfectly plastered ceiling above.

An opened door revealed a walk-in larder filled with white wicker baskets on every shelf, waiting to be filled with food items. A spice rack with only five out-of-date dried herbs looked lonely in amongst tall, empty, glass jars with pine lids that held labels to indicate which ingredient went there. A faint smell of damp wood lurked in the air.

Jake placed the luggage down and opened a barn-like door in the hallway to reveal a cloakroom hoarding outerwear for the body and feet. He took off his boots and placed them inside, which encouraged Anna to do the same. He tossed her over a pair of his black slippers, wafting a smell of dusty material in her direction.

She picked them up and held them close to her chest as she gazed to her right at the opened double doors that led to the living room.

Jake followed her eyes. 'Have a look. I'm going to get rid of all the dustcovers and switch the fridge and boiler on.'

The room was cosy, even without its stone open fireplace alive and burning.

Jake carefully unfolded a dustcover to reveal a long caramel sofa that backed away from the window to face a dark-oak coffee table and a brown rug that was sprawled out in front of the fireplace. High above the log fireplace, pinned to the wall, was a 55-inch TV.

A tall dark bookcase stood at the side of the room, proudly displaying an array of classics in amongst its collection, including a couple of first editions. A tall vintage lamp took up the darkest corner of the room, alongside a small cast-iron table topped with a cream floral vase and a black 1930s telephone. Dark polished wooden flooring followed through to the hallway.

Jake nodded towards the staircase. 'You can choose whichever bedroom you want. I don't mind.'

Anna made her way over to the stairs and then stopped on the bottom step. Her socks sank into the soft beige carpet. 'I wouldn't want to pick your grandparents' room. It wouldn't feel right.'

He smiled at the pawprint pattern on her socks. 'Their room is the first on the right.'

'Which one is yours?'

If you want to be in my room, just say. She doesn't want to be in your room, Jake. Shut up.

He could see that she didn't want to make any wrong moves, but he wanted her to feel just as comfortable in Starlight Cottage as he was.

'Don't worry about that. Pitch your tent wherever you want.'

She placed the slippers on her feet and went to sprint up the stairs but stopped again. 'Is Max allowed upstairs?'

Jake nodded. 'Yeah, he can go where he wants to.' He looked over at the living room again to see Max curled up by the fireplace. 'But I think he's already found his spot. I'll light the fire later on. He'll like that.'

Anna's face beamed. 'I'll like that too.'

Jake felt his body warm.

So will I.

'Once we sort this place out, I'll take you into town to pick up some groceries.'

He watched her falter on the stairs again. 'Thank you, Jake, for bringing me here.'

Her broken voice made his heart melt. He wanted to run up the steps and hold her, but he gave her a warm smile instead. 'You're welcome, Anna.'

14

Anna

The bedroom was light with hints of duck-egg blue, white, and light oak. The view from the square window overlooked a large field that sloped downwards towards a farm.

Anna smiled at the cows she could see mooching around in a green pasture in the distance. She turned towards the double bed and noticed a picture on the dresser to its side.

A man and a heavily pregnant women, mid-thirties, were smiling for the camera on their wedding day. The lady had Jake's smile and dark hair, and the man had Jake's bright azure-blue eyes, jawline, and height.

His parents.

Anna's eyes glossed over. She looked away to scan the rest of the room. It was neat and tidy and didn't look very much lived in. She poked her head around a doorway to see a small bathroom. Its contemporary cream tiled walls, chrome fixtures, and sleek shower cubicle screamed Jake Reynolds. Her eyes rolled to the dustcover on the bed.

He'll be sleeping there tonight. I wonder what he would do if I sneaked in during the night and snuggled up to him? Oh, why can't I have the guts to do something like that? I bet his old girlfriends did stuff like that. Would he reject me? He's brought me here, maybe he does want me. Maybe he is just being kind because he saw me on the roof and felt sorry for me. I hope he does like me. I really want him to like me. Flipping heck! What has this man done to me already?

She quietly left his room to look inside the room next door. It held the same view, a similar bed, but felt warmer, thanks to the autumnal array of colours and dark-wood furniture.

'You like this room?' asked Jake, appearing in the doorway.

Anna jumped slightly. Her body tingled with nerves, which immediately annoyed her. She smiled over at him. 'It feels cosy.' She turned to face the window. 'And I love this view.'

He joined her side, making her even more nervous. His body was so close to hers, all she had to do was lean a little to her right and their arms would be touching.

'That's Pepper Pot Farm. It's a dairy farm. Owned by the Walkers. Joey Walker works in my gran's tea shop. She pretty much runs the place. That shop would be lost without her, and her baking skills. I'll take you there once we've done our shopping. I kind of get the feeling you are going to love Pepper Lane.'

Anna kept her voice light and steady. 'Is that where Edith's Tearoom is?'

Jake's eyes brightened as he nodded. He quickly moved away, much to her disappointment, and whipped off the dust cover that was covering the clean sheets on the bed, then made his way outside.

Anna grinned at the bold yellow bedding.

This definitely isn't Jake's room.

She sat on the floor and unzipped the cabin case that Jake had given her for the trip.

When she had arrived in his apartment that morning holding a black bin bag containing her small number of belongings, she didn't have much of an argument when he had offered the use of his case.

She stared down at the cream silky lining, then over at her faded-red washbag. She hardly had anything to unpack.

Stan had told her not to worry about her things when she told him about her trip. He would keep an eye on her makeshift home whilst she was gone.

Without his advice and encouragement, she would have changed her mind about going off with Jake. It was all well and good making those whimsical, night-time decisions, but when the light of day hit, and she could hear Jake and Max fumbling about in the next compartment of her tent, she'd had a bit of a wobble and decided to stay put.

'Have an adventure, Anna,' Stan had told her. 'It's only a few days. Plus, I know everything about the people who live at River Heights, and he might be the rich playboy type, but he doesn't have a criminal record, or any negative reports about him. Just keep him out of your bedroom. You'll be all right.'

Anna had blushed and averted her eyes.

She glanced over at the window.

Oh, Stan, what am I doing here? I'm not sure this was the right move. I'm living in dreamland. All I keep thinking about is Playboy Jake and how much I want to kiss him. That's not normal. I haven't known him five minutes. I wouldn't mind, every time those dominant eyes flash my way, my cookie crumbles. Like I've got the nerve to kiss him! I feel like such an idiot. I still want to snog him senseless though.

Jake's arm stretched into the room to toss his navy dressing gown onto the bed.

'I brought this, as I thought you might need it here,' he said, walking away.

Anna's eyes lingered on the nightwear. Her stomach flipped at the thought of once more being able to snuggle into his scent.

There was something about Jake Reynolds that she had never experienced with another man before. She felt as though she had known him a lot longer than she actually did, and there was a certain level of calmness and warmth that embraced her every time she was in his presence.

She had never questioned herself about anything to do with Rob, except for the part where she would ask herself daily why she was with him.

Jake seemed familiar, and it unnerved her slightly. The only other time she had felt immediately connected to a stranger was when she met Stan's wife, Marsha.

Marsha had become her best friend on the first day she started work in the bookshop. She had helped Anna to find her smile each day for two years.

Anna had always considered Marsha and Stan her substitute parents.

She smiled warmly at the photograph that she pulled out from her luggage. She had carefully tucked it between a white tee-shirt and plum jumper.

Stan had taken the selfie of himself with Anna and Marsha standing behind the counter at the bookshop on Marsha's second day of work.

Anna swallowed the lump in her throat and rolled back the tears that tried to appear. She didn't want to feel sad when she thought of Marsha. Those memories were precious. She wanted to celebrate them.

Marsha's deep brown eyes gleamed up at Anna. Her cheery face lifting the mood even through an old photo.

I miss you.

She leaned over to the bedside cabinet and placed the picture in front of the orange lamp that was sitting on top. 'There you go, Marsha. Pride of place.' She stood and put away the rest of her things and headed back downstairs to see what Jake and Max were up to.

Max was stretched out upon the brown rug in front of the open fireplace in the living room. His legs were in the air, and his happy face was turned sideways towards the arched doorway. Jake was sitting at the dog's side, rubbing his tummy and talking to Max as though he were talking to a baby.

He doesn't look anything like a playboy. He looks lovely. Perfect. If people really do swoon over other people, then I reckon I'd be up for a big swoon right about now. Do people actually swoon over other people? Someone must have once, else the word swoon wouldn't exist. There was probably a lot of open swooning going on in the old days. I'm definitely not doing an open swoon, but I can live with a secret swoon. Look at him. He is so swoon-worthy.

Anna needed to get her mind off the word *swoon*. She looked at Max and shook her head.

Big goof.

She didn't want to interrupt the bonding pair, but Jake must have sensed her presence.

He turned to face her, and she smiled sweetly. 'I'm ready to venture outside whenever you two are.'

A wave of embarrassment washed over his face, and Anna thought it made him look even more adorable.

He stood up quickly and made his way over to the cloakroom just behind her in the hallway. He started rustling around inside. 'You need a warmer coat than that.'

She glanced down at her black fleece jacket. She always found it quite cosy.

Arms appeared around her shoulders as he placed a hefty grey coat over her back. 'This was Gran's. She was about your size.'

She slipped into the coat and stroked the wool blend fabric. A faded-yellow checked scarf was draped around her neck, and a matching hat was plonked onto her head.

Jake walked around to the front of her and wrapped the scarf up so that it snuggled beneath her chin. He adjusted her hat and tucked away her loose hair. 'There. That's better. You'll be much warmer.'

She raised her eyebrows at the look of satisfaction he had wiped across his face.

His eyes rolled down to her feet and lingered for a while. 'Hmm!'

She glanced down.

'We'll have to buy you some new footwear for around here. Boots and wellies are mostly needed, especially in winter.' He turned back to the cloakroom. 'What size are you?'

I like my trainers, thank you very much. They're comfortable.

'Five.'

He looked over at her. 'Got nothing in here your size. We'll get something in town.'

'I don't have money to spend on footwear. I'm saving up.'

Jake seemed to be avoiding eye contact. He pulled on matted black boots and a long dark jacket that suited his shape. He flung a deep-red scarf around his neck and grabbed a car key from a hook inside the cloakroom.

Anna kicked off his slippers and replaced them with her trainers whilst wondering if he was going to say anything at all. She nodded at the key. 'Do you have a car here?'

One corner of his mouth curled slightly, then dropped as he glanced over at Max. He turned back to the cloakroom and grabbed a blue blanket. 'We'll pop to the pet shop as well to get Max a seatbelt.'

Anna was okay with that purchase. She followed him outside and over to the detached double garage that she hadn't noticed before. It was tucked back from the side of the cottage and looked to be the newest part out of the renovations.

Jake pressed a button on his keyring and the doors to the garage lifted open.

Inside were two classic cars that looked best suited to the 1930s, a bright red motorbike with muddy wheels, and an almost-new black SUV, which only looked slightly dusty.

Anna's car knowledge was little to none, but even she could tell how much money was sitting there. She noticed a pale-blue bicycle that had a front wicker basket. It was leaning against the side wall. 'I'm going to guess this bike isn't yours.'

Jake smiled over at it. 'That was Gran's. She used to ride it every day to get to the shop. That was before she moved into the flat above the tearoom. She loved that bike. Gramps had to look after it more than any car he owned.' He laughed, appearing lost in his own memories.

She liked his laugh and how his eyes sparkled. 'I like those old cars. They're so pretty.'

He stopped smiling. 'They should have covers over them.' He walked around the back of the cream car and bent down to the ground. 'I don't know why these have been left on the ground.' He peered up over the car at her. 'Would you mind helping me pull these covers over the cars, please.'

'Sure.' She grabbed one end and tugged the grey cover all the way to the front of the car, then went to help cover the green car. She glanced over at the motorbike. 'I presume we're not going into town on that.'

'That belongs to my brother. Not exactly safe. No, we won't be using that at all during our stay, but if you're still here in the summer, I'll take you out in one of the old cars. We can go for a picnic up at Wishing Point. It's a lovely spot.'

She smiled inwardly at the thought as she watched him approach the big black 4x4. His nose twisted slightly at the vehicle.

'This needs a wash,' he mumbled.

'You know, you should consider becoming a cleaner.'

His bright eyes flashed her way. 'Is that right?'

'You do like everything clean. Just saying.'

He opened the back door and tucked the blanket down into the black leather seat before encouraging Max to settle there whilst Anna clambered into the passenger's seat and put on her seatbelt. She was surprised when he got in and leaned over to check that her belt was secure.

Is he serious?

'I think I know how to fasten a car seatbelt,' she blurted out.

Jake lowered his head slightly. 'Sorry.' He went to start the engine but stopped. He shifted in his seat. 'I, erm, sometimes, I don't realise what I'm doing. I just act. I know I can be a bit funny about certain things. Safety, for instance. I don't mean anything by it, Anna. Just reel me in when I get too much.'

I plan to.

'If I'm honest, I'm not used to anyone making any level of fuss over me,' she said softly.

His face held no expression as he turned to face her. 'My brother says I'm a bit controlling.'

She arched an eyebrow. 'A bit?'

His face softened. 'Maybe he didn't add the words *a bit*.'

Anna felt the need to say the words that had quickly entered her head. 'I wouldn't let anyone control me ever again. Not after everything I went through with Rob.' She could immediately see how remorseful he looked and wondered if her statement was even necessary.

'I don't make a habit of controlling others.' He sounded uptight. 'I just feel better when I have my own life under control, that's all.' He took a breath and his voice relaxed. 'I guess, sometimes, that might rub off on to those around me.'

Silence loomed for a few seconds.

'Don't worry about it,' Anna said, trying to lighten the mood. 'We've only been housemates for five minutes. I'm sure we'll figure each other out soon enough.'

Max's big head was suddenly on Jake's shoulder, and his wet tongue washed across the side of Jake's stunned face.

Anna giggle. 'Max likes to clean too.'

Jake wiped his cheek on his shoulder and then started the car. 'We'll take it slow all the way to the pet shop. First thing's first. Max is getting strapped in.'

Anna turned to her dog and got him to lie down on the blanket. 'I'm looking forward to seeing the rest of Pepper Bay.'

15

Jake

The bottom end of Pepper Lane was a narrow road lined with small quaint shops on both sides and a large pub on the corner at the top end. The shops were an array of pastel colours, and the pavements were lined with empty flowerboxes, freshly cleaned out, as were the windowsills of the flats above each shop. A narrow conduit ran alongside the road, all the way from the top of the shops down to the small stony beachfront at the bottom.

Anna, Jake, and Max stood at the top end, having just parked the car further away, as no cars were allowed down there.

Anna smiled up at the rows of fairy lights that were strung high up from shop to opposite shop.

Jake followed her eyes. 'We can come back tonight for a drink at the pub, and you can see the lights lit up then, if you like.' He smiled as she nodded.

'It's quite small here.'

'Yeah, just the pub and a handful of shops. It's a good tourist spot. Busy in the summer. People from over in the main town, Sandly, jump on the tram to visit here. Gran's tea shop does especially well then.'

He watched her whole face come alive with excitement as she noticed the pastel-green shop closest to them. He grinned to himself as he looked up at the old hand-painted sign above the entrance.

'Look at this shop,' she whispered.

Jake wasn't quite sure if she was talking to herself or him.

'The Book Gallery,' he said. 'Been here forever. Sells books and local artwork.'

Anna gave a slight gasp, obviously thrilled with her find.

He could see that she was bursting to go inside. 'You want to take a look?'

She was already opening the door before he had finished his sentence. She quickly turned back to her dog. 'Stay there, Max.'

Max obediently flopped to the ground, sniffing the fresh, salty air.

There was an elderly lady sitting behind a pine counter beside the door. 'Is that you, Josh?'

Jake smiled warmly at her. 'No, Mrs Blake. I'm Jake.'

Mrs Blake chuckled to herself. 'You boys look so alike, just like your grandfather. Oh dear. I'm so sorry to hear about John.'

Jake gave a slight nod of his head, and his heart warmed as Anna's arm leant against his.

'Mrs Blake, this is Anna. She's staying with me for a while at Starlight Cottage.'

Mrs Blake's beady eyes gave Anna the once over. 'Hello, dear. You're a lucky girl to be staying up there. Beautiful place that is. Not that the other cottages in Pepper Bay aren't beautiful too. Starlight was always my favourite, well, up until John Reynolds came to town and renovated the place.'

Jake tried not to laugh.

Anna looked around. 'I love your shop, Mrs Blake. It feels so cosy, and look at the paintings.' She moved away from Jake's arm.

His eyes dropped to the floor in disappointment, then quickly back up to look over at the painting Anna was pointing at.

Blues and whites swirled into each other, creating a whipped turbulent sea. A small sailboat was trying its best not to capsize.

'I wish I could paint,' said Anna, gazing dreamily at the picture.

'Look at the one at the back of the shop, dear,' said Mrs Blake.

Anna made the short walk to the back and gasped.

Mrs Blake's old shaky voice called out, 'That's what Starlight Cottage looked like before John Reynolds.'

Anna walked back to the counter. 'Do you sell these?'

Mrs Blake nodded. 'Yes, dear. We have some artists over in Sandly who put their pictures in here for the tourists. I make a small profit from each sale.'

'You should make prints and sell them online,' said Anna.

I've been telling her that for years.

Mrs Blake grumbled something that neither Anna nor Jake understood.

'How much is the Starlight Cottage painting?' asked Anna.

Jake stifled a laugh.

She's interested. Good luck.

The hint of softness in Mrs Blake's eyes quickly changed to dark and stormy. 'That one isn't for sale. My late husband painted that. I won't sell his paintings. They have to stay in the shop.'

Jake watched Anna bring the sunshine to the storm with her sweetness and light.

'Surely he would have wanted people to buy his work,' she said. 'It's so wonderful.'

Oh, Anna. Are you trying to manipulate this little old lady?

He looked at Mrs Blake, interested to see if her expression changed at all.

Mrs Blake gave a slight shrug. Her pallid face softened a touch. 'It's not about him. It's about me.'

Anna stepped closer to the counter. 'I understand, Mrs Blake, but if I could paint such beautiful life-like pictures, I would want to show them to everyone.'

Mrs Blake raised a lightly-pencilled eyebrow. 'You would?'

Hmm, what do you know. The storm is passing. Maybe I'll finally get to own that painting. Gran always wanted it hung in her shop.

Anna nodded. 'I'd make printed copies and give them to everyone I know.' Her sunshine faded. 'I don't actually have many friends, so I guess I wouldn't be showing many people after all.'

Anna, what are you doing? You were almost there.

Mrs Blake reached her wrinkly hand forward to touch Anna's arm. 'I'm your friend now. You could always show me.'

And me. Don't forget about me.

Anna smiled warmly. 'Thank you, that's very kind.'

Mrs Blake gave her a slight nod. 'You like books too, do you?'

'I have a bookshop in London.'

Jake watched her suddenly recoil. 'She's looking for a new job though.'

Mrs Blake's eyes widened. 'You don't want to buy this place, do you, dear?'

Both Jake and Anna were taken aback.

'You're selling?' he asked.

Mrs Blake's eyes glossed over. The one splodge of pinkness in her right cheek faded. 'I'm going to live in a retirement village over the other side of the island. My daughter has arranged everything. I've been holding off, but she's determined to put the shop up for sale.' She nodded upwards. 'And my flat upstairs.'

Anna glanced around the shop. 'Oh, I hope the new owners keep the shop just the same.'

Mrs Blake smiled at her. 'So do I, dear, but you know what it's like these days. It'll probably turn into one of those fancy-schmancy coffee shops where you can't even get a normal black coffee.'

Jake kept a straight face. 'How is Dana these days?'

Mrs Blake waved her hand in the air as though waving her daughter away. 'Same as she always is.'

A horrible, selfish, gold-digging brat who just wants your money.

Mrs Blake nodded back at the wall behind her. 'You going to your gran's?'

Jake looked over at Anna, following her eyes around the shop. 'Yes, that's the next stop.'

Mrs Blake glanced out of the window. 'Is that your mutt out there?'

Anna turned to see that Max was being fussed by a young girl. 'Yes. His name is Max.'

Mrs Blake grumbled something and then said, 'Well, next time you come in, don't leave him out there. It's too cold. He's very welcome.' She pointed to the tweedy carpet below the counter. 'He can sit right there.'

Anna smiled. 'Thank you, Mrs Blake.'

'Call me Betty.'

109

Don't think I've ever seen Betty Blake so friendly before. She's really taken to Anna. Hmm!

Jake opened the shop door for Anna.

'Goodbye, Betty,' she said sweetly.

'Bye, dear.'

Jake turned to the old lady, 'Goodbye Bet…'

'Not you,' she snapped.

Jake laughed to himself as he stepped outside.

The young girl looked up from stroking Max. 'You got a dog, Jake?'

He glanced sideways at Anna as she flashed him an enquiring look. 'No, Robyn. Max belongs to Anna.'

Robyn stood up and tightened the scrunchie holding back her long strawberry-blonde hair. 'He's lovely. I wish I had a dog, but Mum won't let me.' She pointed over the road at the white pub with the dark wooden beams. 'I live there with my mum and grandparents. They own the place, and they all say we're too busy for pets, but I'm thirteen now. I can take care of a dog by myself. They won't listen. You can bring Max in whenever you like. Dogs are welcome.'

'Thank you,' said Anna. 'We're coming back tonight to see the lights.' She pointed up. 'So, we'll bring Max in to see you then.'

Robyn's pale-lavender eyes sparkled. 'I'm going to tell Mum.' She flashed a big smile at Jake and giggled. 'And I'll tell her about your new girlfriend too.'

Jake snuggled his face down into his scarf to hide the hint of a smirk that had appeared.

Thanks for that, Robyn.

Anna giggled as Robyn went back to the pub. 'Kids.'

He rolled his eyes over to her, wanting to tell her that he liked her being called his girlfriend. He had never felt so connected to a woman before. He didn't want to rush in the way he did with the women in his past. There was no way he was going to just grab Anna and kiss her without a care in the world. He glanced down at her mouth.

I could.

He pointed over at a pastel-pink shop that had pretty bunting hanging inside its windows. Proudness filled every part of him. 'Edith's Tearoom.'

Anna's face lit up once again as she clutched her hands together in front of her chest. 'Oh, I just love Pepper Lane.'

16

Anna

Joey Walker was pouring coffee into a tall white takeaway cup when she locked eyes with Jake. Her mouth opened and her perfect smile lit up the whole tea shop.

'Jake, I heard you were in town.' Her voice held a delicate rasp.

'News travels fast,' he said, looking at Anna.

Joey cast him a significant look. 'That's Pepper Bay for you.' She held the coffee cup out to him. 'Here, take this to Betty. She just called me and asked for one. She told me to get *Moneybags* to bring it over. Her words, not mine.'

Jake grinned and took the cup and glanced at Anna. 'Won't be a sec.' He looked back at Joey. 'This is Anna. Anna, Joey Walker. Boss around here.'

Anna watched Jake leave the shop, then smiled over at an approaching Joey.

She is so pretty. She's got that country girl look about her. She looks like she's got the legs to pull off those summer denim shorts. Jeans and gingham. I love that summer look. I'm not quite sure it likes me though. I bet she dresses like that in the summer. I wonder if Joey is a nickname, maybe short for Josephine, maybe Josie. She looks more like a Josie or a Rosie. She's got rosy cheeks. She'd make a good leading lady. There's something about her. Sweet but strong. A Woman of Substance is coming to me. She definitely wouldn't be the damsel in distress in her story. I'd place her in charge of herself and surroundings. She's smiling at me. I bet she's got questions.

'Take a seat,' said Joey, joining her at a table near the window. She flicked her head to look outside, and her blonde mid-length ponytail swished behind her back. 'Is that your dog?'

Anna watched Max follow Jake up the street. 'Yes. Max.'

'Well, there's no one in here but us, so when they get back, he can sit there in the doorway. It's starting to pick up a bit of a chill out there. My gran reckons we're going to have a snowstorm as big as Scotland sees, but when did we ever have their snow worries?'

Anna listened quietly. She wasn't sure what she could add.

'My gran has always been weirdly accurate with her weather forecasts. Think she might be losing her skill now.' Joey glanced at the sky, and then her taupe eyes rolled over to examine the woman opposite her.

Anna knew she was being studied.

'So,' said Joey, 'how do you know Jake?'

A crooked smile hit Anna's face. 'I guess you could say we're neighbours.'

'Could say,' questioned Joey. 'You're not sure?'

What should I say? What would Jake think if I told her the truth? Why do I care what he thinks? It's my story. I can tell who I want, and she's hardly going to tell on me, not if she's his friend. I think I can trust her.

'I live on his roof.'

Joey's big eyes widened. 'His roof?'

'My ex kicked me out a while back. I was sleeping in the bookshop that we still own together, but then he kicked me out of there too, so I pitched a tent on the roof where Jake lives in London. It's just until I have saved enough for a rent deposit for a flat.'

Joey tried not to laugh. 'Well, that takes some guts, Anna.' She dropped her smile. 'That ex of yours though.' She shook her fist. 'Give him five minutes with me. We'll see who gets kicked around then.'

Anna breathed out a laugh. 'He has that effect on people.'

'So,' said Joey, leaning over the table. 'Jake's trying to rescue you, is he?'

I have no idea what he's doing.

'He's being a good friend to me.'

Joey sat back. 'He's definitely changed over the last few years. Since his gran died. I'm glad he finally got rid of that playboy image he had back then. It never suited him. It doesn't suit either of them. Sometimes I wonder where Josh's head is at.' She glanced out the window. 'Is Josh here too?'

'No. Just us.'

Joey's shoulders slumped slightly. She bit in her lip and stared glumly at the pink gingham tablecloth.

'Have you known Jake long?' asked Anna.

Joey raised her head and smiled. 'All my life. Well, when they're around. They mostly only came here in the summer months. A few Christmases as well. They didn't visit as often once they hit their twenties. Josh hasn't been back since Edith died. Well, they all came down for a couple of days for her funeral that was here, but that was the last time Josh visited. That was about three years ago.'

'Their grandmother,' said Anna.

Joey nodded. She looked over her shoulder. 'This is her pride and joy. What do you think of the place?'

Anna felt a wave of warmth fill her body. 'It's lovely.'

Joey agreed. 'Best place in the world to me. I do all the baking out the back there, with some help from Ruby

Morland. We have another girl who works here too, Molly. Together, we make a great team and keep this place just how Edith liked it.' She sank slightly. 'God, I miss her.'

Anna was keen to know more about Jake's life. 'What was she like?'

'She was a tough cookie, but not when it came to her family. Soft as mush then, especially with those boys. Can't blame her. Once she lost her son and daughter-in-law in that car crash, they were all she had left of him. Did Jake tell you about his parents?'

'Yes. He told me about the accident.'

'So sad. They would have had a chance if they were wearing seatbelts. Oh well, no point me going on about that.'

So, that's why he worries so much about safety.

'We were all sad to hear about John's passing,' said Joey. 'He was like a whirlwind when he was around. You were never quite sure what he would get up to next. Stirred a few pots when he renovated Starlight Cottage. Wish he would have renovated Pepper Pot Farm. It needs it. That's where I live with my brother, gran, and niece. You would have passed it on your way down here.'

Anna nodded. 'I saw cows.'

Joey laughed. 'Yeah. That's us. My brother's about to put them inside for the winter.'

'Pepper Bay is a lovely place.'

Joey agreed. 'I wouldn't live anywhere else. We're a really tight community around here. Everyone knows everyone. You're never short of friends here, Anna, and now that Jake has brought you here, you'll be treated as one of us because, whether those Reynolds brothers like it or not, they're considered family around here. They're Edith Marshall's boys, and that's all there is to it. The Marshalls were a part of Pepper Bay for as long as anyone can remember. Edith was the last Marshall, but the boys have her in them, so it's the same thing.' She hesitated, then added, 'You know, Jake's never brought anyone here before, and he was never one for having a girlfriend longer than one night...' She went to add to her statement but closed her mouth instead.

Anna suddenly felt special, and she liked how that felt.

'Hey,' said Joey, making Anna jump slightly. 'Seeing how you're in to rooftops, would you like to see the one upstairs? Edith turned the small area into a, what I like to call, peaceful escape. I stay in the flat some nights. If I've got a lot to do first thing, that is. Most mornings I'm up at half four, so it's easier, and Jake doesn't mind. Not that I ever sleep in Edith's old room. That doesn't feel right, not that she'd care. She was easy-going like that.'

Anna followed her over to the kitchen area at the back of the shop.

Joey guided her to some stairs the other side a dark door. 'Flat's just up here.'

Anna climbed the narrow stairwell and stopped when Joey opened a door to show her Edith's cosy living room. It looked warm and inviting, and like Jake Reynolds hadn't got his hands on it.

Joey closed the door and nodded further up the stairs. 'This way.'

Anna shivered as the cold air hit her face, but she didn't mind the chill. The beauty of the rooftop distracted her.

Oh my goodness. Look at this place. It's so cute.

The small pathed area was lined with potted green plants, fairy lights, and there were flower ornaments attached to the walls. There was a wrought-iron table and two matching chairs, and large chrome lanterns sitting on the sand-coloured floor, holding white candles.

'Lovely, right?' said Joey. 'And look over there.'

Anna turned to her right to face a stunning view of the sea. 'Oh, wow!'

Joey smiled warmly. 'You should see it when the sun sets. It's pure magic.'

Anna sighed deeply to herself and snuggled her cold cheeks down into her scarf. 'You can't beat a sunset.'

'No, you can't,' said Jake, standing in the doorway.

Anna and Joey turned to him. Max was by his side.

Joey walked over to Jake and slid herself effortlessly under his arm, and Anna felt a twang of jealously wash over her. She lowered her head some more to hide any evidence that might give away her thoughts. Jake was hugging Joey tightly. They seemed so relaxed in each other's arms. She wished she was the one being hugged.

I could do that, just slip myself under his arm, snuggle into his chest, place one hand on his back and the other around his neck. I could stroke along his jawline or run my fingers through his hair. Inhale his scent, and kiss his lips, and he would just hold me tightly, never letting me go, and when I went to pull away, he would say, stay, Anna, stay with me, and I would just melt into him once more. Oh God, he's so huggable and kissable. Why can't I look like Joey Walker? I bet she always gets hugged whenever she wants. I wish someone would hug me sometimes.

Max nudged his nose into her leg, gaining her attention. She smiled down and lowered herself to stroke his head, and he smooched her ear under her hat, making her giggle.

'And why are we up here?' asked Jake, watching Anna.

Joey gave a small shrug. 'Just trying to make Anna fall even more in love with Pepper Bay.'

Anna grinned widely as she glanced up at them both. 'I don't need convincing. I'm already in love.' Her eyes twinkled over towards Jake, then quickly turned back down to Max.

17

Jake

The drive back up to Starlight Cottage was pretty quiet. Max was sleeping, Anna was enjoying the view, and Jake couldn't get her words and look out of his head when she had said that she was already in love.

His heart had dropped to his knees, and he was sure that Joey could tell that something wasn't right with him.

She was talking about Pepper Bay, not me. Get a grip.

He turned off the road to pull on to Pepper Pot Farm's driveway.

'I've just got to make a stop to pick up some logs for the fire from Nate.' He glanced at her. 'I noticed we didn't have any, so I called him. He always has loads.' He laughed. 'Nate likes to swing an axe whenever he gets stressed. I've tried it myself. It's good stress relief.'

Anna smiled.

She's quiet. Maybe she's annoyed about something. Maybe you think too much, Jake.

A tall, thickset man wearing dark overalls walked towards the car to greet them. He had obvious muscles and thick dark hair that was in its early stages of grey. He looked around the same age as Jake.

Jake and Anna got out and said hello.

'Nate, this is Anna.' Jake stilled as he watched Anna's eyes trace Nate's body.

It wasn't anything he hadn't seen women do before. He hadn't met a woman who didn't fall weak at the knees at their first sighting of Nate Walker. They would often use words like dreamy, hot, and oh my God!

Nate smiled at Anna. He had the same smile and eyes as his sister, Joey. 'Hello, Anna. I would give you a hug but...' He glanced down at his messy overalls.

Jake stepped forward, creating a barrier between them. 'No one needs a hug thanks, Nate, just some wood.'

Nate peered over Jake's shoulder at Anna. 'You'll have to come back another time, and I'll show you the animals.' He glanced down at her trainers. 'Bring wellies.'

'I've just bought some today,' she replied. 'Well, Jake bought them for me over in Sandly. We went there to buy some food, and then Jake took me to see the shops down the bottom of Pepper Lane.'

Nate grinned over at him. 'Hmm!'

Jake raised his eyebrows. 'The wood?'

'Over here,' said Nate, waving them towards the side of the farmhouse. 'Gran's already put some in a basket for you. Actually, there are two baskets, as she said you need one for the storm.'

Jake frowned as Anna nodded.

'What storm?' he asked.

'The snowstorm,' replied Anna.

He turned to her with an inquisitive look. 'Snowstorm?'

Josephine Walker appeared behind them. 'That's right, Jacob. It's about to hit here.' She handed him a box full with cheese and jam products. 'Take these as well.'

Jake turned to the old lady and smiled. 'Thank you, Josephine, and how are you?'

Josephine shrugged her broad shoulders and moved him out of her way. 'Anna, right,' she told rather than asked. 'My granddaughter called to tell me all about you. You're even lovelier than she said.' She shot a glance at Jake.

'Nice homely look.' She then shot the same sharp look towards Nate. 'See, homely girl. That's what you need.'

Nate's mouth dropped open. 'Gran, really?' He turned to Anna. 'Sorry about her.' He tightened his full lips as he glared at his grandmother.

Josephine ignored him. 'Look at my grandson, Anna. What woman can resist. He's got it all going for him, hasn't he?' Her eyes widened, waiting for Anna to agree.

Jake watched Anna.

Well, Anna, do you agree?

Anna looked flustered. 'Erm...'

Nate interrupted, 'Gran, stop. Take no notice, Anna. She's always on at me to date.' He rolled his taupe eyes over to Josephine. 'When have I got time to date? Between this place and looking after Daisy, I'm pretty full.'

Josephine nudged Anna. 'Daisy's his daughter. Thirteen now, she is. He has time, just too shy.'

'I'm not shy.'

Jake laughed but then stopped when Josephine pointed at Anna and told Nate that there was a beautiful woman standing right in front of him now, and he still hadn't asked her out.

What!

Anna looked as embarrassed as Nate.

'I'm so sorry, Anna,' said Nate. His soft expression hardened when he looked at his grandmother. 'Gran, you're embarrassing Anna, and me, not to mention being disrespectful to Jake.'

Josephine leaned in closer to Jake and placed her chubby arm around his waist. 'Sorry, Jacob. I didn't know she was your girl.' She smiled at Anna, then quickly added, 'Seeing how you never have one longer than five minutes.'

'Gran!' snapped Nate. He ushered her towards the house.

Jake mouthed the words, 'I'm sorry,' to Anna.

'It's okay,' she mouthed back.

Nate froze on his way back to them when his gran called out, 'Just making sure that grandson of hers wakes up.'

He shook his head. 'Take no notice of Gran. She has finally lost the plot.'

Jake laughed to himself as it dawned on him what Josephine had tried to do.

She was trying to make me jealous. Gran, your friends can be a bloody nightmare at times.

'And don't worry about any snowstorms,' added Nate, picking up a basket of logs.

'I love snow,' said Anna, picking up the other basket. Her arms dropped slightly, as she obviously didn't realise how heavy it was.

Jake made sure his hands brushed against hers as he transferred the basket from her arms to his.

What are you doing, Reynolds? Behave yourself.

'Thanks,' she said.

Her cheeks are flushed. She looks cute. Cute? She's beautiful, and Nate can find his own dates.

'Can you open the boot please, Anna?' he asked, avoiding eye contact.

Nate said hello to Max as the back of the car opened. 'What a lovely dog. So, what's your name then, buddy?'

'Max,' said Jake, putting the basket down in the back.

Nate roughed up Max's head and then grinned at Jake. 'A dog, Jake?'

Jake raised his eyebrows at him.

Nate turned to Anna. 'I've got a scruff of one inside, aptly named Scruff. No doubt asleep. My dog could sleep for England.'

Anna smiled. 'Scruff. Good name.'

He nodded. 'Daisy and Robyn named him. That's my daughter and niece.'

'Oh, I didn't know Joey had a daughter as well. She never said.'

He shook his head. 'No, Robyn's not hers. She's not really my niece either. She's our Daisy's cousin, on her mum's side. She's more of a second daughter to me than a niece anyway, but when you're talking to people who don't know your business, you feel as though you have to explain it properly.'

Jake closed the boot. 'Daisy's mum and Robyn's dad were brother and sister. Twins.'

'Small town,' said Nate, rolling his eyes.

Anna looked confused. 'Were?'

Jake let Nate answer.

'Robyn's dad died before she was born.'

'Oh, that's sad. I met a Robyn today. She invited Max to the pub where she lives.'

Nate grinned. 'Yeah, that's our Robyn. Proper animal lover, not that she likes getting her hands dirty around here, and she reckons she's going to be a vet one day.' He looked over at Jake. 'You going down the pub tonight?'

Jake nodded. 'Thought I'd show Anna everything that Pepper Bay has to offer.'

'I'm looking forward to it,' said Anna. 'The Ugly Duckling, right?'

Both the men nodded.

'That's the one,' said Nate. 'Actually, it's the only one in Pepper Bay. If you want any more nightlife, you'll have to go over to Sandly.'

'I'm not really into nightlife,' said Anna, glancing at Max. 'The pub sounds just fine to me.'

Nate gave Jake a knowing glance. 'Gran was right about one thing, Anna. You're definitely a homely girl.'

Shut up, Nate, and stop flashing that ridiculously charming smile you have.

'We'll see you later then,' said Jake, opening the car door for Anna.

Nate gave a slight nod along with a big grin. 'Will do.'

Anna looked over at Jake as he sat in the car. 'Do you really think there is a snowstorm coming?'

He tried not to laugh. 'No, Anna. Josephine's always been a bit quirky.' He hesitated.

Don't say it. Don't say it.

'You know, if you did want to go on a date with Nate, it's okay with me. Don't feel obliged to hang out with me while you're here. We just came here together. It doesn't mean we are together. You're a free agent, and Nate's a really nice man, and he's been single for years. Daisy's mum left him when their daughter was a baby. Her family moved away to Australia after Robyn's dad died. Nate had to raise his daughter alone, not that he's really alone. The Walkers are a good stable family. You'd be safe with Nate.'

The noise of the engine was the only sound all the way back to Starlight Cottage.

18

Anna

Anna felt mortified as she slumped down on her bed, giving the shopping bags on the floor an angry glare. The Chelsea boots, the wellies, all of the goodies bought for Max that Jake was determined to buy.

She thought he liked her, but now she knew he didn't. He was happy for her to date someone else, and as hot and nice as Nate Walker was, he wasn't the one she wanted.

Don't you cry. Don't be silly. Jake made no promises. He's just helping out. Being a good friend. I don't even know him. Not really. He brought me here to help me. I don't know why I thought he would think anything of me. I'm hardly his type. I'm one thing, he's another, and never the twain shall meet. Saying that, Pepper Bay doesn't seem the type of place you would find a millionaire playboy. I shouldn't call him that. I don't know who he used to be. I just know the man I met, and even though it hasn't even been a whole week yet, he seems genuinely nice. I can't get the hump because he doesn't fancy me. I'm being daft. Come on. Get up. Sort dinner out. Right, let's do this.

She went over to the few items of clothing she had hanging in the oversized wardrobe. She needed to get her mind off how this new man in her life was having such a strong effect on her. She distracted herself by remembering how she had imagined Nate Walker poverty stricken, making his way across America during the Great Depression. How he might fit in with the Joad family.

Nah, he looked more like an American wrestler.

Her thoughts turned to Josephine, linking her to one of her favourite book characters.

Agnes Nutter. Possibly?

Her watery eyes came back into focus to stare into the wardrobe. She sniffled and released a deep breath.

'I have nothing to wear tonight,' she mumbled.

Jake's voice came from the doorway. 'Jeans and a jumper are fine for the pub. No one dresses up in there. It's pretty casual.'

Anna hoped her eyes had dried as he approached to look over her shoulder at her clothes. The last thing she needed was to look like a right soppy mare fawning over him.

'That blue jumper with jeans looks okay to me,' he said softly.

She tried holding her breath so that she didn't inhale that familiar scent that she had grown fond of. Her cheeks started to flush, so she exhaled, which came out as a huff.

His hand rested on her shoulder, and a hundred butterflies filled her stomach. She felt in need of a glass of water, or rather, a drop of brandy. Stan always said brandy was great for soothing the nerves.

'Blue suits you,' he added.

Anna focused on his lips being so close to her ear, and the warmth of his breath reaching her skin. She wanted to lean back into his chest so badly. It was all she could do to stop herself.

Breathe, just breathe.

She lowered her head and had a word with her heart as soon as he walked away.

'What is happening to me?' she muttered to herself. 'I mean, I know what is happening to me, but what the hell is happening to me?'

She sat on the end of the bed and attempted to rub away the dazed look on her face.

I blame romance books. They give people like me false hope of ever having anyone like Jake Reynolds fall in love with them. I don't really have anything worth falling in love with. He feels sorry for me and is doing a good deed to get his boy scout badge or citizen of the year award or something. Oh, what am I saying? I know there are good people in this world. He became suicidal once, and it probably made him a spiritual person or something. His grandmother told him he would help people. I guess I'm one of those people. He wants to help others so that they don't ever feel as low as he did back then. I can't let my past make me wary of everyone, and I have to stop putting myself down as well. That's not helpful one bit.

'Okay, wake up, Anna.'

Max appeared by her side.

'It's a bit early, but shall we have our dinner?' she asked him.

On hearing the word *dinner*, Max's tail wagged frantically, and he let out a low bark.

'Come on then, let's get you sorted.'

Max entered the kitchen at least five minutes before Anna. Jake was still putting away groceries.

'Shall I make dinner early?' she asked, picking up a tin of dog food.

He glanced sideways at Max's dinner. 'Well, it's not my usual brand, but I'm willing if you are.'

She tried not to giggle at his joke and carried on sorting out Max. She could feel Jake watching her as she placed the dog bowl on the floor.

Max scoffed his dinner within seconds.

'I'm happy to cook,' said Jake. 'I was going to put on some pasta.'

She gave a slight shrug. 'Okay. I'm just going to take Max for a walk. He likes to pee just after he has eaten. It's his thing.'

That was way too much unnecessary information. Even Max is giving me a funny look now.

Jake quietly pottered around the kitchen whilst Anna took Max outside.

The sun was almost set over the hill, creating just a remaining touch of a beautiful faded burnt-orange colour low in the sky. The air was cold and crisp and filled with a hint of the sea.

Anna inhaled the last of the daylight and smiled to herself as she watched some birds fly off away from the clifftop. Part of her wanted to join them.

Max was enjoying the scenery as well. His big floppy face was filled with joy as he darted all over the green hilly land. He couldn't make his mind up which way to go.

Anna laughed as she raised her arms up in the air and spun in circles. 'Go, Max. Fly, be free.'

I'm free, so blissfully free. Nothing can touch me. The hills are alive with the sound of absolutely nothing. How wonderful is this.

Max thought spinning looked like fun, so he decided to try jumping up her legs whilst she turned. Anna got tangled with him and ended up on the ground, with the big hairy lummox licking her face. She giggled as she rolled with him. 'I love you too, Max.' She rested her head on the grass as he settled down at her side.

I think I could stay here forever. Look how different my life could be. No more busy city. No more crowds. No more bookshop. I'm not sure about that part, but no more Rob.

That's the best part. My life could be as easy as a bird's. I flew here. I'm sitting on a clifftop. I could nest here. How wonderful it would be to just move whenever you felt like it. Not one care in the world. I just did that. I upped sticks and came here, and I have the opportunity to stay. He has offered me that. How surreal. I can't ask for more. I won't ask for more, and I'm certainly not crying over what I don't have, not when what I have just been given is so bloody brilliant. I've got some serious thinking to do. I need to focus.

They jumped up and sprinted back to the house together, with Max leaping into the air every so often to try and catch Anna's outstretched hand.

Her face was fresh and alive as she entered the kitchen to see her dinner waiting for her.

Jake's bright eyes rolled up from his plate to twinkle her way. 'Have fun out there?'

She smiled to herself as she washed her hands at the sink before joining him. 'Dinner looks nice, thank you. Do you like cooking?'

'Not sure if I like it. It's just something I can do. My gran made sure both Josh and I could cook, from baking cakes to frying fish. Actually, I tend to grill mine.'

There was definitely a deep appreciation stirring inside of her that someone had cooked her a meal. She'd never really enjoyed cooking so never put a lot of heart into it herself. Rob always told her she was lousy in the kitchen. She made a mental note to follow a good recipe if she ever cooked for Jake whilst she was there. She didn't want him to think she was useless as well.

Maybe it's best if I'm honest about that now.

'I'm not a very good cook, I'm afraid. I've been told.'

He stopped eating for a moment. 'Well, there are two things we can do about that. One, I teach you everything I know, or two, I'll always cook for you. As you know, I like to clean too, so you really won't have to lift a finger while you are with me.'

Anna twiddled some penne pasta on her fork, enjoying the warm feeling he had just created. 'So, I'll be a lady of leisure.'

'If that's what you want.'

'I'd like to help. I don't want you to see me as useless.'

Why did I say that?

Lines appeared across his brow. 'I would never think that.'

She slowly placed some food in her mouth in an attempt to stop herself from saying anything else she thought sounded pathetic.

He nodded at her plate. 'We'll head down to the pub later on.'

'Okay,' she said simply, then ate her dinner in silence.

19

Jake

All Jake could think about was why Anna had been so quiet. He hoped the trip to the pub would help with whatever was playing on her mind. He knew she had a lot of worries, but he also wondered if she was daydreaming about Nate at all.

He opened the door of The Ugly Duckling for Anna and Max to enter first. The smell of beer, wood, and burning logs entered his nose as the noise of lively chatter and clinking glasses hit his ears.

This place hasn't changed one bit. Feels like I was only in here yesterday.

Max stayed at Anna's side, behaving himself, until Robyn came running towards him. She flung her arms around his neck and kissed him on the head, much to Max's approval.

Jake closed the door behind him and smiled down at them.

Robyn looked over her shoulder. 'Mum, look. This is the dog I was telling you about.'

A woman around the same age as Anna was walking over to the bar, her fingers clasping empty glasses. She quickly placed them down and immediately gave Jake a hug, her slim frame almost getting lost under his arm. She wasn't an inch over five foot, with long red curls of hair, moss-green eyes, and cute freckles.

'Heard you were here.' Her voice was loud, rising above the small crowd of customers. She noticed Josephine was about to pass them by. 'And just in time for the snowstorm,' she added playfully, nudging his arm.

Josephine tutted as she passed. 'I heard that, Tessie Sparrow.'

Tessie held in her laugh. She smiled at Anna. 'Hello, you must be Anna. Joey told me you were here with Jake. I'm Tessie.' She pointed down at Robyn. 'This one is mine.'

Robyn looked up. 'Mum, I want a dog just like Max.'

Tessie shook her head. 'You have shared ownership of Scruff. That's enough.'

Robyn dramatically rolled her pale-lavender eyes.

Nate stood up from a table in the far corner, waving. 'Jake, over here.'

Jake guided Anna over to a small group of people close to the dark-stone open fireplace.

The Walkers were there, alongside a woman in her sixties.

'This is Elaine, my mum,' said Tessie. 'Don't tell her she looks like Annie Lennox, because she never sees it.'

Anna said hello to the woman with the white-blonde hair, who really did look exactly like Annie Lennox, and then shook hands with Tessie's dad when he came over and practically shoved his rough hand into hers.

Jake stared at his shiny bald head. He noticed that Ed was still wearing the same old diamond stud earring in his left lobe. His white shirt was rolled at the sleeves, showing off black rubber bands on both of his thick wrists.

'I'm Ed, Tessie's dad. Welcome to our pub.' His one gold tooth stood out amongst his white teeth as he beamed a friendly smile her way.

He still looks as though he has just stepped off the Queen Anne's Revenge.

Elaine released Anna's hand from Ed's tight grip. 'Let go of the girl, Ed.' She shook her head and turned to Anna. 'Never mind him, Anna. Now, what can I get you to drink? Your one's on me, seeing how you're new to Pepper Bay.' She winked at Jake. 'I want to make sure she comes back.'

Anna hadn't been out for a drink in a long time. Even when she did drink, she didn't drink much. She glanced down at the scratched wooden table. It was already filled with glasses and bottles. 'White wine, please.'

Elaine smiled. She placed one hand on Jake's back. 'Beer, Jake?'

'Yeah, thanks. I'll come with you to pay for mine, seeing how I'm not getting any special treatment.'

Elaine scoffed, nudging his shoulder. 'Cheeky sod. I'll give you a packet of peanuts. That's your lot.'

Nate waved him down to a seat. 'Sit there, mate. This is my round.'

Jake sat next to Joey, and she flung her arms around him, resting her head on his shoulder for a second. 'I'm so pleased you're back.'

He smiled down at his lap, then glanced over at Anna and caught her looking at him. Her eyes quickly rolled away to look over at Nate at the bar.

'Sit down, Anna,' said Tessie, offering her a seat next to Josephine.

Josephine took Anna's hand as soon as she sat down. She turned it over and started to read her palm, and Anna looked worried.

Nate brought the drinks over and plonked himself down on the chair the other side of her. He removed her hand from his grandmother's hold.

Jake's mouth gaped slightly.

He's holding her hand.

'Leave her alone, Gran,' said Nate.

Josephine huffed. 'Was just getting interesting as well.'

Anna's eyes widened.

Jake watched her lean closer to Nate to ask him if his grandmother really could read palms.

Nate beamed his big smile, wrinkled his nose, and shook his head.

I don't know why Nate feels the need to sit so close to her. There's plenty of room, and why is she leaning into him like that? Are they flirting?

Joey whispered to him, 'Not many men let their girlfriend sit next to my brother.'

'She's not my girlfriend,' he whispered back.

Joey tapped his arm. 'Oh, please!'

He forced a smile and rolled his eyes over to see Anna and Nate engaged in a conversation that had them both smiling.

Tessie threw some bags of crisps into the middle of the table. 'Freddy's off tonight, so if you want any food, this is it.'

'Freddy's the pub chef,' Nate told Anna. 'You'll have to come back when he's here and try some food. It's pretty decent.'

'We will,' said Jake, leaning closer.

Nate grinned at him.

Tessie sat down the other side of Jake. 'So, Jake, what brings you here during the winter? Ooh, are you here for Christmas?'

'Not sure yet. At the moment, it's just a few days. Felt like being closer to Gran. Plus, Gramps wanted his ashes scattered here.'

Tessie placed her hand on his arm. 'We were all sorry to hear about John. It's good you came home. We'll look after you.'

He lifted her hand and kissed it. 'I love you too, Tess.'

'Oi, you old smoothie, leave her alone,' said Nate, nodding at Tessie's hand.

Jake grinned at him.

'And what about you, Anna?' asked Tessie. 'It's a surprise to see Jake out with someone, let alone bring someone to Starlight.'

Anna was sipping some wine. She took a bigger gulp and then explained her situation and how Jake was helping her.

All eyes were suddenly on him.

Don't look at me. Great! Now they're all judging my intentions.

He pursed his lips together and gave a slight shrug.

Nate turned to Anna. 'Well, I hope you find work here. It'll be good to have you around. I'll keep my ears open for you. I'd offer you a job on the farm, but things are a bit tight at the moment. I'd give you some babysitting duties on occasion, but they're not really babies anymore. I've got one sitting over in the corner fussing your dog, and another one upstairs reading a book. They pretty much look after themselves nowadays, don't they, Tess?'

Tessie nodded. 'Our girls think they're adults already.'

'Anna will be all right,' said Josephine.

Anna smiled. 'Thanks, anyway.'

Nate put his arm around the back of her chair and leaned in closer to her. 'That ex of yours better not ever show his face around here.'

Jake was struggling to hear what Nate was saying to her. He tried to lean closer to the table to eavesdrop, but Joey pulled on his arm, forcing him back towards her.

'Do you think Josh will show up?' she asked quietly.

He had no idea what his brother was doing. He wished he was in Pepper Bay with him, but he knew that Josh needed time to clear his head after the death of their grandfather. He could also tell that Joey was missing him. He wanted Josh to be with them for her sake as well.

'I don't know, Jo. Maybe in a while. You know Josh. Can't really predict at the moment.'

She lowered her eyes and loosened her grip on his arm.

He pulled her back towards him. 'Hey, ask your gran. She might know.'

Joey tutted and laughed.

Tessie leaned closer to Anna. 'What do you think of Pepper Bay so far?'

Anna's eyes lit up as bright as the twinkling fairy lights outside swinging across Pepper Lane. 'I love it.'

'And Starlight Cottage?' asked Tessie. 'It's magical, isn't it?'

Anna agreed, and Jake felt his heart warm.

'It's always been my favourite cottage in Pepper Bay,' said Tessie.

'Hey,' said Nate, 'I thought your favourite place was Pepper Pot Farm.'

Tessie smiled at him. 'That's not a cottage. It's a farmhouse.'

'Mine's Honeybee Cottage,' said Joey, looking dreamy. 'It's the newest cottage around here,' she told Anna. 'About thirty years old. It's the first cottage you come to as you leave the shops behind. The one closest to the road. It's very modern. I'd love to own that.'

'Well, stranger things have happened,' said Josephine. She got up when she saw Betty Blake enter the pub. 'Ooh, there's Betty. I'm going to sit with my friend, while I still can.' She tapped Nate on the shoulder. 'Before that kid of hers sticks her in the retirement village.'

Nate dropped his hefty shoulders. 'Don't worry, Gran. We're not going to put you anywhere.'

Joey giggled. 'We might, if you keep scaring everyone with your snowstorm stories.'

Josephine waved off the comment and went over to Betty.

Tessie leaned into the group. 'That's Dana Blake for you. Only after her money.'

Joey agreed.

Jake watched Anna getting to know his friends. She seemed relaxed and happy to be in their company. He thought she fitted in perfectly, and he was so glad that everyone had welcomed her into their close-knit community already. He thought that she looked particularly comfortable with Nate, but he tried not to worry too much about that. Nate was the friendly type and a good mate. There was no way he would hit on Anna. He hoped.

Anna glanced over the table at him, and Jake unleashed his best smouldering look, hoping that it would burn through her and distract her from whatever Nate was talking about. He saw her cheeks flush, and he felt the hint of a smirk hit his mouth.

20

Anna

Anna wrapped herself tightly in Jake's dressing gown.

What a day! How is this my life? Yesterday, I was on the roof. Today, I feel like I'm on a different planet. I got to have a shower in Jake's apartment this morning, then I was chauffeur-driven to a helicopter that brought me here. I've been shopping, had dinner cooked for me, and made a bunch of new friends, and then there is him. The man who slept below me. Who bathed my dog. Gave me his dressing gown. I think I might just wake up now before I get too attached to this incredible dream.

She sniffed the material of his robe and smiled to herself, feeling warm and happy. Pepper Bay was more than she dreamed it would be, and Jake's friends were so lovely. She had never experienced feeling part of something or somewhere before. The thought of going home in three days made her feel like crying.

Home! That's a laugh. I wish Starlight Cottage could be my forever home. People actually live in places like this. They are so lucky.

The offer to let her stay in Starlight Cottage whilst she sorted out her finances felt like a crazy idea at first. Now it seemed doable. She thought she might ask Mrs Blake about work in the bookshop, but then she remembered it might not be a bookshop for much longer. There were plenty of shops in Sandly. Maybe she could ask around over there. She was dying to take a trip on the tram.

I have to find a job. I need to have a proper roof over my head. This place has inspired me even more now. I can do this. I really can turn my life around.

Max poked his head around the bedroom doorway to see what she was up to.

'Hey, Max. You tired?'

He sneezed, then headed off downstairs.

She looked out the window. It was dark and slightly eerie. Pepper Pot Farm was the only hint of light in the distance. She picked up the binoculars that were on the windowsill and peered down at the farm. She could see a candle flickering in one of the upstairs windows. She turned her head to see if there was anything going on in the fields, but the cows were tucked up for the winter. She decided to stop looking in case she saw something scary like an escaped murderer, or a lady in white, or some sort of mythical yeti that lived on the Isle of Wight. Her mind was starting to drift towards werewolves roaming around Starlight Cottage. She cursed the day Rob had made her sit and watch American Werewolf in London. It was time to quickly overrule her overactive imagination.

I hope it does snow. It will look even more pretty up here.

Jake's voice floated up the stairs. 'Anna, I've made some hot chocolate and toast.'

She walked down the stairs thinking about how close Jake and Joey had been in the pub and wondered if they had history. She was so glad that Nate and Tessie had kept her mind occupied all night, because she didn't like feeling jealous. She wanted to enjoy her new adventure, and now her new friends.

Blimey, Jake looked hot tonight. He looks so different here. Still hot, but different. More natural. Less tight. How can anyone be so hypnotic? No wonder Joey was all over him. I wanted to be all over him. I wish he had paid me more attention in the pub. I have got to stop thinking of him that way. He's just my new friend, helping me.

She adjusted her mind to think about how much she wanted to show Stan Pepper Bay, knowing he would love The Ugly Duckling. It was just as cosy and quaint as the rest of Pepper Lane.

Her stomach flipped when she saw Jake sitting on the rug in front of the open fireplace with Max. The logs were burning in the grate, creating a golden glow on his beautiful face. Her eyes rolled over his grey dressing gown and navy pyjamas.

Wow, he looks even better in his PJs. He's definitely a perfect ten.

Max didn't bother looking up. He was sprawled out, snoozing.

She walked over to the bookcase to browse the titles to help distract her from any more unwanted thoughts, even if they did fill her with warmth. 'There are some good books here.'

'Gran liked to read.'

'Ooh, *The Bridges of Madison County*. I still haven't read that.'

'You a big reader, Anna?'

'I am. Romance is my favourite genre.'

'Why romance?'

She gently ran her finger down the spine of the book. 'There is destiny and serendipity and fate, and then there is love. The ruler. The intruder. The instigator. The game-changer. Love enjoys messing with the impossible. I like how the direction of two people's lives change.' She straightened and turned to him. 'Look at it this way, love is like a gale force wind. It appears. It picks up. It moves you. It forces your boat east when you were heading west. That's pretty powerful. Love also has the ability to steal words from your vocabulary and oxygen from your brain. Whatever it does, however it feels, it always comes with a story or it creates a new one. Love's fascinating, when you think about it.'

Jake was smiling warmly at her.

Anna smiled back. 'I love getting lost in a love story.'

'How about getting lost in some toast and hot chocolate?' He gestured down at two large mugs of hot chocolate sitting by the fire. 'Marshmallows and cream.'

She joined him on the rug. 'Thank you.' The warmth of the fire reached her cheek, so she shifted back a touch. 'The fire looks amazing.'

He agreed. 'There's always something so mesmerising about fire, don't you think?'

'I do.'

'So,' he said softly, 'how was your first day in Pepper Bay?'

She smiled over at her hot drink. 'I've had a great day. Thank you for doing this for me. I would just be sitting in my cold tent right now. I still can't believe I'm here.'

He looked slightly bashful. 'Thank you for coming. I wanted to come back here, but I really didn't want to come on my own. I don't know why. I just felt a bit weird about coming this time.'

'First time without your family?' she asked, already knowing that was probably the case. She watched him slowly stroke over his thumb.

'Yeah.'

'Looks like we did each other a favour, then.'

He nodded. 'Perfect match.'

Anna could feel her heart beating. She casually glanced down at her chest, knowing she couldn't sit there with him, daydreaming about how his arms might feel wrapped around her. A distraction was drastically needed. She reached for her drink and stuffed a large marshmallow into her mouth and nearly choked straight away.

Jake sat up and leaned over to pat her back. 'Anna, are you okay?'

Oh my God, how embarrassing.

She nodded and spat the splurge of melted marshmallow into her hand.

He handed her a napkin. 'I think we'll get the mini marshmallows next time.'

She cuffed the dribble from her mouth and tried not to look as awkward as she felt.

'Good idea,' she mumbled.

Jake smiled, revealing his laugh lines, which made her feel more comfortable.

They settled into the silence, watching the fire for a while.

'Everyone thinks I'm your girlfriend.' She wished she hadn't said that, as soon as the words had left her lips, but it was out now and there was little she could do about it other than squirm inside. His eyes were filled with confidence as they slowly traced over her mouth, causing her to hold her breath. She wanted to swallow, but held on to that too. She knew she was staring at him for an embarrassing amount of time, but as his eyes weren't looking into hers, she felt she was getting away with it.

'I know,' he said.

Bloody well breathe, Anna, before you pass out.

The slow and steady breath that left her nose wasn't as easy to control as she thought it would be. It sounded like a short sharp whistle, which gave her a second wave of embarrassment to contend with. She distracted herself by stirring the large heap of cream into her drink so that she could take a sip without it sticking to her nose. She was fully aware that his intense eyes were on her and that he had some cream on the tip of his nose.

Should I tell him? I could just wipe it away. No, don't touch him. I really want to touch his face. Why is it so hard for me to hold my hand still? Oh God, look at him. He looks so cute. I'm not going to be able to control my hand in a minute.

She could feel the corners of her mouth rise against her will.

'What are you smiling at?' he asked, revealing his own wary smile.

'You have some cream on your nose.'

His mouth twisted slightly to one side as he wiped away the cream whilst keeping his eyes firmly locked with hers.

I don't know if he's giving me a look or that's just his look. Why does he have to have such a sexy look? I've got to stop staring at him. I'm starting to look like a right weirdo.

'Stan would like it here,' was all she could think to say.

'How do you know him?'

Anna kept her eyes on the fire. 'His wife worked at my shop for two years. We connected straight away. They were like parents to me. I don't know who my parents are, or were. Yep, that's how little I know about them. I had a few foster parents growing up, but no real connections. Stan's all I have.'

'Not anymore.'

She turned to him. 'Yeah, sorry. You're a good friend to me too, and your friends here are great. They made me feel so welcome. I felt really included. I've never felt part of anything before.'

Jake's smiling azure-blue eyes warmed her more than the fire. 'That's Pepper Bay for you.'

'Thank you for bringing me here.'

'You don't have to keep thanking me, Anna.'

I do. I really do.

Her face was filled with the joy she was feeling. It was so hard to hold it back. 'I've had the best time, Jake.'

'So have I, Anna.'

'I've never even sat in front of a real fire before. Well, you know, one that wasn't a bonfire on Guy Fawkes Night.'

A big grin crept slowly across his face. 'Do you know what's better than sitting in front of a real fire? Lying down in front of one.'

Anna felt her heart expand as his hand slipped into hers and tugged her to the rug. Her arm was pressing against his, as he had flopped her backwards to rest at his side. Her eyes were on the ceiling, and her breath was trapped in her throat. His hand was still holding hers, creating a light whirl in her head. She was so glad she was lying down, as she was sure her legs would've given way otherwise. She saw his head roll over to face her, so she turned to meet his smiling eyes.

'See,' he whispered, tucking his free hand behind his head.

'It is nice down here,' she whispered back, wanting the tranquillity of the moment to stay that way.

He rolled his head back towards the ceiling. 'We can do this every night we're here, if you like.'

'But next time take the blanket and cushions off the sofa for comfort. I would get them, but I don't want to move.'

'I know what you mean, but if your neck is aching…'

'I'm okay.'

He released her hand and moved his arm so that it was around the back of her head. 'Lean on me, Anna. You'll be more comfortable.'

No second invitation was needed. She shuffled herself under his arm and rested her head on his shoulder. 'Just for five minutes,' she whispered.

She could hear the smile in his voice as he said, 'Yeah, just for five minutes.'

'It would be nice to have one of those skylight windows right now.'

'My grandparents have one in their room, above their bed.'

Anna smiled to herself. 'Was it really love at first sight when they met?'

'It was for Gramps. I think my gran might have played hard to get for a few days.'

She felt his laugh rumble through her body.

'Gramps wasn't buying any of it. He said she fell for the Reynolds eyes straight away. He reckons we have magic in our eyes that is both a blessing and a curse.'

Anna knew he was smiling. She could sense his playfulness. 'A blessing and a curse is a lot to hold.'

His chest vibrated against her again. 'Yep.'

'Do you think his eyes captured her heart?'

'I once asked her that exact question. She shook her head and told me no, it was his soul.'

'That's beautiful,' whispered Anna.

'Do you think it was fate that brought them together, Anna? Did the stars align for them? Was the universe plotting and scheming, interfering with their journey?'

She knew his question was genuine by his subdued tone.
'I don't know, but I'm glad they met.'
'Me too.'

21

Jake

Creaks in the cottage filled Jake's bedroom every so often. He was used to the silence of his apartment. His plush penthouse never seemed to make any sounds. He guessed he was just more used to that place. He probably slept through lots of noises. As he tossed and turned, trying so hard to fall asleep, thoughts of Anna wrapped in his dressing gown snuggled up to him in front of the fireplace filled his head. He had wanted so badly to lean over and kiss her.

Why didn't I just do it? What's holding me back? It was so nice, just lying there with her pressed against me. No woman has ever just simply snuggled with me before. That's never been good enough for them. This place would never be good enough for those women in my past. Anna is so different. She made something simple seem so perfect.

She'd only been in his life a short while, but he couldn't imagine her not being in it now. Time spent with her didn't seem as new as it was. He already knew how much he enjoyed just being in her company. He really did want to kiss her, but just being with her held rewards too. He'd never experienced that with a woman before. Her presence was comforting and welcome.

The thought of her in the bedroom next door was starting to get on his nerves. He wanted to be in the bed with her, holding her in his arms, breathing in her scent. He flipped his quilt over and flopped his arms over the top.

She's facing that wall in front of me. We're facing each other. I wonder if she's looking at the wall? She's probably asleep. Probably having a great sleep, no doubt. She deserves to have a proper bed every night. I need to make sure she feels safe. I'm going to help her. She's not living on my roof anymore. I could show her the world. A different home in every country. She could choose where she wants to live. It doesn't have to be here. She can live anywhere. I can make that happen for her. I want to make that happen for her.

He stared up at the ceiling. Life suddenly felt surreal.

Where the hell did she come from? The roof, Jake. She came from the roof.

Normally, he was confident enough to make his desires clear within a matter of minutes. He wanted to be that way with Anna. He wanted to tell her how he was feeling. He just had to figure out exactly what it was he was feeling, because the way he was feeling was a whole new experience for him. No woman had ever made him feel muddled, bashful, or at a loss for words before. She stirred many emotions within him and created a few more.

I'm confused. I don't know which way to play this. I want her to know I like her, but I don't want her to know just yet. I want to kiss her, but I can't seem to make that move. I want her to like me. Really like me, for who I am. What am I exactly? What does the world see? A rich playboy who cares little for others? That's what they write about me. I'm not that person anymore. What if they find out about Anna? I can't have them writing anything bad about her. I'll have to protect her now. She's not going to be tabloid gossip. She's safe here. I'm sure she is. I can always fly her away. I'll hire a yacht. Maybe I should buy one again. We can be in the middle of nowhere, and she'll be safe. Maybe I should... Stop, just stop. Breathe. Get some sleep. I'm overthinking. This is too much.

Max's claws tapped on the wooden flooring, gaining attention.

Jake raised his head to look over at him.

'Your bed's in Anna's room,' he whispered.

Max jumped up on the bed and curled up at the bottom and fell asleep, much to Jake's amazement.

'Erm... excuse me.'

He couldn't be bothered to argue with Max. He flopped his head back down on the pillow, quite jealous of how quickly the dog could fall asleep. He glanced over at the window and closed his eyes.

* * *

Jake was having the best dream. Anna was snuggled next to him, breathing heavily in his ear and kissing the side of his face. He heard himself breathe out her name as he woke. 'Anna.' Opening his eyes, he found Max licking his cheek.

Gross!

'Get off me.'

He gently pushed Max off the bed and wiped the slobber from his face as he glared over at the dog.

Max approached the bedside and blew out snot from his nose in Jake's direction.

Jake blinked hard as the spray hit him in the eye. 'Oh my God, I can't believe you just did that.'

Max gave the impression he was about to give an encore.

'All right, I'm getting up.'

Max ran off.

Yawning and stretching, he ran one hand over his face. He'd hardly had any sleep and felt a bit rough around the edges, and the morning wash from Max did little to help. He peered over his shoulder at the window.

Still no snow.

He laughed to himself and then stopped when he stood and heard his knees creak. 'Ooh, I need a run.' He sniffed the air as the smell of fried bacon suddenly wafted into his room.

Now, that's inviting. I haven't had that kind of breakfast in a long while. It's like Gramps is downstairs again.

A warm smile stayed with him as he made his way into the bathroom to take a shower. His plan was to get ready, put on his running clothes, and hit the hills for the next half an hour at least.

Anna standing by the stove, in blue fleece pyjamas cooking breakfast, caused Jake to freeze in the doorway. So many thoughts ran through his mind, and they all involved his body pressed against hers.

She turned to see him standing there. 'Morning. This is one thing I can cook. Do you want a fry up?'

I want more than that. I want this to be real. I want you to be in my kitchen every morning. I want you to be in my life every day. I want this to be who we are. How we live. Where the hell did this feeling come from? Why do I keep wanting so much more with you? Why do I feel as though I have already experienced so much of my life with you? I need to get out of here. I need to run. God, my heart feels as though I've just done a HIIT session.

He lowered his eyes and shook his head, clearing the frog in his throat as he approached the sink to have a mouthful of water. 'I'm just going for a quick run. I'll have a smoothie when I get back. No need to worry about me.'

He stopped in the doorway. 'Thanks, though. Enjoy your breakfast.'

He went outside and ran. Faster than his normal pace.

The view from the edge of the clifftop was incredible. He never tired of seeing the rolling waves of the sea. The salty air was one of his favourite smells, and the cry of seagulls one of his favourite sounds.

He could hear his grandmother calling out to him, and then to Josh, telling them not to go too close to the edge. They would stretch out their arms and run up and down, pretending to be planes.

Jake thought about River Heights. He didn't want to live there anymore. It felt cold and lonely. He had no memories there that he could draw on to make him smile during the unhappy times, except for the small amount of time he spent there with Anna. Pepper Bay was home. Starlight Cottage was home, filled with a hundred and one happy memories. He would have to sort a few things out when he went back to London. Josh was one, and Anna was another.

I don't know what to do first. Should I sell my apartment? No. I'll still need a place in London. Josh might want to stay there as well. How do I get him to come here? This place will help him. He needs to be here. He needs to be with Joey. He loves her. I know he does, and I'm pretty sure she loves him. They spend enough time together whenever we're here. He hasn't been back in three years. I've got to get him to stop running away somehow. Anna. What am I going to do about her? I need to think more about this. I can make this work. I just need to... Oh, I don't know what I need.

The weight of the world fell to his shoulders. He took a calming breath and turned away from the sea to slowly jog back down towards the cottage.

Anna was sitting on the bottom step of the stairs, pulling on her new boots, when Jake was pushed through the front door by a gust of icy wind.

He swallowed hard as he glanced down at her feet. He wanted to act normal. Get out of his head and into the day. 'Boots look good.'

She tugged the second one on. 'Just need breaking in.'

'We should get you some walking boots as well.' He paused, waiting for her to argue about spending money.

She didn't respond.

'How about a trip into Sandly to get you a few more clothes for staying here?' he asked. 'We can jump on the tram. It's so much quicker. Goes straight across Pepper River.'

There was a noticeable spark in her eye.

'I can pay for everything, and you can pay me back when you find work,' he added.

Not that I have any intention of taking your money, but I'll cross that bridge when we come to it.

Anna smiled, and he liked how that made him feel.

'Okay, thanks,' she replied.

22

Anna

Sandly had a large stone-built church, a beautiful park with a children's play area, and a small dome that housed a stage where the local theatre company would hold their annual summer play. There were numerous shops, restaurants, and white-washed hotels that were once sea view homes. Its beach was much bigger than the one in Pepper Bay, and its long stretch of golden sand more comfortable.

Anna and Jake had left Max with the Walkers for a few hours so they could go in and out of the shops without Anna worrying too much about Max being left outside on his own, like she had the day before when they popped there for a few bits. It was quite clear as soon as they dropped him off that Max was happy to hang out with Scruff for a while.

Anna had bought two jumpers, a pair of jeans, some walking boots, and trousers and a shirt that she thought would be useful for job interviews.

Jake had encouraged her to buy more supplies from the chemist and another pair of pyjamas. His words had been full of authority when he told her that she didn't need a new dressing gown. She was secretly pleased. His dressing gown was officially her favourite thing to wear, and she wasn't ready to give it back just yet.

She spotted a hairdressers and asked him if it would be okay if he paid for her to have her hair cut. She saw him glance at her tied-back, long, dark hair. She rarely wore it out of a band, only letting it grow because she couldn't afford to keep going to the hairdressers, but now she felt a change was needed to go with her new upcoming life, and she felt comfortable knowing she would pay him back. She hoped to find a job soon. Surely someone in Sandly would need an extra pair of hands, especially with Christmas around the corner.

Jake sat in a chair by the front window of the hairdressers whilst she had her hair cut into a bob. He ignored the flirting that came his way from the staff members, by staring at his phone and telling them politely that he had work to do.

Anna was smiling outwardly at her new hair style, and smiling inside at the fact that none of the pretty women in the shop could grab Jake's attention.

He looked up when she came over to tell him she was finished. He kept his eyes on her whilst he pulled out his wallet and handed his credit card to the hairdresser.

The hairdresser was trying to make suggestive small talk to him whilst Anna put on her coat, but it was clear that he was oblivious to the woman's blatant seduction techniques.

Anna beamed from ear to ear. 'What do you think?'
Please like it.
He blinked softly. 'I love it. It really suits you.' He cleared the hoarseness from his throat.

She blushed and stepped outside into the cold, and his hands immediately came up around her neck and pulled her scarf up higher towards her chin. His face was so close to the top of her head.

'You smell like coconut, Anna.'

Her heart skipped a beat and a smile built inside as his hands lowered to rest on her shoulders. There was so much disappointment when he moved them to pick up their shopping bags from the ground.

She watched him rest the bags on his wrists and tuck his hands deeply into the pockets of his coat. 'Do you like the smell of coconut?'

His bright eyes hit her straight in the heart as they flashed her way. 'I prefer apple.'

Anna quickly turned away. She hadn't been able to hold his gaze for longer than four seconds since she met him.

'Shall we get some lunch?' she asked.

'Sure. What do you fancy?'

You, is the obvious answer.

Hiding her smile inside her scarf, she turned back to him. A braveness flittered across her eyes, as she suddenly felt bold enough to try out her own seduction techniques.

'I don't know,' she replied, trying to mimic his hypnotic stare. 'What do you fancy?'

Jake's eyes widened slightly. His jaw loosening as he looked down at her.

She held his stare.

One, two, three, four, five… that's enough of that.

She looked down at the shopping bags hanging from his wrists.

Ooh, I did five.

An intense silence loomed. Someone had to speak. 'How about lunch at The Ugly Duckling? We can pick up Max on the way home.'

Home?

Jake gave a half-smile. 'Sure.'

As they walked back to the tram, Anna tightened her grip on the inside of her pockets. She was sure that if she let her guard slip, her arm would move around his. She really wanted to hang off his arm. She found her eyes kept wandering over that way.

Stop looking at him. Think about food. Fish and chips. Fish and chips. I think I'll have fish and chips. I hope they have some at the pub. Stop looking at his arm.

He glanced sideways at her.

Anna swallowed.

He caught me staring at his elbow. Say something before he thinks you're a weirdo.

'Would you like me to carry a bag?'

The corner of his mouth twitched. 'No, thank you. I'm good.'

The tram stop looked like an old-fashioned railway station. It had a small wooden platform, an overhead shelter that was held up by forest-green, ornate, metal pillars, and a ticket office that looked like a garden shed. It just needed three children waving at a steam engine and the look would have been complete.

The old red-and-brown tram was ready and waiting to make its short journey over to Pepper Bay. The seats inside were narrow, short, and made of hard wood. The top half of the vehicle had an open roof, so Anna and Jake sat downstairs to try to keep warm.

She was squished between the window and Jake, and his body heat was passing through his jeans into hers. That arm she was so interested in before was now pressed up against her own. It would have been more comfortable for them both if Jake sat on another seat, but she was glad he chose not to.

His arm suddenly wriggled away from their connection to rest along the back of her seat.

He's got his arm around me. Breathe. It's not really around me. It's resting on the wood, but I can feel it touching my back. Shall I put my head on his shoulder? No, don't do that. I don't know what to do. Oh, flipping heck,

I'm melting. Breathe, Anna. Get a bloody grip. Focus on something else.

Pepper River looked deathly cold as the tram scraped along the track over its calm water. The riverbank had been known to flood during torrential rain, and sometimes cause havoc in parts of Pepper Bay.

Anna was so completely immersed in the view, she didn't hear the conductor tell them they had to get off and walk the rest of the way, because there was a fault in the track.

Jake tapped her shoulder. 'Come on. This happens from time to time. We're almost there anyway.'

Anna thanked the conductor as she stepped off the tram.

'This way,' said Jake, nodding forward.

She glanced down at the river. There was a slippery slope leading down towards its bitter cold surface, and her foot slipped, causing her heart to jump into her throat. Jake's hand immediately caught her arm, giving her back her balance. She quickly shuffled closer to him, away from the edge. She was filled with nauseating embarrassment.

Flipping heck! That's all I need, to fall down there.

Jake swiftly manoeuvred himself around her so that he was the one closest to the slope. He offered out his elbow, and she slipped her arm through before she told herself not to. Their eyes met for a moment, and he looked as though he was steadying his breathing. She wasn't sure if he was angry.

The walk to Pepper Lane only took ten minutes. They were soon sitting inside the much-appreciated warmth of The Ugly Duckling.

Jake had placed his hand in the small of her back and led her over to sit by the fireplace. That one simple touch had launched the butterflies in her stomach into a happy dance.

Anna removed her outerwear and smiled over at the burning logs. 'I'm starting to get used to open fireplaces. I'm surprised your one hasn't got one of those switches that light it up immediately. You control half the house with your phone, why not the fire too?'

Jake laughed to himself. 'My gran wouldn't let my grandfather mess with her fireplace. It's an original feature of the cottage. She loved a log fire and preferred the more natural approach of lighting one.'

'I agree with your gran. Just flicking a switch takes the joy out of it, but I bet you'd prefer a fancy gadget.'

'I can go manual, thanks, but yes, I do prefer fancy gadgets, given the choice.'

'The only fancy gadget I've ever owned is my portable camping stove. That's about as fancy as my life gets.'

Jake smiled up at Elaine as she approached. She nodded down at the bags by his feet. 'Spot of shopping?'

'Yes, and now some much-needed lunch,' he replied.

Elaine handed them both a menu. 'Freddy's made a nice chicken and leek soup, if you're interested.'

Without looking at the menu, Anna asked, 'Do you have fish and chips?'

Elaine chuckled. 'Is the Pope Catholic?'

Jake handed back his menu. 'I'll have fish and chips as well, please.'

Anna was surprised that he would eat something that was greasy.

'Anything to drink?' asked Elaine. She glanced at Anna again. 'Ooh, you've cut your hair. Looks lovely, Anna.'

Anna touched the ends of her bob. 'Thank you.'

'Orange juice for me,' said Jake.

Elaine took Anna's menu back.

'Same, please,' said Anna.

Elaine smiled. 'Won't be a sec.'
Anna caught Jake smiling at her new hair.
'Your hair really does look lovely, Anna.'
She couldn't help the smile that grew widely on her face and inside her heart.

23

Jake

Max wagged his tail happily as Anna appeared in the living room doorway of Pepper Pot Farm, but he didn't move from his spot in front of the fire next to Scruff.

Scruff looked over to see what all the fuss was about, and then he flopped his shaggy black-and-grey head back down again.

Anna huffed. 'I don't know why they call it a dog's life?'

Nate laughed. 'I think they used to work. Now they wouldn't dream of it. Well, not Scruff, anyway.'

'Nor Max.'

Nate reached up towards her shoulders. 'Let me take your coat. You'll stay for a quick cuppa, won't you?'

Jake stepped forward and dropped his shopping bags so that they purposely landed on Nate's feet, causing him to jolt back, and leaving Anna to remove her own coat.

She glanced at Jake. 'Shall we?'

Only if Nate stops touching you.

'Sure.'

Nate noticed Anna's hair as soon as she slipped off her scarf. 'Nice hair, Anna.'

'Thank you.'

Jake wrinkled his nose when they weren't looking, then had a word with himself for acting childish.

'In the kitchen,' called out Josephine. 'There's some tea in the pot.'

They joined her at the kitchen table, where she poured their tea and then watched them sipping the liquid.

'That's enough,' she said, snatching away Anna's cup. She got up quickly and tipped the rest down the sink.

'Gran!' snapped Nate.

Josephine stared into the cup, twisting it around in her hand whilst humming to herself.

Anna glanced nervously at Jake, and he gave Nate a significant look. 'Can we just drink some tea?'

'Oh poppycock,' said Josephine, waving one hand. 'You're just jealous because I'm not doing yours, Jacob Reynolds.'

Nate took the cup away from his grandmother, rinsed it out, and poured Anna some more tea.

Anna was obviously curious. 'Did you even see anything? I thought you have to wait until I have finished.'

Jake arched an eyebrow at her.

Really, Anna?

Anna sank slightly into her chair.

Josephine's face was stern and serious. 'You mind that snow, Anna.'

Nate huffed loudly. 'Oh, Gran, will you stop with the snow.' He pointed out the window. 'Does it look like it is going to snow?'

Josephine sniffed and walked away stating, 'It will.'

Nate shook his head as he sat next to Anna. A little too close, in Jake's silent opinion.

It was clear to him that Anna liked Nate. He wasn't sure how much, but she definitely relaxed more around Nate than she did him, and that bothered him slightly.

He watched quietly whilst Nate made jokes about farming and the weather, and Anna laughed along, enjoying his company.

I'm reading too much into this. Anna is sweet and friendly, and Nate talks to everyone as though he has known them for ten years. He's not ready to start dating again anyway. If he was, I'm sure Tessie would be at the top of his list. What if she's not? I wasn't looking to date anyone until I met Anna. Now I can't stop thinking about her. What if she's the one he's been waiting for? What if my role in this was just to bring her here for Nate Walker. What kind of fate is that? Not one I'm happy with. Look how well they get on. Do they even know that I'm still here?

The short stopover for a polite cup of tea seemed to drag for Jake. At one point, he felt like going to sit with the dogs. At least they might acknowledge his existence.

'We should head back now,' he said, interrupting their conversation. 'You know, in case that storm does suddenly hit.' He added a playful smile.

Nate laughed with him and stood up to show them out. 'Jake, bring Anna here for dinner tomorrow night.' He turned to Anna. 'I'll get Joey to bring a cake up from the shop. You'll love her cakes.'

'Yeah,' said Jake. 'Best baker in the world is our Joey.'

Anna quietly put on her coat and scarf.

Nate pointed over at his dusty pick-up truck. 'I'll drop you home, if you want.'

'There's not enough room in the front,' said Jake, frowning down at the muddy wheels.

'You can sit in the back with the dog.'

Jake raised his eyebrows. 'We'll walk, thanks.'

Anna called Max, and he reluctantly came outside. The icy air hit his nostrils, waking him immediately, and he darted off in front.

Nate waved them goodbye as they made their way down his long driveway, towards Pepper Lane.

Anna kept looking sideways, and he could sense she wanted to say something.

'What is it?' he asked.

'Don't you like Nate much?'

The question threw him. He'd been friends with Nathanial Walker for as long as he could remember. They had always got on like a house on fire.

'Yeah, I like him. Why do you ask that?'

Anna shrugged slightly. 'You just seem a bit narky around him.'

'Narky?'

She nodded. 'Yeah, you know, irritated, a bit…'

'I know what it means.'

'Just made me think you might not like him much.'

I like him. Do you?

'He's my mate. Of course I like him.' He now felt annoyed with himself for snapping at her.

Anna sank into her scarf.

Why did I just talk to her like that? I sounded horrible. She'll want to go home if I keep that up. What's wrong with me? She should have told me not to use that tone on her. Why didn't she snap back at me? She had every right to say something. I feel like shit now. She's gone quiet. Probably hates me. I hate me.

'I'm sorry, Anna. I shouldn't have snapped.'

She stayed silent, and he didn't blame her one bit.

Nothing more was said all the way to Starlight Cottage. The walk felt longer than usual, and the silence awkward, and she didn't hold his arm. Not that he offered. He was too afraid of the rejection.

Dinner was a solemn affair that night. He had made a carrot and parsnip soup, as neither of them was really hungry. Max was the only one that smiled in the kitchen.

Jake had words with himself over his jealousy of Nate with Anna. He knew he was being stupid. He also knew how Nate liked to wind him up.

'You're always so serious, Jake,' he had often told him whilst they were growing up.

Jake knew his downfalls. He knew what areas of his personality he had to work on. He had been working hard on himself since his grandmother passed away. He didn't like the man he was back then. He wanted his gran to be proud of him. He wanted to feel proud of himself.

What would you say to me now, Gran? You wouldn't be very impressed, I know. I didn't mean to bite her head off. I just got a bit... well, I think we both know how I was feeling. It's so bloody frustrating. Why can't she relax around me the way she does around him. What's he got that's so bloody special? Look, now I'm putting Nate down. Like anyone can put him down. He's everyone's mate, a solid family man, he looks like he could be a stunt double for Dwayne Johnson, and I know he wouldn't hit on Anna. He thinks she's my girlfriend. They all do. He was just getting to know her, that's all. I really need to get a grip. I can't go backwards here. I've still got so much to change about myself.

Josh flashed through his mind. His little brother needed to change his fickle ways. Jake wanted his grandparents to be proud of his brother as well. They were the only Reynolds left. They couldn't let the side down.

I'm sorry, Gran. I won't let you down. I'm going to try harder. I guess I just wasn't expecting any of this in my life. One minute, I'm on my own, trying to keep my shit together, and the next thing I know, this woman and dog are standing outside my front door. I even slept in her tent. I still can't get over that. I still can't get over the fact that there has been a woman sleeping on the roof right above me and I didn't even notice. I feel so attached to her already. It's starting to freak me out a bit, if I'm honest. I know Gramps said he fell in love with you as soon as he saw you, but I always thought he was exaggerating. I feel unprepared. It would have been nice to have had a bit of a warning or something. It's like being pushed in the deep end on your very first swimming lesson.

He watched quietly as Anna went to her room. He would have to talk to her about how he felt. There was no way he could keep pretending he didn't have feelings towards her. He just wondered where that would leave him. He'd never dealt with rejection before. He'd never fallen for someone before.

I can't say anything that might scare her off. I don't want to come across as an idiot either. Although, I've probably already achieved that much. I might sort the pool out and go for a swim. That will help me sleep tonight. I can't keep staring at the wall between us. Great! I've just created a bloody great big new wall between us. Why can't I be like a normal person for once? Roll on tomorrow. New day, fresh start. I'll sort this whole mess out then. I can't go on like this. It's not fair on Anna, nor me.

24

Anna

The sun had long set, and Anna felt as though she could join it in going to bed for the night.

The cold air made her cough, so she pulled her head in from outside and closed the bedroom window. There wasn't much to look at when darkness set in. Pepper Pot Farm had the only beacon of light. There were no distracting sounds either, just peace and quiet.

Lights suddenly lit the garden, revealing Jake stepping out of the shadow of the cottage and walking over to the pool house.

Anna took a step back from the window, in case he saw her watching him. He looked peaceful as he pottered around inside the glass-built building. She could see him pressing buttons on a panel, then doing some sort of water test, which involved something that looked like a bottle on a stick. He seemed satisfied with whatever he was doing, then removed all of his clothes.

Bloody hell, he's starkers. Oh my God. How fit is his body. I shouldn't stare. He wouldn't look if it was me, or would he? I wouldn't strip off in a glass building. No one needs to see that. Mind you, I might if I looked like him. I've got to stop staring.

She switched the bedside lamp off and stepped to the side of the window, making sure she was definitely out of sight whilst wondering if she looked like some sort of perv. He was putting on dark swimming shorts, and the small black item of clothing did little to hide his toned physique.

He dangled his legs in the water for a moment before heading off into a front crawl.

He's a good swimmer. Wish I could swim. He's so perfect. Why does he have to ruin it by being moody? He seems to be mostly that way around Nate. What would I know. I hardly know him.

She wasn't sure if she believed him about liking Nate. He did act odd around him. She had noticed how his body tightened, and his lips pursed. How his tone became harsh, and his eyes lost their sparkle.

As far as she was concerned, there was definitely something going on between the pair of them, and she did wonder if it had anything to do with how close Jake and Joey were.

There's probably some family history there. Stuff I don't know about. I won't ask him. He'll just bite my head off again. It's none of my business anyway. I might say something to him though. Not about his business. I'll talk to him about how he made me feel when he snapped. It was uncalled for, and I'm not staying here with him if it continues. I have to look out for red flags. I can't put myself in another Rob situation. I have to admit, he doesn't feel like Rob. There's definitely something wrong, but... Stop thinking about it. You're giving yourself a headache, and stop watching him. Blimey, Anna, all you need is a chair and some popcorn. Right, let's do something else. Read, I think.

As she walked over to the bedroom door, she heard a buzzing sound. She followed the noise all the way into Jake's room.

It's his phone.

She picked it up and was surprised to see Mrs Blake's name on the screen.

She felt rude answering his phone, but because it was Mrs Blake, she felt rude not answering the call.

'Hello, Betty, it's Anna. Is everything all right?'

Betty's rough voice bellowed down the phone. 'Anna, dear. My electric has gone. I've tried calling Joey, but can't get through, and Jake did tell me to call him if I needed anything.'

Oh, poor Betty.

'Don't worry, Betty. I'll come over and see if I can help.'

'Will you, dear? I know what the problem is. It's the electric box. It's happened before. The little switch flipped, and all you have to do is flick it back again, but I get too scared to do it, you see. I worry about getting an electric shock.'

Anna smiled to herself. 'Oh, okay. That's not a problem, Betty. I can do that for you. I'll be right over.'

'Thank you, Anna.'

She put the phone back on the side, feeling glad to have something to do to escape Jake's mood swings for a while. He hadn't even spoken to her during dinner. She was glad she had Max there for company. At least he smiled.

She quietly made her way downstairs and sneaked out the back door.

The side door of the garage was unlocked, so Anna went inside to fetch Edith's bicycle.

The icy wind whipped into her new hair style as she happily cycled along Pepper Lane, feeling free and alive.

The journey was all downhill, making it easy-going for someone who hadn't been on a bike for years.

She lifted her legs in the air as the bike rolled down the hill.

'Weee…' she cried, laughing to herself at herself.

She was glad she didn't tell Jake her plans. He probably would have spouted on about safety or something. She was also glad to have the opportunity to clear her head of him and Joey. She didn't even have Max to worry about.

She glanced out at the darkness of the surrounding fields. Cottages of all shapes and sizes were darted here, there, and everywhere. Some close, some further away from the lane. Light was peeking out from their windows, and smoke wafted from chimney tops, bringing the quaint homes to life. It was a beautiful sight, even at night. She could understand why people came to Pepper Bay to paint pictures, especially of the cottages.

Oh, I just love it here. I want to see what it looks like in the middle of summer. I'd ride this bike every time the sun shines. It's so adorable. Now I know what Edith felt like heading off to work before she moved into the shop. I bet she lifted her feet off the pedals from time to time too and shouted, weee.

She removed her feet from the pedals once again. 'Weee...' She giggled, blowing cold air from her mouth.

The journey down Pepper Lane didn't seem long, and as she hadn't once thought about escaped panthers from the zoo or axe murderers hiding in blackberry bushes, she had enjoyed her unexpected night-time trip very much, especially when light snowflakes began to fall.

She pushed on the door of The Book Gallery to see if it was unlocked. It was, so she steered the bike inside and rested it against the counter. The shop was in complete darkness.

'Betty, it's me, Anna,' she called out.

Betty appeared from the back of the shop. 'Over here, dear.'

Anna made her way over to the fuse box.

'Thank you for coming, Anna. I'm so pleased it's you.'

Anna flicked the switch, and the lights came on. 'That's okay, Betty. Happy to help.'

Betty noticed Edith's bike. 'Did you come down here on that thing?'

'It was so much fun. Pepper Lane looks so magical tonight.'

Betty scrunched her nose up. 'It won't on the way back. All uphill you know. There's no magic in that.'

I hadn't thought about that.

'Oh yeah. Never mind. The walk will do me good.'

Betty frowned at Anna's thin fleece jacket. 'You should have a coat on, Anna. Where's your hat and scarf?' She pointed to the front window of the shop. 'Look, it's snowing now. You'll freeze out there.'

Anna felt quite warm from her exercise. 'I'll be all right, but I'll head back now though, in case the snow gets worse.'

Betty thanked her once more and locked the shop door behind her.

Anna frowned in amazement at the sight of the snow.

Bloody hell, where did all this snow suddenly come from, Canada?

The snow was falling thick and fast. Big heavy clumps had already started to settle on the ground. The wind had picked up, and the temperature had dropped dramatically.

I was only gone five minutes.

She struggled to cycle so got off and walked alongside the bike. Her bare hands had already started to stiffen, and she was pretty sure her lips were blue. The snow was smacking her in the face, stinging her skin, so she lowered her head and squinted her eyes as she slowly plodded uphill.

The sky had opened up and dropped more snow down than the whole of England had ever had in their history of snowfall.

Anna's feet were numb, her ears were burning, and her body wouldn't stop shaking. Her jaw was stiff, and she could barely move her mouth. She longed for her coat, scarf, gloves, hat, anything. She longed for the heater in Jake's car. She kept her mind on the logs burning in the fireplace up at Starlight Cottage, whilst looking down at her feet, willing them to keep moving. They were covered in snow and felt slow and heavy. She couldn't believe how deep the snow was already. She had never known anything like it.

One of Stan's favourite subjects was to talk about climate change. She could hear him moaning about it now. Telling her unusual weather activity was a given nowadays.

Her teeth wouldn't stop chattering, and she was getting a headache and pain in her ears. She could barely see the road before her, and Pepper Lane felt as though it was going on forever.

The icy wind swirled the snow in all directions. It wrapped around her body and blew straight through her clothes to grab her skin tightly. Her chest was constricted, and her thoughts disorientated. The snow reached over the top of her ankle boots and seeped into her jeans, but she could no longer feel her legs so didn't notice.

Anna's eyes almost closed. She kept her head low. Her steps were becoming slower and slower the further uphill she went. She couldn't feel her hands nor could she feel her face or breathe properly. Suddenly, she couldn't walk any further. She dropped to her knees, the bike falling away from her side. Arctic weather consumed her completely.

25

Jake

'Well, would you look at that, Max. A snowstorm after all.'

Max remained curled up in front of the fire. The snow could wait.

Jake rubbed a cream hand towel over his head, then pulled the belt on his dressing gown tighter around him. 'Five more minutes out there, and I would've ended up a snowman.' He laughed to himself as he approached the stairs to glance up. 'Anna, have you looked outside? It's snowing.'

There was no reply.

'Anna?'

He wondered if she might be in the shower so made his way up the stairs and listened at her door.

Maybe she's gone to sleep already. She was awake when I was in the pool house. I saw her watching me from Josh's window. I was hoping she would join me.

He poked his head around her door to find an empty room.

'Anna,' he called.

Silence.

He looked in his own room.

Where is she?

Picking up his phone, he headed back out to the landing.

'Anna,' he called again, only attracting Max's attention.

He searched the house and was starting to worry. He could see how bad the snowstorm was, but he was sure she wouldn't be outside. Looking out of a window, he noticed the garage side door flapping in the wind.

He rushed down to look inside.

'Anna,' he questioned, glancing around the back of his car. His slippers were soaked through, and he was freezing.

Where the hell is she?

He pulled his phone out of his dressing gown pocket when it buzzed, and he frowned down at Mrs Blake's name.

'Hello, Mrs Blake. Everything all right?'

'Yes. I just wanted to make sure Anna got home all right in this snow.'

Jake stilled. He was sure his heart had stopped beating. 'What?'

'She helped me with the electric,' said Mrs Blake. 'She's a good girl.'

His voice was firm. 'When did she leave?'

'Ooh, I don't know. Not too long ago. I think. She was riding that bike of Edith's.'

He hung up the call before Mrs Blake could add another word. His eyes did a double take at the wall where his grandmother's bike usually sat.

Bloody hell, Anna!

He ran back to the house and darted up the stairs to throw on jeans and a jumper. He quickly headed to the cloakroom to fetch his boots and car key. He saw straight away that she hadn't taken her coat or scarf. He ushered Max into the car and headed off down the lane.

The snow was smashing into the windscreen, blinding his view. The windscreen wipers were working hard to clear the way, but the furious snow was winning the battle.

'What is happening out here?'

Max poked his nose forward from the back seat.

Jake quickly stopped, took off his seatbelt, turned to Max, strapped him in, and then turned back and strapped himself back in. 'Sorry, Max. My head's all over the place.'

He moved the car forward, going as slowly as he could.

'She's got to be along here somewhere, mate.'

He drove the whole length of Pepper Lane.

'Where is she?'

His heart was racing as his eyes darted left and right, trying to see through the thick blizzard.

'I can't see a bloody thing,' he yelled to the dashboard, agony filling his voice.

He pulled over and called Nate.

'Nate, I need your help. I can't find Anna. She's along Pepper Lane somewhere. She's got no coat and Gran's bike.'

'I'm leaving right now. Which end are you?'

'Bottom.'

'I'll head up towards Starlight, then back down towards you. We'll meet in the middle.'

Jake took a deep breath as Nate got off the phone. He peered over to the shops to see if any lights were on. Everything looked closed up for the night. Even his gran's flat was in darkness. He knew he wasn't allowed to take the car that far down into Pepper Lane unless loading or unloading, but there was no way he could walk around out there.

'Okay, I guess we're going back up then, Max.'

He slowly pulled away, leant all the way forward, and tried to see where he was driving. He put his headlights on full beam.

'This is ridiculous! Look how deep it is already. Even in this car we're going to get stuck in a minute if this keeps up.'

His phone buzzed on the dash. He pulled over to see it was Nate ringing.

'Jake, I've found her. She was collapsed at the end of my drive.'

Jake felt the blood leave his face.

'I've called the doctor,' added Nate.

'I'm on my way.'

He drove to Pepper Pot Farm as fast as the heavy snow would allow.

Joey held the front door open for him as soon as she saw his headlights coming up the driveway.

'She's in here.' She pointed to the living room.

Jake froze in the doorway at the sight before his eyes.

Anna was sitting on the floor in front of the fire, wrapped in a load of blankets. Nate was sitting behind her, holding her tightly in his big strong arms. Her head was low, and her body was shaking uncontrollably.

Josephine swept past him, holding a pair of Joey's fleece pyjamas. 'We need to get her out of those wet clothes.'

Joey passed her phone to Jake. 'Hold this. It's Doctor Tully. He can't get over here in this storm, but he's telling us what to do.'

Jake stared at the phone that was shoved into his hand.

'Wait in the kitchen till we've got her changed,' called over Josephine.

Nate led Jake away, taking the phone from him.

'Hello, Doc, it's Nate.'

Jake sat down at the table. His mind had gone blank. He didn't know what to say or do. He could hear Nate's voice behind him. It sounded faded.

Wake up.

He shot up out of the chair.

Nate quickly grabbed his shoulder. 'Wait, mate. Let them change her clothes.'

Joey rushed into the kitchen and took the phone from Nate. She pointed at the kettle. 'Sweet tea, Nate.'

Jake followed Joey back to the living room.

Josephine had Anna wrapped in dry blankets and was massaging her legs.

Anna was still severely shaking.

'Her lips are no longer blue,' Joey said into the phone. 'Okay. Okay. Okay.' She looked at Jake. 'Doc says that's a good sign.'

Josephine waved Jake over. 'Get over here. Sit behind her and hold her. She needs body heat.'

Jake did as he was told. He lowered himself to the rug and wrapped his arms around her, just like he had witnessed Nate do. Her rigorous shaking was vibrating his body.

Christ, Anna!

'It's all right,' he said softly. 'You're all right now, Anna.'

'Lift that blanket over her head,' said Josephine. 'Keep her warm.'

Jake raised the blanket so that Anna was wrapped like Little Red Riding Hood. He didn't know how to think or feel. He was so worried. Her body felt frail in his arms, and her shivers were fast and furious.

Nate brought in a cup of hot sweet tea and handed it to his grandmother.

'Sit here, Nate,' she told him, tugging his sleeve down towards her. 'Rub her feet. Get some circulation back.'

The mug of tea was raised to Anna's lips.

Jake was watching over her shoulder.

'Try, Anna,' he pleaded.

Anna sipped some tea.

'Good,' said Josephine.

Joey looked down at Nate. 'He said check her fingers and toes. Black is bad.'

Jake felt lightheaded.

Nate removed Joey's chunky bed sock from one of Anna's feet.

All eyes peered down.

Jake took a deep breath as he started to rub Anna's left arm.

Nate looked up at Joey. 'They don't look like a normal colour, but not black.'

Joey repeated his words down the phone.

All eyes were now on her.

She gave a slight smile and raised her thumb. 'He said she should be all right soon.' She turned away to face her niece, who was walking down the stairs. 'All right, Doc. Thanks.' She hung up the phone. 'Daisy, take the dogs upstairs, will you.'

'Is she going to be all right?' asked Daisy.

Joey smiled warmly at the girl and tucked her blonde hair behind her ear. 'She should be. Let's give her some peace.'

Daisy nodded and guided Max and Scruff upstairs to her room.

Joey sat down on the floor by Anna and started to rub one of her legs. 'Doc said to ring him back if anything changes, but other than that, she should start to defrost soon.'

Anna was still shaking.

Josephine got her to drink some more tea.

'You'll have to sleep here tonight,' she told Jake. 'I'll change the sheets in Robyn's room. She's not here tonight.

You can't go back out in that, and Anna's going nowhere.' She shot a concerned look at Anna before getting up to sort the sleeping arrangements.

Joey leaned closer to Anna and joined Jake in cuddling her.

Nate replaced the bed sock and continued to rub Anna's feet, ankles, and shins.

'You'll be warm in no time, Anna,' he said softly. He leaned over and placed another log on the fire.

Joey picked up the mug of tea and helped Anna to drink some more.

Jake mouthed the words, 'Thank you,' to them both. He snuggled his face into the blanket at the side of Anna's head. 'How are you feeling now, Anna?'

She tried to speak, but her teeth were still chattering.

He gently shushed her. 'It's okay. Don't speak. Just relax. We've got you. It's going to be okay.'

26

Anna

Anna was tucked up in Robyn's single bed. She felt tired and was no longer shaking, but there was a chill in her body that was stopping her from falling asleep. The heating had been turned up, as the temperature outside was below freezing.

The wild snowstorm and bitter cold had caught everyone in England off guard, all except Josephine Walker.

The Walkers were sitting downstairs in the kitchen, listening to the news. The reporter was telling the country what a phenomenal occurrence the amount of snow was.

Upstairs, in Robyn's bedroom, Jake stood at the window, staring at the height of the snow. It had levelled up with the top of his car's wheel arch.

Anna stirred, sensing a presence around her. She could vaguely remember Nate holding her shaky body. How his warmth helped calm her immediately. 'Nate?'

'No, it's Jake.' His soft tone almost echoed around the small pink-and-peach room.

Her eyes flickered to see him sit down in a pink chair at her side.

'Are you okay?' he asked softly, leaning forward to gently stroke her hair away from her cheek.

She had a burning sensation under her skin on her hands that tingled slightly and a chill in her body that wasn't going away. She wished the feeling in her big toes would return.

'I can't get this chill out of me, Jake.'

Her eyes were half closed, but she saw him shift in the chair.

'I can hold you in bed, if you want,' he said quietly. 'My body heat will help you.'

She appreciated his offer more than he would ever know. 'Please, if it's not a bother.'

'It's not a bother, Anna.'

He got up and removed Nate's green dressing gown from his body to reveal the oversized pyjamas he was wearing. He clutched at his tied-but-still-loose waistband and walked around the other side of the bed, pulled back the covers, and squeezed into the small space behind her.

Anna felt the warmth from his body come through his pyjamas. It entered her straight away. She felt too weary to smile when his arm came around her waist and his warm hand held hers, lightly massaging her fingertips.

His face was so close to her hair, and she could feel his breath touching her. He felt so good, and she wished she had the energy to turn around and kiss him.

'Thank you, Jake.'

'Rest now, Anna,' he whispered.

She closed her eyes and relaxed deeply into the arms and warmth of the caring man in her bed.

* * *

Anna was stuck in a hole that was filled with snow. She couldn't breathe properly, and she was sinking fast. Her heart was racing as panic took over. She couldn't see. She couldn't hear. Every part of her was numb. She wanted to cry out for help, but her voice had disappeared. All sound had disappeared. She was alone and scared. Suddenly, Nate was calling her name. His hand was reaching down to her, grabbing her. He pulled her up, and she was safe in his arms. He was carrying her somewhere. Somewhere far away. Somewhere warm. She felt her body suddenly jolt back to life.

'Nate?'

The arm resting over her waistline moved.

'It's Jake,' came a soft voice from behind her.

She opened her sleepy eyes. 'Jake?'

'Yes.'

Her body relaxed, immediately feeling safe and warm.

I'm so glad you're here with me.

His arm went to slip away. Without thinking, she moved her hand and held his tightly to her stomach. She felt him still.

Please, don't go. Hold me. Just stay holding me. I just want us to stay like this.

'How are you feeling?' he asked. There was something about his tone that sounded slightly off.

The full force of last night's events hit her hard, as she suddenly remembered every detail. She took a calming breath as a twinge of guilt came over her.

'Embarrassed,' she replied.

Jake's body adjusted itself to hers as she stretched out her legs.

'There's no need to be, Anna. It's not your fault.'

She watched his arm leave her body. She could feel him struggling to sit up behind her in the small bed.

'I need to check your fingers and toes this morning,' he said flatly. 'The doctor told us last night.'

He doesn't sound happy. Probably because he had to spend the night babysitting me.

She rolled over onto her back as he left the bed, placing her hands upon the top of the cover to glance down at them.

He reached over and softly stroked her fingertips as he examined them.

Hold my hand again, Jake. Please, get back in bed with me.

'They look okay,' he said.

She watched his eyes roll towards her head as his hand reached up to remove her hair away from her brow. There was a gentleness in his face, and his light touch was so soothing, she closed her eyes until she felt his hand move away. She sighed inwardly and scrunched her toes. 'One of my big toes feels a bit numb.'

A thin line appeared on his forehead as he moved to the bottom of the bed and untucked one corner to study her feet. 'One toe looks bruised. I'll call Doctor Tully. See what he says.'

She watched him quietly manoeuvre around the small room. He pulled on a dressing gown, turned his back on her, removed the pyjama bottoms, tugged on his jeans, and swiftly left without looking back.

I've upset him. I've made a fool of myself. All those people had to save me. What a complete idiot. What are they going to think of me? The whole of Pepper Bay will know by the end of the day. Great! I want to go home. I wish I never came here now.

She got up, once she was sure Jake wasn't coming back, and went off to find the bathroom. She dithered inside, prolonging the agony of facing everyone downstairs. There was a folded beige hand towel and flannel with a lilac toothbrush still in its wrapper sitting on top of a shelf above the sink. An orange sticky-note was attached with Anna's name written on it in blue ink. She washed her face and brushed her teeth and tucked her hair behind her ears. She stared at her gaunt face in the mirror.

Oh God, what a mess. Why me? Why did this have to happen to me?

Making her way downstairs, she could hear voices coming from the kitchen. She took a breath and entered.

Joey jumped out of her chair and rushed forward. 'Anna, how are you?' She wrapped her arms around her, drawing her into a huge hug. 'You scared the life out of us last night.'

Anna felt the blood hit her cheeks.

Josephine smiled over at her from the stove. 'She's got some colour back in her face. She's all right.'

Joey guided Anna to the table and sat her down next to Jake. 'We've dried your clothes, and Max has been fed. You don't have to worry about him. He's outside with Nate and Scruff. It's a bit milder out there this morning. Nate's out clearing a pathway. Have you seen how high the snow is? It has broken records. They're saying so on the news.'

Josephine placed a hot cup of tea in front of Anna. 'I'm making you some porridge, young lady, and you're going to eat every last bit.'

'She will,' said Jake flatly, looking into his coffee.

He can't look at me. I feel so stupid.

Joey released Anna of her hold. 'Jake spoke to Doctor Tully just a minute ago. The doctor isn't worried about you. He thinks you're fine. Lucky, but fine. He just said to keep an eye on your toe. It should look a lot better tomorrow. He said you're to stay home and keep warm.'

Anna could see the relief in Joey's eyes.

Jake abruptly got up from the table. 'I'm going outside to see if I can help Nate.'

Joey pointed to a door. 'Put on some of those waterproof overalls and boots in there, Jake. There are some gloves and woolly hats in there too.'

Anna glanced sideways to see that he was dressed to go home.

He's not going to speak to me now that he knows I'm okay. I've really embarrassed him in front of his friends. Don't cry. It's all right. Everything will be fine.

She waited for him to leave.

'I'm sorry,' she whispered into her tea.

Joey placed her hand on Anna's arm. 'Hey, you have nothing to apologise for. It's not your fault a planet's worth of snow fell on you.'

'I did warn you,' said Josephine.

Joey narrowed her eyes at her grandmother. She softened her face as she turned back to Anna.

Anna could feel tears welling up. 'I'm so sorry.'

'It's okay, Anna,' whispered Joey.

27

Jake

Jake's eyes widened at the height of the snow. The path between the back door of the farmhouse and the outbuilding where the cows were had been cleared by Nate, but the driveway leading to Pepper Lane was still full. He knew the lane would be untouched as well.

Great! How am I supposed to get Anna back to Starlight? She needs to be home where I can look after her properly. She needs me. I'm supposed to be helping her. I'm so glad she isn't on the rooftop. What if she was still there and I didn't know about her? I can't think like that. She's here. She's safe.

He looked over at the big barn. Nate was still clearing snow and creating pathways. Jake knew that his old friend had been up since before the crack of dawn, seeing to the cows, the henhouse, and, no doubt, weightlifting for an hour in the small gym he had set up over in another barn.

Max and Scruff were mooching around Nate in any snow-cleared space they could find.

The air was milder than the night before but still bitterly cold. It burned into the back of Jake's throat as soon as he inhaled. He raised his hand to cover his mouth as he coughed. He narrowed his eyes and lowered his head and made his way over to Nate.

'Hey, Jake, nice look,' said Nate, eyeing the overalls whilst handing him a shovel. 'How's Anna doing?'

'She's going to make a full recovery.'

But if I have to hear her say your name one more time… Shut up, Jake. It's not his fault. Look at him. Of course Anna's going to be smitten. All women are. They always were, ever since we were kids, way before he had that body.

Nate held a puzzled look. 'You okay, Jake?'

Jake ignored his damaged ego. 'Yeah. What do you need me to do?'

Nate laughed out at the mound of snow surrounding them. 'Not sure where to start. Gran says there's another load coming later on, so, apparently, I'm wasting my time, but I had to get to the cows.' He nodded towards the main road. 'There's no point trying to shift that lot if we've got more on the way. I was thinking of trying out the tractor to get you and Anna back up to Starlight.' He glanced sideways. 'Or you could stay here another night.'

'We'll try the tractor,' said Jake abruptly.

Nate chuckled out a waft of cold air. 'Oh, I won't take offence.'

Be nice, Jake. The Walkers are like family. Nate saved Anna.

'Sorry, just want to get home. You know how it is.'

'Yeah, I know, mate. Let's get over to the tractor now, see if we can make a pathway from it to the lane.'

A faint crease appeared between Jake's brows, just beneath his woolly hat. 'Hey, Nate. Thanks for coming out last night and finding Anna.'

Nate's face stiffened a touch. He gave a slight nod and patted Jake on the arm. 'No worries. That's what friends are for. I'm just glad she's okay.'

* * *

The ride inside the small enclosed cabin of Nate's wine-red tractor was slow and not as easy as they thought it would be. They had jumped out a few times to clear some snow from Pepper Lane, then they had to clear the driveway that led to Starlight Cottage.

Jake went inside whilst Nate went back to Pepper Pot Farm to fetch Anna and Max, as the tractor wasn't big enough for them all.

His face and hands were burning from the snow, so the warmth in the cottage from the heating being left on all night was appreciated. He glanced over at the dead fire that had burned out during the night. His eyes dulled, and he sighed deeply.

Bloody snow. Why did I come here? I could have gone to New York with Josh, or The Bahamas would have been better. I'm not going to allow this to bother me, and I'm not going to allow Anna's obsession with Nate bother me, and I'm definitely not going to let that mess in the kitchen bother me.

He glanced at the washing up that needed doing.

Sometimes, Jake Reynolds, I really bloody hate you.

He sat down on the bottom step of the stairs and removed his boots. He wanted a hot shower but wanted to wait till Anna returned.

I'll run her a bath.

He trotted up the stairs and into the biggest bathroom Starlight Cottage had, because it had the best bath. An oval, shiny, walnut wood tub sat against one side of the room. He rinsed it out and then sat on the floor beside it whilst the water poured out of a gold waterfall tap attached to the cream wall.

Her body was in my arms all night. Where the hell did those goosebumps come from? I've never had goosebumps from holding a woman before. Never held one all night before either. First time I've slept in a single bed since I was a kid too. I really wanted to stay in bed with her.

His face shined in the steam from the water.

She felt so frail. I've only just found her, and I could have lost her. I don't care about Nate. I'm going to have to talk to her about this. I need her to know how I feel. I need to get this off my chest.

With his eyes glossed over, he cleared his throat and got up to fetch Anna some pyjamas and his dressing gown.

She can have a pyjama day.

He glanced down at his jeans.

We both can.

The navy dressing gown was carefully placed on a cream wingback chair in the corner of the room. Jake peeked out of the window at the settled snow.

Christ! We've got more of this to come later on? There's no way I'm letting Anna out there again. Frank won't want to land the helicopter in this for at least a week. She won't be able to go back. If this is all over the country, her tent will be covered. I'll call Stan, see if he can take it all down. He has spare keys to the apartments. He can leave her things in mine.

He turned the tap off and wondered if he should light the three candles that were inside the large white storm lanterns that were clustered together on the floor.

Edith loved candles. She always had one in every room. Some scented, some plain. Jake had never lit a candle in his life, with the exception of birthday candles.

He glanced over at the cupboard.

I bet there's a lighter in there somewhere, knowing Gran.

He opened the door and rummaged through the white baskets that lined four shelves.

Ah ha!

He glanced once more at the lanterns, narrowing his eyes. His hand dithered before the first candle. There wasn't much left of it, but enough for a long hot soak in the tub. He lit the wick and then decided he might as well light the other ones.

A small transparent box filled with rose petals caught his eye in the cupboard as he replaced the red lighter.

Bath petals was printed on the box.

His eyes rolled over to the steaming bath.

Too much. She'll like it. Will she? Would you? No. It's a bit anniversary. No, it's too much. I'm not doing it. Would Nate do it? Josh would probably do it just for a laugh. It's not funny. I'm not doing it. Gramps would do it, but he loved romance, so did Gran.

He picked up the box and twiddled it around in his hand. He flung it back into the cupboard and closed the door.

I'm not doing it.

28

Anna

Anna waved goodbye to Nate from the doorway of Starlight Cottage, then closed the door.

Max ran straight into the kitchen to have a drink of water from his new bowl that Jake had bought over in Sandly.

She felt sluggish and really wanted to get out of her clothes and just flop on the sofa for the day. She slowly made her way up the stairs to be greeted by Jake at the top.

'Everything okay?' he asked. His voice seemed lighter, and his eyes more relaxed.

Nothing feels okay about my life, if that's what you're asking, but I know you're not.

She nodded and offered a weak smile. 'Tractor was fun. Bit of a tight squeeze, especially with Max on my lap, but at least he kept me warm. I still don't know how we managed to fit.'

Jake's smile was just as weak. 'I'm glad you're back now. I've taken the liberty of running you a bath.' He pointed towards the bathroom. 'I've put some pyjamas out. Thought we'd have a PJ day. Eat, watch movies, if you like.'

She glanced towards the bathroom door.

That's so thoughtful.

'Thank you. I get the feeling I'm going to be nice and warm today.' She suppressed a laugh.

'Yes. You are.' His voice sounded commanding, and his face looked as stern as it was at the farmhouse. He must have realised, because his expression softened. 'The heating is on, and I'm about to light the fire, and then I'll wash and dry all your clothes ready for the week ahead.'

The week?

'It doesn't look as though we're going anywhere for a few days, Anna,' he added, walking away.

I didn't think about that. Rob's going to have a fit if I don't turn up at the shop, even if it's snowed in, he'll still expect me to take my shift. Great, that's all I need, him on my back. He'll go on and on about it forever. I can't think about him right now. Right now, I'm in Pepper Bay, and he doesn't exist.

She idly wandered into the bathroom. Her eyes met with the burning candles first, and then they rolled over to the pink and white rose petals floating in the most beautiful bath she had ever seen.

Oh my goodness! How lovely is that. Don't cry. Don't be silly. It's just a bath. A lovely bath. He did this for me. He doesn't hate me. He has given me rose petals. I've never bathed with rose petals before. I've never been in a bath like that before either. I think I'm actually in heaven.

She leaned over and placed her hand in the water to feel that the temperature was just right, then removed her clothes and looked over her body in the tall, dark-framed floor mirror over by the window.

I need to eat more. I'm fading away. I'll ask Jake if I can have some of his vitamins this week. I know I need a boost. Everything about me needs a boost, preferably starting with my mind.

She turned to the window, knowing full well there wasn't a single soul around to see her naked body through the glass. The view was of the pathway that led up to the clifftop.

The whiteness of the snow outside filled the room with a dull light, only lifted by the three lanterns on the floor. The steam from the bath mingled with the heating from a long chrome radiator attached to the wall near the door. Anna could smell the faint scent of something creamy.

She enjoyed every single touch the water made on her bare skin as she entered the inviting tub.

Her blue eyes sparkled as they rolled over to a dark wooden stand that stood next to the bath. Almond milk shampoo, conditioner, and bath cream filled the top slats, along with the book *The Bridges of Madison County*. A coral sponge, cream face cloth, and a new disposable razor sat on the second shelf. Down the bottom was a back scrubber, a face cleanser, and her own bottle of apple shampoo.

He's thought of everything. I really am not gonna cry.

She quickly wiped away a falling tear as she smiled softly at the comfort and care now in her life. She took a moment to absorb her idyllic surroundings once more, and then she sank down further into the heated liquid, submerging her head.

Oh, I can feel my body again. Thank you, Lord, universe, guardian angel, whoever looked after me last night. Thank you to the Walkers, and Doctor Tully, and Jake. Thank you so much for Jake Reynolds.

She took a calming breath as she came up for air, then reached over for the almond milk shampoo.

* * *

Jake was holding a plate full of pastries that Joey had given him to take back with him that morning. He smiled warmly as Anna entered the living room.

She watched him place the food down on the coffee table and sit down at one end of the comfy sofa.

Feeling refreshed and happy, she gazed at her slightly pruned fingers from her long stay in the bath. She did wonder at one point if Jake might knock on the door to see if she was okay, but he had left her alone. She hadn't felt rushed or awkward. Her time spent in the bathroom felt as comfortable as home. She had enjoyed a few chapters of the book he put out for her, and she had felt snuggly slipping into her pyjamas and his dressing gown. Her new hair had dried nicely, which she was surprised about, as she was sure she would turn the cute bob into a bushy mess, and she now smelled just like Jake and that made her smile from the inside out. Although, she still preferred the smell on him.

He nodded at her dressing gown. 'That's going to need a wash at some point.'

Anna sat at the other end of the sofa to him and raised one shoulder to sniff the material.

I'm never washing it. It still smells like you.

'It's okay,' she said, trying not to look at him with dreamy eyes.

'Did you enjoy your bath?' His voice seemed steady, and his eyes submissive.

He looks so sweet when he drops his guard.

'Yes, thank you. It was the best bath I've ever had.'

He glanced at her and held eye contact for a moment, and then he looked down at the plate. 'Joey made these first thing. She knew she couldn't get to the shop, but she still has to bake, especially if she's nervous.'

He knows her so well.

'Are you going to eat one?' She already knew that he preferred fruit or a vitamin as his snacks.

'Hell yeah! Joey's baking is the best.' He picked up a cinnamon swirl and bit into it straight away, catching the flaky pastry in his hand.

Anna thought about how Stan would often bring pastries into River Heights for her breakfast. She always favoured the cinnamon swirls. She was pleased to see another one sitting there. She swiped it up and stuffed it in her mouth, without one stiff or awkward movement about her.

Jake smiled over at her. 'Nice, eh?'

She agreed.

Wow! Joey really can bake. This is mouth-watering.

'You're very close with Joey,' she mumbled, licking a flake from her top lip.

Jake's eyes were on her mouth, and the flicker of intensity in his eyes didn't go unnoticed. He nodded slightly and continued to eat.

She felt her heart return to her chest with a thud as he looked away.

He stood up. 'I'll make us some tea.'

'Could I have some orange juice instead, please?'

'Sure.'

Anna passed Max a piece of croissant as soon as Jake was out of sight.

Max gently took the offering, ate it, and then snuggled back down on the rug with Kermit.

She was surprised he hadn't wolfed down the whole lot.

'You all right, Max?'

Max made a low rumbling noise and closed his eyes.

29

Jake

Jake handed Anna a glass of cold orange juice and placed his own down upon a cork coaster on the coffee table.

She nodded towards her dog. 'Max is quiet.'

Jake got himself back into a comfortable position on the sofa. 'Probably got a bellyache from eating Scruff's breakfast before eating his own.'

Her eyes widened. 'He didn't?'

'Yep, he did,'

She shot a look down at Max. 'How embarrassing. What will that family think of us?'

Jake arched his brow. 'I think they like you both.'

Anna seemed to smile to herself.

Are you thinking about Nate again? Oh, Jake, this has to stop. Get a grip. What is it with you and this girl? Come clean. Say something. It's not as though she can run off. We're stuck here for the next few days at least. Did she just lick her lips again? Great! Now she's chewing on her bottom lip. Does she realise how sexy she looks when she does that? Don't look at her. Turn away. Look at the dog.

'Do you need to call your shop to let someone know that you won't be back in time for your shift?' He nodded towards his phone on the coffee table and turned in time to see the pinkness in her face fade away.

She hesitated, clearing her throat. 'No, that's okay, thanks.'

I don't like that look. Compressed and submissive. Well, okay, I might like the submissive part a bit. I can work with that, but crushed? That's a nope. I bet it's that ex of hers, Rob. That was his name. I'm going to have to do something about him. I should buy the shop and kick him out, or maybe just punch him in the face.

He glanced at the fire. The log was burning nicely and didn't need any extra help. 'How are you feeling? Are you warm enough?'

A slight pinkness re-entered her cheeks.

That's better.

'I'm fine, thank you, but can I talk to you about something?'

He felt his stomach suddenly churn. He wasn't sure about her low tone or the serious look that had appeared in her eyes. 'Sure. What do you want to talk about?'

'I didn't like it when you snapped at me. I know it doesn't sound like much of a big deal, but my ex was… Well, he's not a nice person, and when you got angry at me, it triggered old memories, and I know that's not your fault, but I didn't like how it made me feel, so I would just appreciate it if you…'

'I'm so sorry, Anna. You didn't deserve the way I spoke to you, and I'm sorry it brought back bad memories for you. I was going to suggest we talk about it as well but then the storm hit and, well.'

'I needed to get it off my chest. I don't want to feel that way again. I suffered years of abuse, and now I just want some peace in my life. I'm not trying to sound dramatic or anything. I just thought that perhaps if I mentioned it to you, at least then, you would understand why I don't engage in that kind of behaviour.'

Jake felt his heart break into thousands of tiny pieces. A lump had wedged in his throat, and clouds filled his mind.

'I'm so sorry,' he managed to say again.

'You don't have to apologise again. I said what I wanted to say. You know now. I don't want things to turn weird or awkward, but sometimes explanations are needed. Shall we just put it behind us?'

I'm going to struggle with that, now that I know I made you feel unsafe. That's what you're trying to say, aren't you? I made you feel scared.

'Only when you're ready, Anna. I'm totally up for spending more time apologising.'

Her eyes brightened as they peered above the fireplace at the television attached to the wall. 'How about we watch a film instead?'

'Sure.' He picked up the remote and started to flick through channels. 'There are loads of films stored, thanks to Gran and Josh.' He glanced at her and smiled. 'They loved watching movies together, and then they'd have a big debate about them and give a review.'

Anna was reading through the titles.

This should be interesting. I wonder what she'll pick. Maybe I should steer her towards something soppy, make her think about love. No. She'll just start dreaming about Nate again. Why did I have to introduce her to him? I know what women are like around him. Shut up, Reynolds. He saved her life. Stop feeling insecure. I don't normally feel like this. This really has to stop. My moods need to stop. I can't have Anna feeling unsafe again.

He took a peek at her out of the corner of his eye.

I want to put my arm around you, Anna. Hold you and never let go. I hope she doesn't put on a love story. I'm the only idiot it's going to affect. She was in my arms all night. Oh God, get over it already.

Anna gasped. 'Ooh, I love that car.' She was leaning forward, pointing at the TV.

Jake met with the title. 'Herbie?'

She sat back, pulled the chunky grey blanket down from the back of the sofa, and spread it out so that it covered them both. Her slim body snuggled further down beneath the soft bobbled wool.

I guess we're watching Herbie Goes to Monte Carlo. Lucky old Herbie.

Jake pressed play.

After the film ended, Anna asked him if he wanted to talk about the movie, like Edith and Josh.

Not even if my life depended on it.

He gazed over to the window. 'It's started snowing again.'

Anna followed his eyes. 'Do you think we should ring round to make sure everyone is all right?'

He stared warmly at her delicate face, then glanced down at his phone as she turned back to face him.

'Everyone's okay. Tess would have called everyone in Pepper Bay to check. We would have heard by now if anyone needed any help. Everyone's probably hibernating for the next couple of days, like us.'

She pursed her lips. 'They probably all know about me.'

'And they're probably all relieved you are okay.' He nodded at his phone. 'I've no doubt got loads of messages on there from well-wishers.' He handed it over to her. 'Here. Take a look.'

Anna peered into the small screen. 'Flipping heck, you have as well.'

'Pepper Bay is a small community, and everyone cares about everyone here.'

She read aloud. 'OMG, heard about Anna. Glad she's OK.' Her eyes lingered on the phone. 'That's from Tessie.'

'Any more on there?' He knew there would be.

She nodded. 'Yep, there are a few. They're pretty much all asking after me.'

Jake smiled to himself. 'Well, you'll have to reply. Tell them about your bruised toe. Speaking of which.' He leaned towards her, lifted the blanket, reached out for her foot, whipped off his bed sock that she was wearing, and examined her toes.

Anna peered down at him.

'It's looking okay,' he said softly.

She still feels warm from the bath. Don't stroke her skin. What are you doing?

He carefully replaced the sock and blanket, making sure she was tucked in.

30

Anna

'Do you want to watch another movie?' Anna asked, glancing around at how settled Jake and Max both looked. She didn't want to go anywhere. She only wished she was snuggled under Jake's arm, or even curled up with him in bed. Spilling the beans about her past had triggered something in him, because he had looked ready to cry before the film, and now she was wondering what he was thinking.

The film had been a good distraction for her, and she hoped for him too. She wanted things to go back to normal between them. To happily daydream over him again, not worry that he was worrying she thought he was some kind of monster. There would always be people who would shout at her again one day, or bite her head off, especially as she worked in a shop, she just didn't want Jake to be one of those people. She wanted him to be nice and kind and to like her the way she liked him. That was why his snap had affected her so much.

She decided to think about the things she liked about him, and within seconds, she was right back there in the single bed with him, lying in his warm arms. It was the best feeling she had ever had. She was sure of it.

I bet he's good in bed. I bet he wouldn't use me for sex. He would love me. Look after me. Make sure he's not hurting me. I know he would be caring. I just know.

The temperature in the room had risen, or maybe it was just her. She hoped it didn't show on her face.

A compelling look washed across his eyes. 'I'd like to talk to you about something, Anna.'

Sounds ominous. I bet he wants to pull me up on something now. Have I done anything to upset him? Maybe he wants to pick at my past. He might have questions. I might not want to talk about it. He might want to ask me to leave now. I can't leave now. We're snowed in. I've made him feel uncomfortable. I know I have. What does he want to talk about?

'Okay,' she said, feeling her stomach flip.

He moved closer to her, and she braced herself, and then his phone started to vibrate.

She watched him still. He appeared aggravated at the interruption as he leant away to answer his call.

'Yes, Josh, I'm fine. I know. It's the most I've ever seen in this country. Where are you. Still? Are you coming home anytime soon? What? Really? Okay. Speak soon.'

I feel sick. My head feels light. Don't cry. Please, don't cry. Oh no. Don't start shaking. Hold it together, Anna. Come on, you've got this.

As he leaned back to place his phone on the table, Anna felt a full-on rush of emotion hit her whole being.

The snowstorm had scared her so much, especially when she had given in to its dangerous hold. Allowing herself to fall was haunting her. There was a moment where she felt she had little to rise for. A moment where forever peace was an option. She had seen Jake and Max whilst she was on her side, numb in the snow. Then Marsha's voice had hit her hard, telling her to breathe. Just keep breathing. Something stirred within her. Something came back to life in amongst the numbness. The roaring in her ears had returned, and then arms were carrying her.

Hold it together, Anna. Oh no…

She burst out crying.

Jake's face was filled with concern.

'Christ, Anna, what's wrong?'

She tried to speak, but her sobs turned her words into an incoherent babble. 'Jake... I'm... The snow... Sorry... Thought I was going to...'

His arms were suddenly wrapped around her, holding her tightly.

'It's all right, Anna,' he said softly. 'You're safe now. I promise you. You are safe. I'm not going to let anything happen to you ever again. Please, don't cry. You're safe.'

Tears soaked into his shoulder as they rolled down thick and fast. She couldn't control the flood. It was all too much. Her head was in a whirl. Her heart was pumping too fast. The nightmare was haunting her. Everything about her miserable life was haunting her. She had been needing to cry for so long. She had needed arms to hold her for years. Her mind needed to release a whole heap of bagged-up rubbish. She didn't know she had been holding that much within her until it all came flooding out.

Jake was making gentle shushing noises and rubbing her back with one hand.

She tried to catch her breath, to relax her tight lungs, to settle herself.

'It's okay, Anna.' His voice was soft and soothing. 'It's okay.'

Come on, Anna. Breathe now. Calm yourself. It's going away. It's all going away. The past is over. It's done. You're moving forward. You're okay. Everything's going to be okay now. I have to stop crying on him. He's going to see me with puffy eyes, a blotchy face, and snot bubbles. I feel worse now.

She slowly took a deep, shaky breath. Her eyes felt heavy, and her body tired, and she no longer cared about snot bubbles. The tight hold on her body loosened as Jake shifted on the sofa. Blinking through her damp eyelashes, she watched him rearrange their bodies.

He climbed behind her, flapped open his dressing gown, and gently lifted her into his arms, where he held her like a baby. Her cheek pressed against his navy tee-shirt and settled there, embracing his warmth and scent.

He lifted the sides of his dressing gown and wrapped them around her, then leaned forward to grab the blanket, which he pulled up so that it covered them both.

Anna sniffed and took the tissue that he had taken from his pocket and was holding in front of her face.

I can't believe I just did that. I just cried and snotted all over him.

'I'm sorry about that, Jake,' she murmured.

'Shh. Rest now, Anna.' His tone was almost a whisper.

She wiped her eyes and her nose, all the while remaining glued to the comfort of his chest. She could feel his breathing. It was steady, reassuring. Her face softened as his hand gently traced over her hair, removing a strand from her face and tucking it behind her ear.

She wanted to apologise again for crying on him but knew it would be waved away. Plus, she felt too weary.

He's holding me. Caring for me. I want to sleep here. I don't want him to let go of me. I'm so tired.

Their weight shifted on the sofa as he shuffled them both further down to an almost lying position, and then his mouth pressed lightly down onto the top of her head, soothing her instantly.

31

Jake

The tapping noise of dog claws upon wooden flooring caused Jake to stir from his sleep. He slowly opened his eyes and took a moment. Anna was still in his arms. They were both stretched out on the sofa, on their sides. He realised they had snuggled down further during their nap. The chunky blanket was still covering their warm bodies. He felt hot, but there was no way he was moving, not whilst he was holding her.

How long have we been asleep for? I can't reach my phone. I don't care. It doesn't matter. All that matters is this.

The snow outside was falling harder, but the inside of Starlight Cottage was cosy and unaffected by the harsh winter that had set in early.

Jake looked up at the ceiling. He could feel Anna's calm breathing on his chest. The protectiveness he felt towards her had doubled, and the affection he felt had hit the roof.

The crackling fire was the only sound in the room, and the almost-silence soothed his soul. His face was damp with sweat, but the softness of Anna's body snug in his arms held off his need for a glass of water.

His mind drifted back to his first impression of her in the lift.

Greasy hair. Dowdy clothes. Wet-dog scent. Ashen skin. Ice-blue eyes. Sweet face.

The corners of his mouth creased as his eyes rolled her way. He lowered his nose to her hair and inhaled.

Fresh hair. My dressing gown. Flushed cheeks. Peaceful. Lovely. Beautiful.

He closed his eyes.

I'm not going anywhere, Anna. I'm going to stay by your side for as long as you want me. I'll help you. I'll make all those wrongs go away. You're going to smile again. I'll show you the world. Give you everything you want. You will feel safe again. You will know love. I'm never going to let you face anything alone ever again. I've got you now. Please, feel safe.

Max barked in the kitchen, making both Jake and Anna jump.

He tightened his hold on her as she shifted, and he watched her face roll up his chest and her eyes look into his, giving him a sleepy smile. He stilled.

Don't move, Anna. Stay with me. I want you.

She blinked slowly, looking as though she were gathering her thoughts.

'How are you feeling?' he asked quietly.

She looked slightly bashful. 'Better, thanks.'

Their eyes remained locked. He didn't want to look away. He wanted her to stay looking at him the way she was. She looked happy resting on his chest.

What do you want, Anna? What are you thinking? Tell me. Tell me what you need, and it's yours.

Max barked again, jolting Jake out of his intense gaze.

Anna moved first. 'His water bowl is probably empty.'

He felt his hands gripping the blanket around her back. He knew he had to let go. He just didn't want to.

She frowned. 'You're sweating, Jake.' She sat up and placed her hand on his forehead. 'Are you all right?'

'I'm fine,' he replied, sounding croaky. 'I think the heating is up too high. I need some water as well.'

She went to get up, but he reached out his hand to stop her.

'Please, rest. I'll go.'

He needed to move. His body felt tight, his head a bit light, and he wanted her to stay on the sofa.

It was no good. As soon as he got up, she did too.

'I'm just going to the bathroom,' she said. 'Will you get me some water too, please?'

He smiled gently. 'Of course.' He watched her head off to the downstairs toilet, and then he sleepily walked into the kitchen, stretching his arms up, rolling back his shoulders, and clicking his neck.

Max was standing by his bowl, looking disgruntled.

'Sorry to keep you waiting, sir.'

Max grumbled and quickly lapped away at his fresh water as soon as it was placed at his feet.

Jake joined him by leaning over the sink and drinking straight from the faucet, something he was told off for doing as a child.

Edith would scold him. 'Use a glass.' She would also tell Josh off for drinking a whole pint of milk straight from the bottle whilst standing at the fridge.

Jake was grinning as the cold tap water poured down into his mouth and ran down his cheek. He cuffed his mouth as he straightened up.

Anna was watching him.

His laugh lines appeared as he waved her over to the sink.

'Drink?' he offered.

She stared down at the tap, then slowly lowered her head to drink from the faucet.

He quickly reached down and grabbed her hair, holding it out of her way as she gulped down the refreshing liquid.

Anna straightened and smiled playfully and then copied him by cuffing her mouth.

Max ran over and dripped water from his mouth down onto Jake's bare feet.

Jake laughed. 'Cheers, Max.'

Anna giggled, and everything was perfect.

32

Anna

'Jake, wake up.'

It was eight o'clock in the morning, and Anna was leaning over his bed, gently nudging his arm.

'Jake,' she whispered.

She was feeling slightly nervous of her close proximity to his bed, so she went to straighten up, but his hand reached out and grabbed her arm.

He groaned. 'Anna.'

Her eyes were wide open. Goosebumps filled her arm. With a sudden tug, her body was propelled forward. Her footing unbalanced, causing her to stumble down flat onto his chest. The thump made his eyes quickly open. He stared up at her, curiosity burning in his sleepy eyes.

Oh my God!

She felt slightly giddy. Even half asleep, he was drop-dead gorgeous.

'Anna, what are you doing on top of me?' His husky voice was filled with charm.

'I… erm…'

She was flustered, and he was silently waiting for her to respond, but words failed her for a moment.

A slow smile built on his face as if he couldn't hold it back any longer. 'Do you want to get in my bed?'

Yes, please.

'Tell me what you want, Anna.'

I want you, and you know exactly what you're doing to me, don't you?

She couldn't allow herself to get caught up in her imagination. She steadied her breath as her frazzled mind snapped back into play.

'I was trying to wake you,' she just about managed to say.

'I can see that.'

Trying not to lose her train of thought wasn't easy whilst sprawled out on top of him, especially with the intensity he was holding in his eyes. Even the butterflies in her stomach were clinging on in anticipation, unsure of their next move. She tried to produce some moisture in her mouth, and when she did, she swallowed hard and composed herself.

'It's Max,' she said. 'I think there's something wrong with him.'

Jake's eyes disconnected with her immediately, and she squirmed her way off his body and bed as he slowly sat up.

'What's wrong with him?'

She tried to hide the agony in her voice. 'He won't eat his breakfast, and he couldn't go to the toilet. I cleared some snow outside the backdoor for him, and he tried to go to the toilet right there, but he couldn't do it. He just kept whining. He looked like he was in so much pain. It was horrible.'

Jake flipped the covers off him to get up, revealing long black bottoms and no top. 'That doesn't sound good. I'll call the vet.' He paused. 'I don't have a vet.'

Anna moved over to the doorway as he stood. She watched him rake his hand through his dishevelled hair, and then she rolled her eyes over his ironing-board stomach.

Oh Lord, what's happening to me right now? Now is not the time for this. I need ultimate control, and some oxygen would be good right about now.

'I'll call Nate,' he said, flashing her a quick smile. 'He'll know the best vet around here.'

They both stared down at his phone sitting on the bedside cabinet.

'I'll just go and check on Max while you're doing that.' She pointed behind her and watched him nod her way before she went back downstairs, glad to leave his bedroom. She needed to focus on Max, but Jake's ripped body and intense eyes had been making that extremely difficult.

Sprawled out in his favourite spot by the fireplace, Max looked tired and sad.

'What's wrong, boy?' She sat cross-legged on the rug by his side and gently stroked his back.

Max was silent, but she knew he wanted to tell her what was bothering him.

'I wish you could talk, Max,' she whispered.

Jake was in the doorway. 'Nate said Pepper Lane has been cleared a bit. Well, apparently, it's drivable. He's bringing my car back in a minute. We can see if we can get over to Sandly. There's a vet there who Nate recommended. I've already called the clinic. I was told they would see Max if we can get there. Everyone is snowed in.'

'Okay.'

He walked over to the window. 'Christ! It hasn't gone down.' He turned back to her. 'I'll take Max. You can stay here in the warm.'

No chance!

'I'm coming as well. There's no way I'm not coming,' she said quickly.

She could see the immediate aggravation in his eyes. She had come to realise that it wasn't something he was very good at hiding.

'You're not going out in this weather, Anna.' There was a slight furious undertone to his commanding voice.

Who does he think he is?

'Don't speak to me like that. Max is my dog, and I'm taking him to the vet, whether you like it or not.'

A submissive look flashed across his eyes as he lowered his head slightly.

'I'm sorry.' He sounded genuine. 'I'm just worried about you. You need to be inside, resting.'

She felt her body come alive with nerves. Her hand that was resting on Max was shaking.

He is not bossing me around. Use your voice, Anna.

She took a calming breath to compose herself. 'I'm not having anyone tell me what to do anymore, Jake. That includes you. I'm not going to be controlled.'

His thick lashes flickered. 'I'm not trying to control you,' he said quietly. 'I'm just trying to control me.'

What the hell is he talking about? You know what, I don't care. I don't have time for this. Max is sick, and he needs to see the vet.

She stood up quickly and glared over at him. 'I'm taking my dog to get help. I'm going to get dressed now. I suggest you do the same.'

Oh my God, I sounded just like him.

'Please,' she added softly. 'So we can leave.'

Jake avoided eye contact as he turned and headed up the stairs to his room.

33

Jake

What the hell, Jake! Talk about express yourself incorrectly. She's sitting there, worried out of her mind about her dog, and you go all dictator on her.

He huffed into his wardrobe and pulled out some jeans, a tee-shirt, and a brown jumper and carelessly threw them on the bed. He made his way into the bathroom and headed straight for the shower.

The hot water washed over his sombre mood. He closed his tear-filled eyes, rested one arm on the wall in front of him, and slowly released his shaky breath.

* * *

'Nate's already cleared the path,' said Anna, handing him the car key. 'He said the road to Sandly is blocked, but if we head down to the beachfront, Freddy Morland will take us around the bay in his dad's boat. Apparently, it'll only take five minutes. We just go around in a semi-circle. The animal hospital is along the seafront on the other side.'

He followed her hand movements circling the air. 'Where's Nate now?'

'He went back to the farm.'

Jake glanced down at Anna's socks. 'How is your toe feeling today?'

'Much better. Nate told me to wear the walking boots out there. He said the bitter wind has gone now, so not as cold.'

He took a slow and steady breath, then headed over to the cloakroom. He winced as he shrugged on his coat, making sure Anna didn't notice.

His arms felt sore from vigorously scrubbing them clean in the shower. The fact that Anna and Max needed him made him finally pull himself together and stop.

The disappointment in himself from his lack of control in the shower was haunting him. Therapy had worked well for him in the past. He knew how to lower his anxiety levels and settle his racing mind. He was frustrated that he had allowed his stress levels to build over the last couple of weeks. It was time to put his demon back to sleep.

Anna wrapped herself up, ready for outside. She gently coaxed Max down the pathway towards the waiting car where she strapped him in and then stood back.

Jake knew she was expecting him to check that the seatbelt was secure. He didn't double check. He just climbed in his seat and waited for her to get in.

The drive down to the seafront was quiet. Max didn't stir, and neither Jake nor Anna so much as looked at one another. Pepper Lane was empty, and all of the shops were closed.

He pulled up beside the pub. Cars weren't allowed down that far, but Tessie had told him to park around the side. He was far too worried about Max to think about parking arrangements. He glanced out of the window to see Freddy waiting in the side doorway.

Freddy looked warm wrapped in a dark-green fishing coat and black woolly hat. His apricot hair poked out the sides and back.

'Thank for this, Fred,' said Jake, getting out.

Freddy gave a slight nod. Cold air wafted from his thick lips as they parted. 'No worries, Jake. How's the poor fella doing?' He peered through the window to the back seat.

Jake shrugged. 'Not sure.'

Anna was out of the car and helping Max to the pavement. She glanced over at Freddy.

Freddy smiled. 'You been on a boat before, Anna?' he asked, leading them down to the shingles.

Jake watched her shake her head. 'No, it's my first time.'

Freddy led them over to a narrow, concrete-looking walkway that was covered in slimy seaweed. 'It's my dad's boat. We live just the other side of the bay in Sandly. It's the quickest way for me to get to work.'

'You're the chef, right?'

'That's right. You've had my fish and chips, but next time, I want you to be more adventurous.' He flashed them both a goofy grin.

'After what you're doing for us, we'll happily eat the whole menu,' she said, glancing at Jake.

Jake forced a smile towards Freddy. 'We certainly will.'

Freddy looked down at Max. 'You're going to have to carry him along here to the boat.'

Jake immediately bent down and effortlessly lifted Max. He balanced himself along the slick slab and carefully placed him down inside the small blue-and-white fishing boat. He turned to see Anna's worried eyes examining the wet walkway.

She needs help. Don't ignore her.

He took a breath and then went back along the slime to stand in front of her.

'Will you let me help you?' he asked, sounding indifferent.

She hesitated. 'Thank you.'

He took another steady breath, and then he swooped her up into his arms and carried her to the boat, ignoring his painful arms. He could tell by the surprised gleam in her eyes that she wasn't expecting to be carried.

Freddy's mouth twitched as he chewed on his thick bottom lip whilst watching them.

Anna's face was flushed as she sat down on the cold seat inside the small cabin at the front of the boat.

Jake stood portside and took a deep breath to inhale the salty air. It instantly soothed his mood and relaxed his stiff body. He glanced up at the shaded sky to see the sun struggling to make an appearance.

Freddy pointed out at the cliff that divided Sandly from Pepper Bay. 'You can walk along there when the tide is out,' he explained to Anna, shaking his head. 'But it's so dangerous. Falling rocks. There are signs up, warning people not to attempt the short journey from Sandly to Pepper Bay, so mostly you don't see anyone along there. Years ago, someone died right there when a piece of the cliff broke away. Sad story.'

Jake looked to the bottom of the cliff. He knew the story about Robyn's dad, Henry Evans. He removed his gaze from the cliff to look down at the calm, icy water gently splashing against the side of the boat below him.

The dark liquid was mesmerising for a few seconds, taking his mind to a place of emptiness. The cry of seagulls jerked him from his vacant daydream, and he glanced over at Anna to see that she had her arms tightly wrapped around herself, trying to keep warm. He wanted to hold her, help keep out the chill of the sea air that was blowing through the boat.

Freddy started the engine and effortlessly steered the vessel around to Sandly.

Misty spray hit Jake, causing him to lean back. He balanced himself as he made his way over to Anna to sit at her side. He wouldn't put his arm around her, but he figured his close proximity would emit some body heat her way. He watched her worried eyes widen as Sandly came into view.

A beautiful long stretch of golden sand lined with colourful, snow-covered beach huts filled the near distance.

Freddy pulled the boat around to a small harbour where the pontoon had been partially cleared of snow and was a lot wider, dryer, and easier to walk along than their last walkway. He pointed towards a row of tall white terraced houses lining a street over the road from the harbour. 'You want the one with the purple door. Brook Brown, that's the vet's name. She's really good.'

Jake gave him a slight pat on the back on his way off the boat. 'Thanks, Fred.'

Freddy nodded at Anna. 'Call me when you're done, and I'll take you back.'

Jake held out his hand to help her cross over to the platform and was pleased she took it. He watched her turn to thank Freddy as Max leapt off the boat to run over to a patch of grass that had been cleared of snow.

Max tried to go to the toilet but stopped after letting out a faint cry.

Anna looked as though she was about to cry.

'Come on,' said Jake, nodding towards the road. 'Let's get this sorted.'

They knocked on the purple door and was greeted by the friendly face of a frail-looking old man, who was barely the height of Anna's shoulder.

'You must be Max,' he said, looking down.

Max didn't look up.

The old man then smiled up at Jake and Anna. 'Come inside. My niece is expecting you.'

They entered the clinic, where a smell of disinfectant filled the air. There was no one else inside the cool white waiting area.

Jake looked over at shelves filled with animal accessories. A large brown dog's bed on the bottom shelf caught his eye. His thoughts about buying it for in front of the fireplace were interrupted by the old man guiding them straight through to a small side room to the right of the pine reception desk.

'Is that Max?' called out a female voice.

A second door in the consultation room opened and in walked Brook Brown. Her pink pixie hair style, pale-blue jeans, and purple David Bowie tee-shirt were not what Jake was expecting.

She smiled at the worried pair in front of her. Her big smile was perfectly designed for calming nerves. She poked her black glasses back up to the bridge of her nose, then stretched out her hand to shake Anna's first.

'Hello, I'm Brook. So what's the problem with Max?' she asked, bending down to stroke his back.

Max lowered his head.

'Oh dear,' she said, looking into his eyes. 'Someone looks sad.'

'He won't eat,' said Anna. 'He struggled to go to the toilet this morning and just now outside.'

Brook was listening to Max's breathing through her stethoscope. 'Any changes recently?' She glanced up. 'Apart from all this snow,' she added, rolling her dark eyes.

'He ate another dog's dinner,' said Jake. 'I thought it might have unsettled him.'

Brook started to feel around Max's stomach. 'What's his normal diet?'

'I just buy the cheap tins from the supermarket,' said Anna.

'And what was the other dog eating?'

Jake watched Anna's eyes roll his way.

'I believe the same sort of thing. I have no idea what Scruff eats,' he replied.

Brook smiled. 'Scruff, you say. Nate Walker's dog?'

He nodded. 'That's the one.'

'Hmm,' she mumbled

'What is it?' asked Anna, her voice almost a tremble.

'Scruff often picks up small bones around the farm. I'm just wondering if Max has done the same thing. He's not fed the raw diet, so it's unlikely he'll know what to do with a bone. He could have just swallowed it.'

Jake saw the pink blush that the sea air had created leave Anna's face. He turned his attention to the vet. 'What should we do if he has swallowed a bone?'

Brook stood up. 'That depends on the bone and where it's stuck. I'd like to do an X-ray.'

Jake nodded. He thought that was the sensible thing to do.

'Have you got insurance?' asked Brook, turning to her computer screen.

He watched Anna swallow hard.

'No,' she said quietly.

'Is it needed?' he asked. His voice was more stable and in control. 'Are we allowed to just pay you direct?' He really had no idea how a vet clinic worked. He had never used one before.

Brook was tapping away on her keyboard. 'You can pay cash or card here.'

'How much will it cost?' asked Anna.

Brook glanced over her shoulder. 'I'll just work that out for you.'

'No need,' said Jake quickly, his commanding voice filling the room. 'Just see to Max.'

Both women stared at him.

'Please,' he added softly.

Brook nodded towards her uncle. 'Why don't you take a seat outside, and Uncle Miles will make you both a cup of tea.'

Jake felt himself being ushered out of the room by the little old man.

'I should be with Max,' said Anna, digging in her heels. 'I'll be able to settle him for the X-ray.'

Brook gently placed her hand on Anna's shoulder. 'He'll be all right. We're only out the back, and Max will be sedated.'

Anna was led by the old man to a long wooden bench by the street door. 'You sit here, dear. I'll bring you a nice biscuit to go with that cuppa.'

She stared blankly at him. 'Thank you, Miles, but I have no appetite.'

'Call me Uncle Miles, everyone does. I'm not just Brook's uncle, I'm an uncle to all of our pets that come here, including their owners.'

Jake looked sideways at Anna as she sat down next to him.

'He's in good hands, young lady,' said Uncle Miles softly. 'Your fur-babies are our fur-babies.'

'Thank you,' said Jake, as Anna hadn't responded.

Uncle Miles went off to make some tea, leaving Anna to stare absentmindedly out of the window over towards the boats.

Jake lowered his hand, reached over, and held hers, hoping she wouldn't pull away.

She didn't.

34

Anna

Max was sleeping peacefully on his new soft bed that Jake had bought from Brook. Its plump brown material blended into the soft fireplace rug. Anna was slouched on the sofa, staring his way. 'He looks so tired.' She watched Jake carefully place Kermit down to nestle beside Max's front paw.

'He's sleeping off the sedation.' His voice was low as though raising it would disturb the dog.

She sighed quietly.

Oh, Max, you'll be the death of me.

Jake went to the kitchen, then swiftly returned with a dark wooden tray that he placed down on the coffee table. He nodded towards her. 'Eat something, Anna.' His tone was a lot softer than it had been all morning.

She glanced down at the soft brown bread cheese sandwiches he had made. She had skipped breakfast, eager to get Max over to see the vet. She didn't even eat the Jammie Dodger that Uncle Miles had brought her.

Jake sat down at the other end of the sofa. 'I'm just glad he'll be able to pass that bone by himself.'

She agreed. 'I can only imagine how much an operation would have cost.'

He frowned. 'That's not what I was thinking.'

She took a sandwich and sat back, flopping it in her hand, and he handed her a white paper napkin.

'Thank you for paying for Max.' She looked only at her sandwich.

'You're welcome.'

'I'll pay you back as soon as I can.'

'Let's not think about that right now.'

Anna bit into one corner and forced herself to chew the tiny morsel she had bitten off.

Jake cleared his throat slightly. 'I'm sorry for the way I spoke to you this morning.' His tone was low and gentle, revealing a hint of guilt.

I don't know what to say to you, Jake.

A moment of silence sat between them.

'How is your toe?' he asked, glancing over at her foot.

Anna scrunched her toes. 'Feels okay. Those walking boots were really warm. Thank you for buying them for me.' She watched his face soften into a smile.

I really hate this atmosphere. I have to say something. I just hope it doesn't cause any confrontation.

'Sometimes, Jake, you sound so…'

'I know. I'm sorry.'

She wanted to explain more about her past. Lowering her sandwich to her napkin, she shuffled so that she was facing him.

Concern stiffened his brow.

'When I was with Rob,' she said, taking a moment to swallow, 'I wasn't allowed to do anything without his permission. He controlled everything, and I reached a point where I lost myself.'

Jake's eyes were firmly on her.

She continued, 'Sometimes he would lash out, and I still have some psychological scars from that time. I've been slowly healing since I've been away from him, and I like my life now. You know, apart from living on a roof.' She stifled a laugh, trying to lighten the conversation. 'I don't want to have anyone like that in my life ever again. I don't want people telling me what I can or can't do. It's too much. It's not how I'm going to allow the rest of my life to go.'

Jake lowered his head. 'I understand.'

Not sure you do. Not sure anyone who hasn't experienced that kind of life would ever be able to fully understand. I think you're hearing me though. I can see you're listening.

She lifted her sandwich and reluctantly nibbled at the thin crust. Any appetite she did have completely evaporated.

He slowly looked up. His eyes were despondent, quite lost. 'When my parents died, my mental health declined, but I didn't know what was happening to me at the time. I have a need to control my life. It makes me feel calm. Only, it doesn't, not really. Fighting to stay in control often leaves me exhausted.' He paused and took a deep breath. 'I've never hurt anyone, Anna. I would never hurt you. I just want you to be safe, that's all. I didn't want you back outside in this weather. You being hurt messed with my control. It messed with everything.'

Oh, Jake, I'm so sorry you have all that pain.

'You can't control some things in life, Jake. Most things, probably, and trying to control others only destroys them. It's like wanting to protect a small bird, so you put it in a cage. The bird is protected, but it's now sad because it's not allowed to fly anymore.'

'I know how it works. It's not always easy for me to control the control. I sound nuts.' He shook his head into his hands.

Anna laughed through her nose. 'We're a right pair.'

He raised his head, with serious eyes focused on hers. 'I've never cared so deeply for anyone outside of my family before, and I've never opened up to anyone before, who isn't a therapist, that is.'

Her heartbeat accelerated as his gorgeous smile appeared for a second.

He kept perfectly still. Hardly blinking. 'It's weird how I feel about you, Anna. I haven't known you long, and yet, I feel as if you've been in my life forever. When you were missing in the snowstorm, I thought I'd lost you. I can't fully explain how that made me feel, but it wasn't pleasant.'

Breathe, Anna. Just breathe.

He leaned a touch closer towards her. 'I just want you to know, holding my feelings in hasn't been good for me. I'm not expecting anything back from you, and I haven't told you this to make you feel awkward or sorry for me. I want you to understand me as much as I want to understand you, and I just want you to know how much I want you to stay in my life. I like you in my life. Everything makes sense when you're near me.'

Anna thought she had good conversation skills. She would happily chat to her customers about all sorts when they came in her shop, but now, all words had left her head. She had no conversation. No thought process. Her brain had turned to mush, and her heart had expanded so much, it had clogged up her throat.

Say something, you idiot.

Jake looked away.

'I…' she tried. 'I…'

His compelling eyes were back on her, holding a puzzled expression.

'Jake, I…'

'It's okay. You don't have to say anything. I kind of got the feeling you have already set your sights on Nate, but I had to tell you. I had to know if I stood a chance.'

Wait! What? That's why he's been acting strange around Nate? He's been thinking I had feelings for his mate. He's actually been jealous. Flipping heck. I don't know what to say. What should I say? How do I react? I can't breathe properly.

Jake continued, 'I've offered you this place to stay, and I can see you love Pepper Bay, so I want you to know that even if you start seeing Nate, I would never take any of my offer back. Starlight Cottage is still yours for as long as you want, Anna. You don't owe me anything.'

35

Jake

That conversation didn't go as expected. I should just leave. Let her get on with her life. She's got a good chance of happiness here. The last thing she wants is me and my issues. I can't blame her. I don't want them either.

He looked down at Max, trying to avoid eye contact with Anna, as she didn't look too happy.

His body felt as lifeless as the cheese sandwiches he could see on the coffee table, and he wondered if what he had said was a bit cringeworthy. Bringing Nate into the mix made him feel like a kid. He could have explained himself better, but his stomach had churned, and his heart had toyed with his tongue.

You're so stupid, Reynolds. Talk about overshare. I don't think I explained myself properly at all. I just don't want her to feel afraid of me. Say something else. Do something. What is she thinking? What do I look like in her eyes? I know I look as though I've just acquired a strange fixation with the rug. Look somewhere else. Just move.

Glancing at Anna through his peripheral vision, he wondered what kind of reaction he had provoked.

Judging by her silence, an awkward one. Perhaps I should put the telly on. At least we'll have something to focus on. I guess this is what rejection feels like. Can't say I like it very much. The first woman I've ever actually wanted, and she doesn't want me. I wish she wanted me. I wish she loved me. How has this happened to me? I've only known her five minutes. Feels like a lifetime. She hasn't even gone and I miss her already. I don't know what to do. Just put the telly on. Change the subject.

He leant forward to pick up the remote control from the table.

'Jake.'

Her soft voice caused his body to still. He swallowed hard as he sat back to look her way.

She looks teary.

'Are you okay, Anna?'

'I want to say... I just... You just said... You want me to stay in your life.'

He was too deflated to be amused by her bumbled words. He was also too busy holding his weeping heart in his hands, wondering what the hell to do with it.

'Yes,' was all he could manage at that moment.

Her voice was barely a whisper. He couldn't make out what she had just said.

He leaned closer. 'What was that?'

Her head was low, and her voice even lower. Her hands were trembling on her sandwich, and he thought he caught a glimpse of a falling tear.

'Anna?'

He shuffled closer to her. His knee pressed up against hers. He folded her sandwich inside the napkin and placed it on the table, then gently lifted her head so that he could see her face.

A tear rolled down her cheek to land upon his hand. He used his thumb to brush away the next one. 'Anna, what's wrong?'

She took a shaky breath and sniffed. 'I'm so sorry, Jake.'

She's going to give me the polite brush off.

'I don't mean to cry,' she added.

Oh! I was expecting her to say something else like, it's not you, it's me. It's Nate Walker.
'I just got a bit overwhelmed.'
'It's my fault, Anna. I was a bit full on.'
She reached up and took his hand away from her chin. The coolness of her skin against his fingers caused his breath to catch in the back of his throat.
Holding his now clammy palm in her lap, she quietly said, 'I want you to stay in my life too.'
Jake felt a thump hit his chest. His brow furrowed, and his body stilled as time seemed to slow. 'Anna, I…'
She raised her free hand, pressing her index finger lightly onto his lips, and he immediately felt every part of him jolt back to life. He removed her finger, leaned closer, cupped his hands around her face, and gently kissed her mouth. He half-expected her not to kiss him back, but her lips were with him all the way, and a surge of emotion swept through him, taking him by surprise.
It was the first time he enjoyed having control over himself. He took his time exploring her tongue, her lips, her cheek, and then he trailed down to her neck.
Anna gasped quietly close to his ear, and the heat from her mouth tingled his skin.
His mouth came back to hers and picked up the pace as his heartbeat accelerated. He couldn't get any closer to her face. They were pressed against each other so tightly. His fingertips were tangled in her hair, and their kiss was deepening every second.
Her soft voice vibrated on his lips. 'Jake.'
Control was slipping away. One of her hands was on the back of his neck. The other was clasping the side of his face. Her fingers then traced his jaw and swiftly moved up to his hair. He felt her grip tighten, and he was lost in her.

Oh God, I want her so much. Slow down, Jake. Take it easy. Enjoy her. Love her. Breathe. You've got this.

He pulled his face back so that he could look at her. He needed a moment where he could just study her ice-blue eyes. See her wants, her wishes, her needs.

She was breathing heavily as her dreamy gaze met his wondering eyes.

What are you thinking?

'Tell me what you want, Anna.'

She blinked slowly and then placed one hand on his top, gripped it into a ball, and pulled him back towards her whilst attempting to remove it.

He quickly helped lift his top over his head, and then he saw her eyes flicker. She was staring at his sore arms.

'Jake, your arms,' she questioned, her tone almost as broken as he was now feeling with her staring at his self-inflicted wounds.

He glanced down at his right arm whilst catching his breath. 'It's okay.'

Anna was frowning with concern. She adjusted her position so that she was upright and even closer to him. Her gentle touch traced his stinging skin. 'We should put some cream on this.'

He wanted to ignore the pain. He didn't want a reminder of his lack of control that morning in the shower. His eyes were avoiding his skin. He raised her hand and kissed her knuckles.

'It's okay,' he whispered.

She slowly shook her head. 'It's not okay, Jake.' She lifted his arm and lightly kissed a sore. 'Please, don't do this to yourself again.'

He lowered his head to rest upon her shoulder. 'I'm trying, Anna.'

She held his hand and kissed his palm with affection whilst rubbing her other hand gently down his back. Her loving touch was too much for him to bear. He wanted to kiss her bare arms. To see all her unbroken skin. To love all of her body. He went to remove her top, but she stopped him.

'Jake, you're sore.'

A slightly shaky breath left his mouth. 'I don't care right now, Anna.'

Her voice was as quiet as his. 'I know, but I care. I don't want you to be in pain.'

He gently swept his hand across her cheek, brushing her hair behind her ear. 'I'm not in pain. Not now.' He leant towards her and lightly kissed her lips.

'The next time you feel like hurting yourself, will you come and talk to me instead? I don't know how these things work, but maybe somehow I could help you through it. Even if I've got the hump with you, you can still talk to me. I would listen. I would try my best to help. You talked about suicide with such ease, but this… Not that I ever expected you to tell me anything about your life, but…'

'Anna, I'm fine. Please don't worry about this. Things have just been a bit tough lately, that's all. I'll get this back under control, but thank you for offering to help.'

'How long have you been doing this for?'

'It started after my parents died. I felt dead too, but I knew I wasn't because of the excruciating pain that was ripping through my heart. I never knew it was possible to be alive and not breathe.'

Anna combed her hand lightly through his hair. It felt soothing and filled with love. 'I wish I could take away your pain.'

He closed his eyes for a moment and sighed deeply, absorbing the contact. 'Your touch is like a thousand bandages.' He opened his eyes to see hers glossed over. 'Would it be okay if I went back to kissing you now?'

She nodded and slowly removed her top.

He moved closer, tracing his hands over her bare back whilst kissing her neck, feeling her body weaken in his arms. Her head tilted to one side, allowing him more access to her neck and shoulder, which he willingly took.

36

Anna

The heat from Jake's body was warming every part of her. She closed her eyes as he removed his jeans and then hers, kissing the inside of her thigh whilst he was down there. She could feel herself trembling beneath him, but she wasn't afraid. Every touch he made was soft and gentle, kind and loving. She felt loved. Not used, not unlovable, just simply adored.

Her name was brushed against her skin from time to time, electrifying her pulse. If it weren't for the fact that she was so conscious about touching his arms and hurting him, she would have happily moved around his body as easily as he was moving around hers.

'Anna,' he whispered close to her ear. 'I have a condom in my wallet. Do you want to use it?'

'Yes,' she whispered back, feeling the catch in her breath.

'Are you sure? This is our first kiss, and I feel I've taken this too far.'

'I want to do this, Jake.'

This isn't my first kiss with you. I've kissed you a hundred times in my mind.

She watched his hand reach down to the floor for the pocket of his jeans. He pulled out the small wrapper from his wallet and placed it on the arm of the sofa above her head.

'Aren't we using that now?' she asked.

He slowly traced her mouth with his fingertip. 'No, Anna. I'm not going to have sex with you. I'm going to make love to you. We won't need that for a while.'

A tingling sensation flooded her body. 'You're just getting prepared,' she managed to say.

A hint of a smile hit his lips. 'I'm just getting started.'

Anna felt every part of her immediately surrender to him. She closed her eyes and gasped quietly as his soft lips met her neck once again before slowly moving down her body towards her waist. She tried to keep her breathing steady, but her heartbeat had accelerated as her need and desire for him intensified. Her hands were tangled in his hair, gripping him, holding him, unable to let go.

Jake's naked body was lightly pressed down on hers. His familiar scent surrounding her. She arched her back and softened into his arms as his mouth lowered to greet her hip.

* * *

Anna woke on the sofa, snuggled into Jake's warm chest. She could hear his heart steadily beating, and it soothed her soul. She raised her head slightly to glance over at Max.

He was still sleeping off the sedation, looking as warm and relaxed as she felt. She smiled at him and then gently placed her head back down upon Jake.

She felt dazed at her new life. It was like a dream. Meeting him, the night he slept on the roof with her, Starlight Cottage, being in his arms, the whole lot. She couldn't believe how happy she felt.

What did I do to deserve any of this? My whole life, I have never been seen or heard or loved. No one has ever shown any need for me. No one's ever wanted me. Why now? Why him? I can't believe any of this. Nothing feels real. I'm lying on him, naked, and he feels so good, but I don't think I'm really here. This is so surreal. Things like this don't happen to me. People like Jake Reynolds don't enter my life. I'm just going to close my eyes and hang on to every moment with this man before it's taken away from me, because I'm not this lucky.*

The chunky sofa blanket moved up. Jake had tugged at its end to cover her shoulder. He squeezed her body closer to him, and his hand gently stroked her back.

Oh God, this man's touch. He just makes me melt. I'm just going to stay right here for as long as I can.

'How are you feeling?' His voice was low and husky, barely audible.

Anna could feel the pull in her cheeks from the large smile stretched across her face.

Blissful. Ecstatic. Wonderful. Take your pick.

'Happy,' she replied.

She felt his lips kiss the top of her head and his arms tighten around her body.

'How are things on your side of the fence?' she asked.

There was a slight breathy laugh, then the word, 'Perfect.'

She had a sudden thought. She rolled her face up to look at him. 'You know how you thought I liked Nate? Well, I thought the same thing about you and Joey.'

Jake raised an eyebrow. 'Joey's like a little sister to me. Her history lies with my brother.'

She smiled as she blushed. 'I'm not gonna lie, I did feel a small amount of jealously.'

He softly stroked her hair. His eyes were filled with a gentle gleam. 'You don't have any competition. All I want is you.'

Anna felt her heart melt. It was all she could do to stop herself from blurting out those three little words.

He stopped staring deeply into her eyes for a moment. 'We really should eat something. We've hardly had a thing all day.'

Food is the last thing on my mind right now.

'I'm not hungry.' A mischievous look washed across her face. 'Are you hungry, Mr Reynolds?'

A flash of humour entered his bright eyes. 'Are you flirting with me, Miss Cooper?'

Oh God, I am. I totally am. Can I do that? Yes, I can. Bloody hell, now I sound like Bob the Builder. Shut up, Anna, and get on with it. Pout your lips. Flutter your eyelashes. Do something sexy, just don't laugh. Too late.

She giggled. 'What if I am?'

The corner of his mouth twitched into a crease. 'That's dangerous grounds.'

Anna felt bold. His endearing eyes no longer intimidated her. She suddenly felt in charge of herself, and the situation. 'I live on a rooftop in London. Danger is my middle name.'

'Oh, is that right?'

She giggled again and turned her face back to his chest when his dominating eyes fixed into her soft stare.

That's enough of that.

'Oh no, don't you hide. Not now.' He lifted her face.

Anna blushed. She stretched up and gave him a quick peck on the lips.

He closed his eyes and pulled her up closer to his face. 'I think I'm going to like finding out more about the dangerous Miss Cooper.'

37

Jake

Jake woke early the next morning, stretched out his arm, and frowned with disappointment when his hand sank into the plump pillow next to him. He opened his eyes, wondering why his bed was empty, and looked across the room to see Anna standing at the window in his dressing gown. The winter sun shone through her hair, lighting the side of her face with a warm glow.

What an incredible sight to wake up to. How did I get to be so blessed? She's so perfect.

'Hey, beautiful,' he called over. 'What you up to way over there?'

Anna turned away from the view and smiled warmly. 'Just looking at the snow. It's so lovely when viewed from the warmth of a room. It doesn't look like it has gone down much on the fields.'

'What time is it?' He picked up his watch from the bedside cabinet and groaned. 'Why are you up so early?'

'I've hardly slept,' she replied, approaching the bed. 'I kept checking on Max every hour. I've not long fed him, and I took him outside. He managed to go to the toilet, and it hurt him, but the bone is out now. He seems happy enough. He's gone back to bed.'

Jake flipped the covers over on her side. 'Where you should be.'

Anna removed the dressing gown to reveal her naked body and quickly climbed in and snuggled down beside him, where he pulled her closer into his warm arms.

I think this could quite possibly be my most favourite moment of all time.

'Let's just go back to sleep for a couple more hours,' he whispered, closing his eyes.

She nuzzled her nose into the side of his cheek and kissed his warm skin. 'Or…'

He opened his eyes and turned his head to face her, shooting her a sleepy, sexy grin. 'Yes, I much prefer *or.*'

* * *

Jake came down to the kitchen for breakfast. He was wearing a dark tracksuit, which he chose on purpose because he already knew that Anna liked his loungewear look. He could tell by how the look in her eyes changed slightly whenever he was in his nightclothes. He knew now that he hadn't imagined it, as he had talked himself out of the thought many times.

Shower fresh and looking forward to a banana smoothie and preferably a kiss and a cuddle, as he was already craving her touch, he stopped in the doorway, leaned on the framework, hooked one leg over the other and watched her for a moment. She had her back turned to him and was eating a bowl of cereal.

She's so beautiful.

'Morning, once again,' he said happily.

Anna glanced over her shoulder, and he grinned at the dribble of milk that dripped from her bottom lip.

Stepping forward, he leaned over and kissed the top of her head. She raised her hand to stroke his hair, and his face gravitated towards her palm for a few seconds. He closed his eyes and sighed deeply to himself, relaxed in her hold.

'What are we going to do today?' she asked, once he had straightened up. 'It just said on the radio that everywhere is still struggling with the amount of snow. It'll take a few more days to melt.'

I hope it never melts. I hope we're stuck here for the rest of our lives. Just you and me, snowed in together.

He picked up his silver blender and rinsed it under the tap. 'We can spend another day on the sofa watching films if you like.' He looked over at her through his lashes. 'Or we can spend the day in bed, which is my preferred choice.'

The slight pinkness that hit her cheeks always caused a jittery feeling low in his stomach. He wondered if his own face held a glow.

She smiled softly down at the table. 'I was thinking of looking on your laptop to see if there are any jobs around here.' She gazed back at her food. 'If I'm going to stay here, then I need to find work.'

He raised one side of his mouth as a fizz of excitement filled him from head to toe. 'So, you've decided then?'

Anna nodded. Her eyes looked dreamy as though she were seeing something magical for the first time. 'I love it here, Jake. It's perfect. If I could stay here forever, I would.'

Okay, it's time.

'Anna, there's something I need to tell you.' Stalling for time, he walked slowly over and sat down opposite her at the table. 'It's about you working.'

I don't know how to break the good news.

He felt his heart rate accelerate, and his palms were suddenly clammy.

'I wanted it to be a surprise, but I might as well tell you now,' he added, a touch of nerves catching in his throat. 'I'm hoping you'll like it.'

Curiosity burned in her eyes as her smiled widened. 'What is it?'

He tried not to look too proud about his achievements, opting for cool and composed. 'I bought you The Book Gallery in Pepper Lane, and I got you out of your... situation with your ex. You're free of that bookshop in London now, you don't have twenty percent...'

'You did what?' Her tone was low and unforgiving.

She doesn't look or sound one bit happy.

'I... I thought you'd be pleased.'

Anna looked far from pleased. Her brow wrinkled down, creasing the bridge of her nose, and there was no trace of a sparkle left in her eyes, and he was pretty sure he heard her swear under her breath.

'Anna, what's wrong?'

'What's wrong?' she snapped. 'What's wrong? I'll tell you what's wrong. How dare you take control of my life. You said that you only control you, but you've spoken to my ex... you've taken away my only income. You've bought me a shop. Decided my whole future without even a word to me. Where was the discussion? Where was the permission? I should have been part of this idea because it's my life, Jake, not yours. Mine.'

He watched helplessly as she shot out of her chair to leave, knocking it over in the process. He quickly followed her to the stairs.

What just happened? This wasn't how the conversation was supposed to go.

'Anna, wait, please. Let me explain.'

She turned on the bottom step. 'I won't let you control me, Jake. No one is ever taking over my life again. Get that through your thick head. I thought that you listened to me. I thought that you heard me. I thought you actually understood. Obviously not. I'm leaving. I want to go home. I don't want to be around you any longer. Leave me alone.'

Jake felt his heart fall to the floor. 'Anna, you can't leave. The snow. It's everywhere.'

Why am I talking about the bloody snow?

'I can do what I want,' she snapped.

Angry tears were in her eyes. He needed to talk to her and calm her somehow, but there was no way she was in the mood to listen. It was written all over her face.

Where would she go? She has nowhere to go. I'll go. Give her some space.

'Wait, don't leave. I'll go. Pepper Lane is drivable. I'll go and stay at my gran's flat.'

She scoffed. 'Fine!'

He watched her sprint up the stairs, and he desperately wanted to run after her, but she needed to cool off. There was so much more he had to explain.

Max's nose nuzzled into his ankle.

Jake's disheartened eyes glanced down at him. 'Yeah, mate, I know. I messed up.'

38

Anna

Tears flooded her eyes. Her body trembled, and her heart raced. She paced up and down by the window, her blood boiling from pent-up rage. She felt overheated and frustrated and just wanted to scream, to cry, to hit something.
How bloody dare he. What a control freak.
She sat on the bed and crossed her legs and pulled a tissue out from the pocket of his dressing gown that she was wearing and blew her nose. Her shoulders were rigid, and her face flushed.
I knew it was too good to be true. What's wrong with me? Am I cursed or something? Why do I pick the controlling men? My shop. My little bookshop. It's gone. How's it gone? How has this happened to me? When did he do this? I haven't even signed anything. He can't do this. Rob can't do this. I'll get a lawyer. I'll fight them. They're not taking away my life. This is my life. What am I going to do?
She took a deep breath, as her stomach was churning, and she didn't want to throw up. Her blood pressure shot up, causing a surge of heat to fill her head. She frantically waved her hand in front of her face.
I need to calm down. Focus, Anna, come on. There's not much I can do right now. Breathe. Breathe. Nice and steady now. Oh, why is this happening? Bloody snow. I wish it wasn't here. I'm trapped now. I want to go home. As soon as it clears, I'm out of here. But I want to stay. I love it

here. *I was going to get a job, and have Rob just send me my share of the takings once a month. I don't know what to do now.*

The thought of facing Rob filled her with dread, but she knew she had to. She couldn't live on a rooftop forever, and if she didn't sort her mess out, that's exactly where she would have to stay for a very long time.

I wish I never met Rob. I wish I never met Jake Reynolds either. Why is this happening to me again? It's not fair. It's so not bloody fair.

Flopping backwards on the bed, she closed her eyes and took a much-needed calming breath. She felt ill and needed the unwanted feeling to subside. Everything inside her mind became quiet as numbness took over her heart. She turned on her side, squashing her face into a plump pillow, and a lone tear escaped through her eyelashes to roll slowly down her cheek.

* * *

Anna's body jolted as a noise interrupted her light sleep.

That was the front door.

She got up and made her way downstairs to see Max waiting for her in the hallway. He wagged his tail, and she lowered her hand to pat his head.

'Where is he, Max?' she whispered.

The engine to Jake's car rumbled in the distance. He was gone, and her heart ached immediately, but she pulled herself together as their last conversation washed through her mind.

She went into the kitchen and peered out of the window, just to double check that he really had gone. There was little to see but snow. She glanced back at the kitchen to see that everything had been tidied away from breakfast. It felt as though their argument hadn't taken place there at all.

A note on the table caught her eye. She unfolded the notepad paper to see Jake's message.

I'm sorry, Anna. I'll be at the tea shop if you need me.

There was that sinking feeling again. She wanted to cry but felt too angry to do so. She wanted to hate him, really hate him, but it was a struggle.

Do not put him first. Do not let someone else control you. Come on, Anna. Wake up.

She glanced over her shoulder at her lonely surroundings and sighed. Max nudged Kermit into her knee. She smiled down at her faithful friend. 'At least I've still got you.' She took his toy and tossed it out to the hallway. 'Go on, go fetch.'

Max mouthed her sleeve, tugging her forward.

'Oh, I'm fetching, am I?'

She allowed him to lead her into the living room, picking up his toy along the way.

Now I'm being controlled by my dog.

She sat down in front of the fireplace with him and watched him curl up on his bed. She tucked Kermit into his side. 'Well, I'm glad one of us is happy.'

Max made a low murmuring noise as he rolled his dark eyes up to look at his owner.

'What's that look for?'

He sneezed and pressed his nose into the side of his bed.

Anna looked up at the ceiling and took a deep breath.

Did I overreact? He just bought me a shop. I don't know what's happening in my life anymore. Everything's moving so quickly.

'What are we going to do now, Max?'

Max lifted his mouth and flipped Kermit over to her lap.

She glanced down at the green frog. 'We both know who bought you that.'

Max whimpered and lowered his head.

'You like him, don't you?'

Max barked a quiet bark, but it still made her jump.

'You're supposed to be on my side.'

One front paw reached forward to settle on her knee.

Anna smiled at her dog. 'I love you too, Max.'

39

Jake

Joey's eyes widened as Jake entered the tea shop. She looked straight down at the black holdall clutched tightly in his hand.

Jake gave a slight shake of his head. 'Don't ask.'

She bent over to check the timer on the oven. 'I've got forty minutes. Come on.' She waved him towards her.

Stepping forward, he headed for the door to the flat and made his way up towards the faint gleam of light that was visible in the shadow of the staircase.

Warmth filled the air with a hint of vanilla as they entered Edith's flat. Her belongings hadn't been touched since she died. The small, cosy living room made it look as though she were still alive.

Jake could hear his grandmother's voice echoing up the stairs as she happily chatted with her customers. He could smell the faint aroma of her freshly baked cakes and bread.

His smile reached his eyes as he saw her favourite chair sitting in the corner of the room by the back window. A puffy, floral, cream armchair that his grandfather complained about because he struggled to get out of it whenever he sat there. Josh loved that seat. He'd sit there for hours reading his comics.

Lowering his bag to the floor, all he wanted to do was go into the kitchen and bake soda bread with his gran. He wanted to feel her soft arms cuddling him and hear her soothing words telling him that everything was going to be all right. Memories of her singing along to the radio warmed his aching heart.

I miss you so much, Gran.

Joey swiped past him and headed for the small kitchen to his side. 'I'll pop the kettle on, and you can tell me what you did to Anna.'

'Why do you assume I did something?'

She looked over her shoulder and grinned.

He pointed at himself. 'Jake, not Josh.'

'Fair point.' She shrugged and went back to making the tea.

Deciding to get the weight off his chest, he sat at one end of the pine table-for-two that divided the kitchen from the living room and took a deep breath. 'All I did was…'

Joey laughed.

He cuffed his growing stubble. 'All I did was try to be helpful.'

'Yeah, people kick people out for that all the time.'

'She didn't kick me out.'

Joey gestured at his bag.

He followed her eyes. 'I agreed to leave. She needed some space, and she can't go anywhere. She's better off at the cottage.'

Joey joined him at the table. 'Start at the beginning.'

'To be honest, I don't really know what happened. I thought I did something good, but apparently I'm just controlling.' He studied her face, trying to figure out what she was thinking, as her expression wasn't giving away any clues.

'Hmm,' she mumbled.

'Hmm? What does that mean?'

'Well…' She paused.

'Spit it out, Jo. You know you can be straight with me.'

She slowly raised one shoulder to her cheek. 'You can be a bit... bossy.'

Bossy? I'm not bossy. Am I?

'You're not so bad nowadays,' she added, getting up to make the tea. 'But I can see why people who don't really know you might take you the wrong way.'

Was I being controlling? I guess I did try to organise her life for her. She had every right to be angry about that. I would hate that.

Joey placed two brown mugs filled with steaming tea on the table and sat back down. 'What exactly happened?'

The faint flicker of amusement in her eyes didn't go unnoticed to him.

'I bought The Book Gallery for her.'

'Oh, wow, really?'

'Mrs Blake only sold it to me because she knew it was for Anna. Plus, Dana was on her back to sell.'

Joey gave him a knowing look. 'I bet Dana put the price up when she knew you wanted it.'

He nodded and sighed deeply. 'Yep.'

'She is such a bitch. I still hate her for what she did to Nate. I swear to God, if she had actually married my brother and then sold our family home from under us, I don't know what I would have done to that woman. I'm just so grateful that Tessie found out before it was too late for us.'

'Dana Blake never was a nice girl, was she?'

Joey shook her head and blew into her tea. 'So, anyway, you bought Anna the shop. That's actually a nice thing.'

He raised his palms in the air. 'I thought that too.'

Her eyes narrowed. 'What else did you do?' She swallowed hard. 'Oh God, please don't tell me you had to kiss Dana as part of the deal or something. I wouldn't put that past her. You didn't sleep with her, did you?'

The thought of doing anything at all with Dana Blake made his stomach churn, and not in any good way. He scrunched his nose. 'Dear God, no.'

'There's more to this story,' said Joey, hurrying him.

Jake sighed. 'Okay, so I might have arranged for someone from Gramps' team to pay her ex a little visit.'

'You had him beat up?'

'What? No. Of course not, but now that you mention it, that is an idea.'

'Jake,' she scorned, her voice low and meaningful.

The corners of his mouth twitched. 'I'm joking. I sent Mike over to see if he could get her ex to buy her out of her twenty percent. Mike made him an offer to do so. A generous offer, as it turned out, but then the solicitor found something out.'

Joey sat forward, completely engrossed in the story. 'Oh, what was that?'

'Turns out, Anna didn't own any of that shop.'

'What do you mean? What about her twenty percent?'

'She signed it over to him some time last year without knowing that she did.'

Joey's mouth gaped. 'He tricked her?'

'Yep.'

She sat back and frowned with confusion. 'So, wait. This isn't making any sense. Why would he pretend she still owned some of the shop, and more to the point, why did he let her continue working there? She told me he wouldn't even let her sleep in the shop after he'd kicked her out of his house.'

'He wanted to keep some form of control over her.' The mere thought burned the lump that had appeared in the back of his throat. He unclenched his fists and tried to relax.

Joey shook her head. 'Wow, that's pretty messed up, Jake.'

He agreed.

'So, what did she say about that?' she asked, hugging her mug and blowing the hot tea.

'She doesn't know that part yet. She wouldn't let me explain. She just wanted me out of her face.'

'You have to tell her, Jake.'

'I know. I will. Let me just give her time to calm down. She thinks I've taken away her only income. She thinks I've taken charge of her life. She thinks I'm just like her bully of an ex.'

Joey smiled weakly. 'I can see where she's coming from.'

Slumping further into his wooden chair, he sighed. 'So can I now.'

Joey screwed her face up as she tightened her grip on her cup. 'I don't even know him, and I hate him.'

'Join the club.'

'Poor Anna. She doesn't own anything now.'

Jake held a hopeful smile. 'She does. She owns The Book Gallery. Well, I do, at the moment, but she will, as soon as I can get her to sign on the dotted line.'

'Do you think she will?'

I hope so.

'Right now, Jo, I really have no idea.'

'I'm going to get Nate to bring her to the pub tonight. She might talk to you again if there are other people about.' She studied his face for a moment, then smiled softly. 'I'm glad you've found someone to love, Jake.'

He stared into his tea and thought about Anna's sweet face. It wasn't just the smell of baking bread wafting up the stairs that was warming his heart.

40

Anna

Having lost her appetite, Anna was mindlessly prodding at the pile of mixed salad on her plate that she had decided to have for her dinner.

Max barked at the door, as someone had knocked.

Before she had a chance to get up, the front door opened, and Nate walked in.

'Hello, Anna?'

I guess they just walk in each other's houses around here.

'Hello, Nate. What are you doing here?'

Nate entered the kitchen, flashing his big smile, forcing her to return one. 'I've come to take you to the pub tonight for a nightcap.'

She was in no mood to socialise, having spent the whole day brooding, reading *Little Dorrit*, and feeling very much alone.

'Come on,' said Nate. 'It'll help take your mind off things for a while.'

She rolled her eyes his way with an enquiring look. 'Do you know what happened?'

He shrugged one shoulder. 'Jake's not good with people, Anna. He's always been like a king who sits around barking orders, expects those orders to be carried out, and then wonders when people have questions. What can I say? He's just Jake. He has started to show some human qualities the past couple of years or so.' He laughed to himself.

Anna didn't find it funny.

'Look,' he added, losing his grin, 'come out with me, have some fun with the locals, they'll all be there, and forget about Jake Reynolds for the night.'

It was tempting, and he had made it sound as though Jake wouldn't be there, but she didn't want to go out.

'Sorry, Nate. I don't want to come out tonight.'

'Are you sure?'

She nodded.

'All right.' He headed for the door. 'But you know where we are if you change your mind. Just call me, and I'll pick you up. You don't want to walk down the lane in the cold and dark.'

Anna waited for him to leave, then went into the hallway and picked up the house phone that was sitting on a stand next to the stairway. She removed the receiver, sat on the bottom step, and called the only number she knew off by heart.

I don't know why Nate told me to call him. I don't even know his number. Jake has that in his phone.

'Oh, hello, Stan, it's me, Anna.'

Stan's voice was full of cheer. 'Hello, Anna. How are you getting on down there? Have you got all this mad snow as well?'

'Yeah, it was so high. I've never seen anything like it before. It's gone down a bit, but not much. How are you?'

There was no way she was going to mention her near-death snowstorm experience. He would only worry, even though she was now safe and well.

'Not too bad. They gritted all the streets round here, so I still had to go to work.'

She heard him huff.

'Anyway,' he added quickly, 'that was a turn up for the books, wasn't it? I always hated that man, but even I didn't think Rob could stoop that low.'

The sudden change of conversation threw her for a moment.

Rob?

'What are you talking about, Stan? What about Rob?'

'Conning you, that's what I'm talking about. He'd better hope I don't see him again…'

'Stan, I don't know what you're going on about.'

'The shop, Anna. Didn't Reynolds tell you?'

He told me he had sorted my so-called situation.

'He said I was free of the shop, and…'

I didn't give him a chance to say anything else. What have I missed?

'What do you mean, conning me?' she asked slowly.

Stan didn't sound too pleased. 'You didn't own twenty percent of the shop, Anna. Rob had somehow got you to sign it over to him last year. He was pretending you still owned some so that he still had a hold over you. He is such a…'

'I did sign some paperwork for him last year. He said it was to do with our joint bank account.'

Bloody hell, I believed him.

'Well, that was probably it,' said Stan.

She felt as though her heart had turned to stone and dropped so far down in her body it had whacked her on the toe. The jolt made a shiver run the full length of her spine.

I really don't own that shop anymore.

Stan's voice echoed into the silence. 'Anna, are you all right?'

'I don't know how I feel, Stan.'

'Well, it is a bit of a shock, I guess.'

Now what? The roof?
'Stan, my things on the roof…'
'It's okay. I had all your stuff removed. It's all packed away in Jake's apartment, like he asked.'
Jake Reynolds taking control again.
'Anna, do you think you'll stay there?' Stan's voice held a hint of sadness.
'I want to, Stan. It's lovely here, and the people are so nice. I was wondering if you might consider coming to live here as well, once I get things sorted for us.'
He sounded delighted. 'Really? Well, I wouldn't say no. I'd love to get out of London, and that poky bedsit. Where would we live though, and what about work?'
Anna rolled her eyes over to an approaching Max. 'I don't know yet, Stan, but I'm sure we can figure it out. You're close to retirement now, and I can get a job, and…'
The Book Gallery.
'Stan, Jake bought me a shop here. A bookshop.'
'Blimey! It sounds like he's thought of everything.'
'I didn't accept.'
Stan scoffed. 'What! Why not?'
'It's a bit much, don't you think?'
'Do you know how much money that man has? That's pocket change to him.'
'It's not about the money, Stan. He has taken away my bookshop with Rob, replaced it with his own, moved me to another part of the country, and taken down my tent.' She paused to take a deep breath.
Stan was quiet for a second, then said, 'Sounds like he's changed your life, Anna.'
That's the problem!
'Don't you think that's controlling, Stan?'

'It's unusual, that's for sure. He hasn't known you all of five minutes. I guess he is really taken with you. Probably his way of showing he wants to help. I don't know. He's always been a hard one to read.'

Anna scratched a fingernail along her knee. Her lips pouted, and her eyelids drooped. 'Do you think I'm an idiot to turn down his offer?'

Stan laughed. 'You're not an idiot, kid. You're just cautious, and who can blame you, after everything you've been through. I do think you should consider it though. Don't make any hasty decisions. Sleep on it, that's what Marsha would say.'

Anna smiled, thinking about her dear old friend. 'Okay, I'll take Marsha's advice. I wonder what she would have made of Jake Reynolds?'

'She'd probably like him if he was treating you well.'

'I don't know if he's treating me well or just trying to own me, like Rob.'

Stan scoffed. 'He might be a few things, but he's no Rob, that's for sure.'

A sudden silence lingered in the air between them.

Stan cleared his hoarse throat. 'Only you know if he's good or bad, Anna. You're the one with him. Go with how he makes you feel. He'll either make you feel scared or safe to be around, or maybe when you're around him, you don't feel anything at all.'

41

Jake

The burning logs in the fireplace inside The Ugly Duckling crackled steadily, warming the small group of customers sitting close by. The slight fragrance of beer and recently cooked sausages filled the air whilst cheerful, raised chatter boomed over the top of the 1960s music playing quietly in the background.

The door to the pub opened and in walked Anna and Max, creating a two-second silence.

Jake looked over at Tessie as her surprised eyes met with the door. He peered over his shoulder to see why everyone had stopped talking, and his body stilled as Anna sheepishly entered the pub.

Joey was the first to greet her. 'Anna, glad you came,' she called out, waving her towards their table by the fire. 'Come and sit with us over here.'

Jake watched Anna as she made her way across the thin grey carpet. He looked down at his beer bottle when she arrived, knowing full well he was being a coward about the situation.

'What you drinking, Anna?' asked Nate.

'White wine, please.'

Jake tensed his jaw as Joey practically shoved Anna down into the seat next to him. He took a peripheral peek at her coat.

At least she's wrapped up. I wish she hadn't walked though. She only had to call. Someone would have picked her up. Nate said she wasn't coming.

'Same again for everyone?' asked Nate, pointing at the table.

Freddy swigged the dregs of the cider in his glass. 'Yep.'

Jake swiftly stood up. 'I'll help,' he told Nate, following him to the bar.

Nate gave his order over to Ed, then turned sideways and grinned.

Jake rolled his eyes. 'What?'

'Nothing.'

'Clearly, it is not nothing.'

Nate was grinning widely, revealing long laugh lines and thick eye creases. 'It's just… your face when you saw her.'

Jake furrowed his brow. 'What about my face?'

'Made me laugh.'

'I'm glad I amuse you.'

Nate put a couple of beer bottles on a tray, keeping his eyes on Ed.

Jake leaned closer to him. 'Do we have to sit back there?'

'What's a matter with you, gone shy all of a sudden?' Nate glanced over his shoulder at their full table, giving Tessie a quick wink.

'I'm giving Anna some space.'

'Obviously, she doesn't want any, else she wouldn't be here.'

'She probably didn't think I'd be in here.'

Nate turned back to the drinks that Ed was bringing over. 'Sit down and talk to the girl.' He glanced over his shoulder. 'Too late, Gran's in your seat.'

Jake turned quickly to see Josephine practically snuggled up to Anna.

Great! She's probably telling her about her future, which, no doubt, doesn't include me.

'Take this tray,' said Nate, nudging his arm.

Jake reluctantly headed back to the table and placed the tray down in the middle.

Josephine looked up at him. 'I was just telling your girl here that we're all glad The Book Gallery isn't being turned into one of those fancy coffee shops you own.'

He saw Anna's face flush, and this time it didn't amuse or excite him.

'Take your coat off, Anna,' said Tessie, waving her hand across the table at her. 'You won't feel the benefit when you go back out otherwise. God, now I sound like my dad.'

Nate laughed as he delivered another tray of drinks. 'You look like him too.'

Tessie slapped his hand away from her face as his fingers tickled her ear. 'Get off, cheeky.'

Anna quietly did as she was told and removed all of her outerwear.

Jake felt Max rub against his leg. He bent over to greet him. 'Hello, boy.' Max enjoyed the fuss, then went to lie down behind Tessie.

'How's he been?' Freddy asked Anna.

She smiled and nodded. 'He's okay now, thanks, and thanks once again for all your help, Freddy.'

'No worries, and stop thanking me. You must have said it ten times over coming back on the boat.'

Jake wanted to add that he felt grateful too but decided to remain silent.

Josephine got up and pushed him down into the chair. 'I'm going to have another sausage sandwich, if there is one left.' She shot a sharp glare at Freddy.

He spluttered his drink. 'Yeah, go and look.'

Jake tried to control his breathing. He wanted to look perfectly natural sitting next to the woman who refused to talk to him.

Joey got up, barging his shoulder, causing him to lean into Anna. The touch of her arm on his sent a shot of electricity straight through him, which he didn't appreciate.

'Sorry,' was all he could think to say to her.

She didn't respond.

She really isn't going to say anything to me.

Giving up thinking about it, he watched the others talking and laughing around him, and even forced a smile and a laugh when appropriate.

Anna suddenly leaned over his chest, causing him to still. She asked Joey how she was managing with the tearoom.

He sat still whilst the two women chatted in front of him about the problems the snow had caused. A waft of apple shampoo became too much for him to bear. He quickly stood up. 'Excuse me,' he told them both, and then moved out of the way.

Elaine came over, smiling towards Anna. 'Come out the back for a sec. You're the only one who hasn't seen my new lights in the beer garden. Come and have a peek. Tell me what you think.'

Tessie laughed. 'Mum, leave her alone. Not everyone needs to see your lights.'

'Oh, hush,' said Elaine, waving Anna towards her.

Jake watched her stand up and walk over to the back door with Elaine.

She hasn't taken her coat.

He quickly snatched it off the back of the chair and rushed over to her, feeling her body tighten as his arms came up behind her to drape the coat over her shoulders.

She glanced at him, and he caught her soft gaze.

You have no idea how hard it is for me to stop my arms from wrapping around you and holding you close. God, Anna, I want to kiss you so much.

He wanted to say something, but he thought it best if he quickly went back to the others before she had a chance to call him controlling again.

42

Anna

A warmth that didn't come from her coat tingled Anna's skin. She figured Jake was trying to be nice. She knew he worried about her being cold.

Why did he have to touch me? I miss him so much. It was all I could do to stop myself from turning around into his embrace and snogging him senseless. Listen to Marsha. Sleep on it. No decisions tonight.

She gasped with delight as she stepped into the beer garden.

Elaine was beaming at her. 'Beautiful, right?'

'Oh, Elaine, it's magical.'

Along each winding pathway that led to a wooden table and bench were small colourful lamps poking out of the snow-filled grassy verge. Bottles filled with white sparkling wires sat on each table, and tall Victorian streetlights stood either end of the decking area right at the back. Multicoloured fairy lights draped across the rope rails, stretching from each upright sleeper to the other that held the rope in place.

'I've got a snow machine up there as well,' said Elaine proudly, pointing up to the balcony above the doorway. She giggled. 'Bought it before all this snow. Who knew! Oh well, it'll be a nice gimmick for Christmas if we don't get any more snow. I've also got some black-and-white buffalo check tablecloths, but they're for the dry days. I've also got some jam jars to go around the decking. They look nice with some fake candles inside them.'

'Do you get many customers during the winter?' asked Anna, trying to get a business feel for the area.

'Mostly locals, but there's a Christmas market over in Sandly for one day every year. We have a beer tent there, so make some money that way, but what happens is, a lot of the tourists who come for the market jump on the tram to come here. They'll have to come by boat this year, if they want to come. Wes will sort that out. Also, there's a big hotel in Sandly, Hotel Royale. It hosts tours for its guests, and over the last three years they've been bringing them here for Christmas Eve, so that's a busy lunchtime for us now. As if we don't have enough to do that day. Oh well, mustn't grumble. It really helps fill the purse. Plus, it's always a nice atmosphere that day. Pepper Bay is well liked because it's so quaint, and people love quaint. That's our gimmick.'

Anna smiled to herself. 'It is lovely here.'

'Yeah, I remember the first time I came here. I was swept away too, Anna.'

She could see that Elaine was a bit teary-eyed. 'You're not from here?'

Elaine sniffed the cold air. 'No, I'm from Kent. I met Ed in Portsmouth. This is his home. His grandfather used to own this pub.' She turned to face Anna fully and reached out to hold her arms. 'You stay here, love. Turn that bookshop into something even more special than it already is. I, for one, would love to see you move here, and just between you and me, I've never seen that lad look so happy before. You're good for him, and you'll be good for that shop.'

Anna smiled warmly at her. 'Thank you for your support, Elaine.'

Elaine sighed. 'Just wish I could get my Tessie to settle down, preferably with Nate.'

'Isn't she interested in him?'

'I don't know, to be honest. They're always together. Tess and Nate have been friends since they were kids. There were four of them in their group. Those two, and the Evans twins, Tori and Henry. Thick as thieves, they were. The girls decided they wanted to have kids at the same time, and so they both ended up pregnant. They were all happy enough, but then Henry died. Freak accident. Falling rocks from the cliff. Had to go and hit him, didn't they.'

Anna touched Elaine's arm as she watched her take a breath.

Elaine smiled softly. 'It's all right, Anna. Long time ago now. Happened while Tess was still carrying Robyn. Tori had Daisy, and she walked away straight away. Nate didn't know what hit him. He tried to get her to come around, but she wasn't the same girl anymore. She really took her brother's death badly. So did her parents. They couldn't cope with living here anymore, so they all upped and left. Australia. Our Robyn's never heard a peep from any of them. Nate and Tessie drifted apart for the first few years, then they started to get to know each other again. I had great hope for them back then, but then this other woman came on the scene, and that was the end of that. She's long gone now, and our Tess and Nate have been joined at the hip for the last five years. They're like a proper little family with their daughters, but still, nothing else has come of it. You see, you're not the only one with relationship problems, Anna. Happens to the best of us.'

'At least you and Ed seem happy.'

Elaine glanced back at the pub and smiled to herself. 'Did anyone here tell you about our story?'

'Now I'm intrigued.'

Cold air wafted from Elaine's mouth as she breathed out a laugh. 'I'll give you the short version. He grew up in a pub, and I grew up in a mansion. I had to choose between him and money. I chose Ed. My mum disowned me. Here I am.'

'Bloody hell, Elaine. That's like book material.'

Elaine flapped one hand. 'Ah, it is what it is. My mum wasn't a nice person, Anna, and money isn't everything. Sometimes, you have to make choices in your life about stuff you didn't expect to come into your life. I didn't need much time to think it over. I loved Ed with all my heart. Nothing was going to stop me being with him. I still love him. He gave me the one thing I never had in my life. Love.'

Anna felt her heart warm. 'Oh, Elaine, that's lovely.'

Elaine's smile broadened. 'He also gave me some of his accent. Kind of rubbed off on me over the years.'

Anna giggled. 'My accent is from the East End of London, but I use my phone voice a lot so that people understand me, and I speak even clearer when I'm around Jake.'

'I had an extremely posh accent before I met Ed.' She nudged Anna's arm and winked. 'I've gone right downhill now.'

'That's all right, Elaine. It's quite nice in the valley.'

'That's a good one, Anna. I'll add that there's lots of love to be found at the bottom of the hill too. I always tell my Tess to never shy away from love. That's the one thing that deserves a chance.'

It's bloody scary though.

Elaine rubbed Anna's arm. 'Come on, let's get you back inside before we both freeze.'

Anna met with Jake's soft gaze as soon as she walked back in the pub. She felt he was waiting for her return. Her eyes rolled down to his lap to see Max's big face snuggled there.

Traitor!

Joey's arm came around her shoulder. 'You probably need a brandy after that. Come and stand by the fire.'

Anna removed her coat and placed it on the back of Nate's chair before enjoying the glow of the fire on her hands. Max brushed against her legs. She smiled down at him, then glanced over her shoulder at all of the new friends she had made in Pepper Bay.

Stan would love this.

She imagined Marsha standing at her side.

'What a wonderful opportunity you have been given, Anna,' she would say. 'Enjoy your life.'

She came out of her daydream to notice that her glossy eyes were lingering into Jake's. She blinked and turned back to the fire.

A sausage sandwich came into view. 'Eat this, dear,' said Josephine. 'These sausages are the best in the world.'

She really didn't want a sausage sandwich but politely took the plate. 'Thank you.'

Josephine patted her on the shoulder and whispered in her ear. 'Edith likes you.'

Anna didn't know how to respond and was glad when the old lady walked away.

Nate was at her side, his hand on her plate. 'You don't have to eat that, Anna.' He removed the plate, leaned back to put it on the table, and then put his arm around her shoulder. 'Are you going to say anything to *old misery guts* tonight?'

Anna stifled a laugh.

He grinned and squeezed her shoulder. 'That's all right. He gives me the hump sometimes as well.'

She tapped her head on his shoulder. 'You do make me laugh, Nate Walker, just keep your bones away from my dog.'

He widened his eyes. 'Oh yeah, sorry about that. Scruff picks up all sorts on the farm.'

'I guess we'll have to get used to it, if I do stick around.'

He removed his arm from her shoulder and went to speak but stopped when he noticed Jake standing behind him. 'Your round, is it, Jake?'

'Yes, same again?'

Nate patted him on the arm and went back to sit at the table to talk to Tessie, leaving Jake looking at Anna. 'Another glass of wine?'

She glanced at her almost full one still on the table. 'I haven't finished that one yet.'

He gave a slight nod and lowered his head submissively. 'Would you like some crisps to go with your sausage sandwich?'

Anna bit her bottom lip, in an attempt to stop a smile building. 'No, thank you.'

His husky voice came close to her ear. 'Please don't bite your lip in front of me, Anna. It's hard enough being around you and not being able to touch you, without you making it worse.'

Her lip pinged back into place. Her cheeks flushed, and her hands trembled.

He went to walk to the bar but stopped and turned back to her. 'I'm sorry. I shouldn't have said that. It's your lip. Chew away. It's none of my business.'

Anna's mouth gaped slightly.

Is he winding me up?

Deciding to take control of the jittery feeling fluttering in her chest, she sat back down at the table to join in with the lively chatter. She had come out for the night to help clear her head, not realising Jake would be in the pub, but there he was. It was time to act normal, ignore the lightheaded feeling and smell of his scent, and start being part of a community that seemed to want her around.

She leant over and started up a conversation with Freddy about the food on his menu.

This will keep me distracted for a while.

Jake's arm accidentally brushed hers as he sat down next to her.

Or maybe not.

43

Jake

The noise of the sea floated through the open window of Edith's spare room in the flat above the tea shop. Seagulls cried, filling Jake's sleepy mind with happy childhood memories. He squinted his eyes over at the window. The winter sunlight peered back. He wondered why he had left it open all night, then remembered how he had enjoyed the smell of the salty, night-time air.

He turned his head to look at the empty pillow beside him. Thoughts of Anna came flooding back. Just for a moment, he imagined her there. Her dark hair was brushed against her cheek, and her eyelids flickered as she quietly stirred. Her slim body stretched as sleepy ice-blue eyes smiled his way, awakening his senses. The sensation of her hand upon his chest made him move his fingertips slowly over his tee-shirt.

I wish you were here. I miss you.

Joey was the designated driver last night, so he knew that Anna had got home safely. He wondered if she was awake yet. If she was thinking of him.

I'm holding your hand, Anna. Feel me holding your hand.

He sighed into the top of his quilt. Anna had been so distant towards him in the pub. Max was the only forgiving one. Even his friends talked to her more than him.

You have really blown it, Reynolds.

A waft of sweet air drifted into his bedroom. He tilted his head up and sniffed.

Is that cake?

He smiled warmly. He knew Joey must be downstairs in the shop, baking, but just for a moment, he pretended it was his grandmother.

'Time you was up, Jake. You too, Josh. Don't waste the morning. It's the best part of the day,' she would say.

Reaching over, he picked up his phone and tapped the screen, then placed it to his ear. 'Josh, you'll never guess where I am right now.'

Josh sounded half asleep. 'Jake, do you know what the time is?'

Jake stretched and yawned. 'I don't know, seven?'

'Maybe where you are...' Josh paused. 'Where are you?'

'In bed...'

'You'd better not be calling me to tell me you're in bed with some woman, because I really don't give a...'

'No. Shut up. I'm in Gran's flat.'

Josh sounded disgruntled. 'Are you in Gran's bed?'

'No. I'm in the spare room. I can smell the sea and hear seagulls.'

'I'm still in New York, Jake, so I really don't care.'

'You should be here. Come for Christmas. You, me, dinner at The Ugly Duckling, all the trimmings, just like old times.'

Josh's voice grumbled down the phone.

Joey called out from the living room, 'Jake, I've got a fresh cinnamon swirl with your name on it, and I've made you a coffee.'

Josh was immediately back on the phone. 'Was that Joey?'

Jake grinned to himself. 'Yep.'

'Why is she making you breakfast?' he asked, sounding annoyed.

Got him.

'She likes me.'

Josh huffed. 'No, she doesn't.'

'Well, little brother, I beg to differ. After all, I'm the one she's alone in the flat with. I'm the one she's making breakfast for. I have to go. Joey's waiting for me. Wait, do you think I should put on some clothes first?'

'Jake, I swear to God...'

Jake hung up on him and laughed. He got up, wrapped his dressing gown over his pyjamas, inhaled the cool air coming through the window, and then walked into the living room.

Joey gestured at the coffee mug on the table. 'I made it strong. You had a lot to drink last night.'

He sat down and took a sip, still grinning to himself about Josh.

'What are you grinning about?' she asked, dunking half a digestive in his coffee.

He frowned up at her as she munched the soggy biscuit. 'Can you not?'

She ignored him and sat down. 'And who were you talking to in there? Was it Anna? Have you made up?'

Jake had a slight headache. 'Joey, please. I've just got up.'

She stood up and rummaged around in a cupboard in the kitchen. She placed a packet of paracetamol down next to his pastry.

'Thank you. I think it was the whisky chasers Nate made me drink that did it.'

She raised her eyebrows. 'Made you?'

'Well, I was fed up. Anna ignored me all night, and most of you lot did too.'

'You were the one being quiet and moody.'

He raised his bloodshot eyes to glare at her. 'I wasn't moody.'

She nodded. 'You were.'

He swallowed a couple of tablets with his coffee and groaned as the hot liquid burned the back of his throat. 'Oh that wasn't a good idea.'

Joey leaned forward with the other half of her biscuit, and Jake quickly swiped his cup away. 'That's disgusting. Keep your biscuit away from my drink. Make your own.'

'I've had one already. Anyway, I was wondering, regardless of Anna, how long are you sticking around for?'

Curiosity filled his eyes. 'Why? What do you want?'

She frowned. 'Who says I want anything?'

'Your face.'

She smiled widely. 'Well, I was thinking, if you're going to be here for a bit longer, maybe you could help out on Gran's stall at the Christmas market tomorrow. I'll be on the cake stall all day while Ruby and Molly work here, so Gran will need help. I can't ask Tess, because Ed's staying at the pub, so she'll be helping out her mum in the beer tent. I didn't think we'd be able to get over there this year because of all this snow, but Wes Morland said he'll help us with his boat, and a lot of Sandly has been cleared.'

'You want me to sell jam?'

She tapped his hand that was flat on the table. 'Don't say it like that.'

He murmured something into his coffee.

Joey huffed. 'What did you say?'

'I said, what makes you think I'd be any good at selling jam?'

'It's not just Gran's jam. We're a dairy farm, as you well know. We sell our cheese there, and eggs.' She beamed a cheeky smile. 'I think we'll get loads more sales with you as front of house.'

Jake tried to hold back his grin. Then a thought crossed his mind. 'Wait, why won't Nate be there?'

He'd better not be out with Anna.

'He's Santa this year.'

They both laughed.

'Now that, I'd pay to see,' said Jake.

Joey smirked. 'We could put you in one of those kissing booths. We'd raise loads of money for charity with that. That's something I'd pay to see.'

Jake's brow furrowed.

'Oh, come on,' she urged. 'Just look at those full lips.'

'Leave my full lips alone. I'll sell the jam.'

She got up, ran behind him, and threw her arms around his neck. 'Thanks, Jake. This is why you're my favourite big brother. Don't tell Nate I said that.' She laughed as she made her way over to the door. 'I've got a feeling it's going to be a good Christmas this year.'

Jake smiled over at her. 'For you, Joey, I think it just might be.'

44

Anna

Sandly Christmas Market was set up in Hope Park for December 1st every year without fail. Snow had been cleared to make way for boarded walkways to be placed over the grass, and the surrounding roads and nearby car park had been gritted, ready for visitors. Rows of wooden alpine huts filled the squared-off area, awash with food, drink, and Christmas gifts. Swaying lanterns hung above, and a large twinkling Christmas tree sat proudly at the entrance to the yearly event.

Tessie tugged at Anna's arm and nodded over at Santa's Grotto. 'Nate's doing Santa this year.' She giggled to herself. 'He'll probably hand out lumps of cheese to the children.'

Anna laughed. 'I've not tried their cheese yet.'

'Really? Next time you're in the pub, order Freddy's cheesy chips. That's Nate's. Actually…' She pulled Anna down a pathway of huts. 'Let's rectify that right now.'

'Where are we going?'

'The Walkers have a stall here every year. Josephine likes to sell her jam, and they sell their cheese here too. You can try a sample. There are always samples on offer.'

Anna stopped just short of the Walkers' Christmas stall. Her body stilled.

At the back of the wooden hut were rows of shelves lined with wicker gift baskets filled with curly woodchips, small jars of jam, and large jars of chutney awaiting the wrapped cheese from the cold counter. Along the countertop were foil trays holding cheese samples and crackers, and boxes of organic eggs that sat neatly piled to one side. Serving a small group of customers was Josephine, and just behind her was Jake.

Anna felt a flutter of nerves fill her stomach. 'Jake's working here?'

Tessie smiled and squeezed Anna's arm closer to hers. 'He won't bite,' she whispered. 'Come on.'

Anna was reluctantly led over to the hut.

Jake's eyes peered over the customers' heads to look at them.

Tessie beamed at him. 'I didn't know you were helping out.'

Jake's expression said that he could tell that she one hundred percent knew. 'Blame Joey.'

The customers cleared and Tessie stepped closer to the counter, taking Anna with her.

Jake gestured over to the opposite side of the walkway. 'Joey's got her cake stall over there, and Nate's Santa this year.'

'And I'm not being left all day on my own,' chimed in Josephine, unfolding a black chair at the back and sitting down.

Jake smiled at the ladies in front of him. 'So, here I am.'

Tessie held back a laugh. 'Working suits you, Jake.'

He scrunched his nose up at her. 'I'm actually having fun, thank you.'

She picked up a chunk of cheese and stuffed it into her mouth. 'Anna,' she spluttered, 'try some.'

The creamy yellow cheese looked freshly cut and small enough to eat without choking, which Anna was sure would happen if Jake didn't stop beaming his bright eyes straight into her face.

She reached her hand down and picked out the smallest morsel and slowly placed it in her mouth and chewed.
Stop watching me.
As though reading her mind, Jake looked over her head.
'So, what are you ladies up to next?' he asked casually.
Tessie's flushed face broke out into a big grin. 'Helping Mum in a minute, but first, Santa's Grotto to take as many pictures as I can.' She turned to Anna. 'You can sit on Nate's knee. That'll wind him up.'
There was an aggravated glare in Jake's eyes that didn't go unnoticed.
He's not the only one who will be wound up.
She breathed out, what she hoped was, a relaxed laugh. 'I won't be doing that.'
Jake's face softened, and she felt better that he wasn't imagining her snuggled up on another man's lap.
Joey's voice rang out across the walkway, calling Tessie over to her stall.
Tessie turned and slid her arm from Anna's. 'Won't be a sec.' She sprinted over to Joey.
Anna took a slow and steady breath as she found herself alone with Jake.
I need to talk to him.
She rolled her eyes up to find his waiting for her. 'Jake...' She was suddenly interrupted by four women standing at her side.
'Jake Reynolds,' said the tallest woman. 'I heard you were over here.'
Anna found herself pushed out of the way as the women huddled closer to the counter. She stepped back as one of them trod on her foot.
Ow! She did that on purpose.

It was clear within seconds that none of the women wanted to buy any of the items on offer. They were only interested to see if Jake was on offer.

Anna felt awkward listening to them flirt with him, finding their blatant seduction techniques cringeworthy. She twisted her nose and muffled a huff every so often.

They look like they've just jumped straight out of a Jackie Collins novel. Look at her stupid heels. They'll sink in the grass when she leaves here. Good bloody job. Oh my God, did she just touch his hand? What did she say? I'm sure I heard her say bed. What is she saying about a bed? She wants to take him to bed. Flipping heck! Talk about play hard to get. What did he say? He's not saying much. He's smiling at them. His eyes aren't smiling. Ha! He's not interested in them. Suckers! Ruddy heck, could that woman's top be any lower? It's winter, for crying out loud. I swear to God, if she steps on my foot one more time...

Anna's train of thought was broken by Jake's voice rising in volume.

'Ladies, you know I'm expecting each of you to purchase a gift basket while you are here. If only for my sake. Please, don't make me look bad.'

The women pulled out their designer purses and each bought a gift basket, except for the tallest woman. She bought two.

Of course she bought two. Look at her flashing around fifty-pound notes like they're worth a penny. Keep the change, Mr R. Who does she think she is?

'Drinks at the Royale tonight, Mr Reynolds,' said the tall woman.

Anna frowned in disgust as she watched the woman lick her ruby-red lips at him.

I think I just threw up in my mouth.

Jake was looking over at Joey and smiling, and Anna turned to see Joey give him both thumbs-up.

Tessie waved Anna over to the cake hut.

Anna was happy to have somewhere else to go.

'Ignore old Coca-Cola lips over there,' said Tessie. 'She might be loaded but she's sure as hell cheap.'

'All fur coat and no knickers,' said Joey.

Anna quickly lowered her face into her scarf, releasing an eruption of giggles.

Joey grinned at Tessie, then turned to Anna. 'Hey, you couldn't give me a hand for a bit, could you? I've got a pain in my lower back, so it would be nice to sit down for a sec. Tess is due over at the beer tent soon to help her mum, so you'll be doing me a huge favour. Although, I can't afford to pay you.'

Anna smiled. 'You don't have to pay me, Jo. I'll help.'

'Great. The door's around the side.'

45

Jake

Joey's cake stall was filled with trays of muffins and scones, cupcakes and shortbread, vanilla biscuits and raisin cookies amongst other tasty bits. She had been busy all morning, and obviously desperate for lunch.

'Jake, I'm going to get us something to eat. Pulled pork bun okay?' she called over.

He turned to Josephine, who nodded her approval. 'Yep, that's fine.' He pulled out his wallet, but Joey waved him away as she went off to the food tent before he had a chance to take out any money. He glanced over at Anna. She was sitting down behind the counter, looking quite lost.

God, I miss you, Anna, so much. You have no idea how much I want to jump over this counter right now and kiss you. Say something to her. Something that doesn't sound controlling. Oh, I can't second guess everything I want to say. Just be yourself, Jake. Yes, because that works out well for me, doesn't it! Stop talking to yourself and get on with it.

'Have you eaten yet, Anna?'

She raised her head. 'Joey's getting me a bun as well.'

He bit his lip and nodded.

Okay. Now what?

Anna lowered her head.

Great! She doesn't want to talk to me. I hope she doesn't think I was coming on to those women earlier on. I was only getting them to buy Joey's stock. Oh God, this is so hard. Why is this so hard? She's right there. How am I supposed to cope with not having her in my life? I really need to hold her right now. This is insane.

He smiled at a customer and served the middle-aged woman some wrapped cheese. He then glanced over at Anna, as Brook Brown had approached the cake stall, holding hands with another lady, who Jake thought looked a lot like Beyoncé. He watched them all happily chat to each other.

Probably asking after Max. Where is he?

He waited impatiently for the vet to disappear so that he could ask Anna about her dog.

'Hey, Anna,' he called over. 'Where's Max?'

'Daisy and Robyn have him and Scruff.'

He watched her look left and right down the walkway.

'They're around here somewhere,' she added.

'How's he been?'

She nodded and held a weak smile. 'He's okay. Thanks for asking.'

How are you? Don't ask. Keep it casual.

Two customers stood at her counter buying chocolate muffins, so he glanced back at Josephine. She was taking a nap.

I'll do all the work, shall I? You just sleep. I bet you find this funny, Gran. To be fair, your friend Josephine hasn't been that bad today.

He bent below the counter to pull out some more gift baskets to replace the ones he had just sold off the shelves. When he turned back to see what Anna was up to, his mouth twitched slightly in annoyance.

Oh, you have got to be kidding me!

Wendall James, the local estate agent, was standing at her stall, beaming his shiny dental veneers her way. His long dark coat, skinny jeans, and black boots were smartly put together, making him look as though he had just stepped out of a clothing catalogue.

Anna was smiling back at him.

Stop worrying. She's only being polite. But it's Wendall. That man's smoother than velvet. He's a pretty decent man. At least he won't sleaze on her. He is hitting on her though. He thinks she's interested. Well, she's not, Wendall, so move along. Find someone else to chat up. God, how long is he going to stay there for? I bet he's reaching for all his best lines. Look at that, he's doing the thing. I've seen him do that before. Ooh, Anna, I like your hat, can I feel the material? Stupid line. He's touching her hat. He's touching her hair.

'Oi!' The yell had left Jake's mouth before he had a chance to think and remain silent.

Oh shit! They're both looking at me now. Quick, think.

Grabbing his phone out of the back pocket of his jeans, he waved it over at her. 'I'm going to ring Joey to get some hot drinks. Do you want one, Anna?'

'Hey, Jake,' greeted Wendall. 'How's it going?'

It would be going a lot better if you kept your hands off my girlfriend.

'Oh, hello, Wendall. Didn't see you there.'

Wendall's cheery face was filled with charm. 'Working suits you.'

Yeah, yeah, that joke's been done.

Jake forced a laugh.

Wendall glanced over at Josephine, then back at Jake. 'Where is Joey? I want to talk to her about something.'

Jake pointed to his left. 'Food tent.'

'Cheers,' said Wendall. He turned to Anna. 'I guess I'll see you around, Anna.'

Not if I can help it.

'Bye,' she said. Her eyes then rolled over to Jake.

Jake held the same look he had whenever Edith caught him eating biscuits before dinner. He pursed his lips and faced the back of the hut.

Think I handled that well.

'I'll have a hot chocolate,' she called over.

He turned back to face her. His eyes brightened, and his heart lifted. 'There's a hot chocolate stall here. I'll get some for us when Joey gets back. No big marshmallows for you though.' He let out a short playful laugh.

Anna smiled softly, turned her eyes away, and sat back down.

He felt fed up. All he wanted to do was go over there and hold her in his arms. He sighed deeply to himself.

Oh, it's going to be a long day.

46

Anna

Nate had finished playing Santa for the day. He had helped Joey to pack up their stalls, then arranged for Freddy's dad, Wes, to take Josephine and Elaine home with Scruff and Max and the rest of their things.

He beamed widely at Daisy and Robyn. 'Who's ready for ice-skating now?'

The girls both smiled and rushed off to the outdoor ice-rink that had been set up at the back of Hope Park just for December.

He turned to Anna as she departed the hut that she had volunteered at all day. 'We're all heading there now, Anna. I'll not take no for an answer, you're coming too.' He waited for a reaction. He could see she looked tired. 'If you want,' he added. 'No pressure.'

Anna could see that Jake was waiting in the walkway for her to answer. She smiled and nodded. 'Okay, why not.'

She saw Jake nod as though talking to himself.

Tessie and Joey quickly linked arms with her, leading her over to the cold ice.

The makeshift winter scene sparkled in the darkness with white and ice-blue lights. Tall, white, fake trees with leafless branches were dotted here and there around the perimeter of the rectangular rink. They were covered in twinkling blue lights. Benches sitting beneath the trees had a lighting system embedded into their plastic that created a rainbow of colours that faded in and out of the seats. Snow covered the rest of the park, creating even more of a winter wonderland. A tall, thin Christmas tree stood proudly in the middle of the bright white ice. A log cabin was attached to the side of the rink. Inside, skates were for hire on one side, and hot chocolate and mulled wine for sale on the other. A seating area flowed from indoors to a small veranda outside that overlooked the skaters.

Anna stepped onto the slippery ice and nervously held the wooden rail around the side to help balance herself. She looked around the rink at the magical sight surrounding her.

This is beautiful.

She watched the cold air leaving her parted lips as she raised one hand to her mouth. She didn't feel as cold as the air, as she had a warm and cosy feeling swirling through her veins.

I can't believe I'm here. I could be stuck in the snow up on the roof right now, or in a hospital bed with hypothermia, but no, I'm here instead.

Joey tapped her on the shoulder. 'Come on, Anna.'

Anna smiled as she watched Joey wobble her way around the rink.

I see her back pain has miraculously disappeared. I'm starting to think she pretended to need my help just so I was close to Jake all day. It was nice being near him. He was so jealous of Wendall. I thought he was going to jump over the counter at one point and punch him. He's not very good at hiding agitation. We really need to talk at some point.

Tessie and Nate were holding hands as they passed her by, laughing loudly at their daughters trying to put them off balance.

Anna had only been ice-skating once, as a kid with a foster family, and she didn't take to it very well. She looked out at the ice and smiled to herself at all of the fun she could see. She thought she would attempt to go around at least once.

Holding tightly to the rail, she inched her way along the ice. After a couple of minutes, she felt brave enough to let go and try to slide forward unaided. She wobbled a bit, only moved slowly, and kept her arms out to her sides, but she was rather impressed with her effort, because she was doing it. She was skating.

Before she knew it, she had ventured a little bit too far from the safety of the handrail. The worry of seeing it out of reach combined with Daisy whizzing past her caused her balance to shift.

Argh!

She felt her stomach fly up into her mouth as she headed face first towards the ice. Just as she was certain her moment would end with a bruised elbow or worse, someone had swooped in behind her, grabbed her around the waist, and brought her back up to a stand.

She looked over her shoulder to meet the owner of the arms wrapped around her.

'Jake?'

He didn't smile. He just stared into her surprised eyes with his hypnotic come-to-bed look.

Kiss me.

'Mind how you go, Anna,' he said simply.

He removed his arms and skated off.

Her heart galloped off with him. She watched him glide around on the ice like he was Christopher Dean.

Of course he can skate. I bet he can do everything. He's perfect. Why can't I be like Jayne Torvill? I reckon I could do the end of Bolero with no problem. That's certainly where I'm heading any minute. Oh God, look at him. He really is perfect, and he was just holding me. Why didn't he kiss me? He should have kissed me.

She shuffled forward another inch whilst watching Jake help Robyn stand up from sitting on the ice. Robyn smiled and carried on as though her fall didn't even hurt. Anna was pretty sure her own fall would have hurt.

Tessie arrived at her side, holding out her hand. 'Come on, Anna. I'll help you.'

'Thanks, Tess. This is my second time ever on ice.'

'Really? Oh, well, you're doing great.'

Anna wobbled and quickly grabbed a hold of Tessie's arm. 'Oh, Tess, I might take you down with me.'

Tessie went to speak, but it was too late. They both slid down to their bottoms.

They looked at each other and burst out laughing.

Nate came to a halt in front of them. 'Don't stay down there too long, you'll get a numb bum.' He practically threw Tessie into the air as he lifted her from the ice, as she was so light and he was that strong.

Anna placed her gloved hand down onto the ice to help herself up whilst Nate was helping Tessie. Suddenly, her body weight lightened. Jake's arms were wrapped around her again, effortlessly bringing her to a stand.

'You okay, Anna?' he asked, close to her ear.

Her throat tightened, her mouth dried, and her brain barely registered where she was as she attempted a noncommittal nod.

He pulled her yellow hat down a touch to cover her ears. 'You sure?' His tone was the smouldering, husky one that always gave her jelly legs.

She really hoped that for once she wouldn't blush around him. She gazed down at his hands attached to her elbows, then up into his smiling eyes. 'Yes, I'm all right. Thanks for helping me.'

He gave her a cheeky wink. 'It's what I do.'

Anna tried hard to fight off a smile as he skated off, taking her heart with him.

47

Jake

It was cool inside the ice-rink's woodland-themed bar. Cold air blew in from two opened doorways, causing a few shivers here and there from its customers.

Jake was sitting at a round pine table with Nate and Tessie, watching Anna and Joey at the bar, getting the drinks.

'It's colder in here than out there,' said Tessie, rubbing her arms.

Nate stood up and removed his blue puffy coat and wrapped it around her. 'There's nothing of you, that's why you feel the cold.'

Tessie looked like a cocoon. 'No, Nate, it's because it's cold. You just can't feel it because you're built like a buffoon.'

Jake breathed out a laugh. 'I think you mean buffalo.'

She raised her eyes over the top of the large coat that had swamped her. 'That's the one.'

Joey and Anna each placed a tray down on the table, and Joey giggled at Tessie. 'What do you look like?' She glanced outside at the ice. 'I didn't bother getting the girls a drink yet. They're still having fun out there.'

'That's all right,' said Nate, leaning forward for a cup of mulled wine.

Anna placed hot chocolate in front of Jake, then removed one from the tray for herself.

'Thank you,' he said quietly, looking out for any giant marshmallows.

'I said no to the marshmallows,' she said, following his eyes to her large white mug.

'What's wrong with marshmallows?' asked Nate. 'I would have had them.'

'Speaking of food,' said Joey. 'We'll grab something to eat at the pub when we get back. Hopefully, Freddy will have left us something as a late-night snack. He normally does.'

Tessie giggled as she struggled to free herself from Nate's coat to get her mulled wine. He leant forward and passed her the cup, and she snuggled back inside her cocoon to sip her warm drink. 'Ooh, this is nice and cosy.'

'For you,' said Joey. 'The rest of us are freezing.' She glanced over her shoulder. 'I wish they would shut the doors.'

'There's no point. People keep coming in and out,' said Nate.

Tessie sat up. 'You can all fit in here with me, if you like. There's room enough for a herd of elephants.'

Nate playfully frowned. 'Hey, I have a lot of muscles.'

'Joey, do you want my coat?' asked Jake.

'No, I'm all right, thanks, Jake. Unlike Tessie, we don't all need to wear two coats.'

Jake looked past Joey to speak to Anna. 'Are you cold, Anna?'

Anna removed her mouth from the rim of her not-so-hot chocolate. 'I'm okay,' she replied quietly.

Jake stared at her for a moment before glancing into his drink. He heard Nate make a joke about Anna and something to do with being cold, and then the voices around him started to fade from his ears as he slipped away into the shadow of his mind.

Hey, Mum, Dad, Gran, Gramps. I hope one of you can hear me. I wish one of you were here right now. I need some advice. I don't know what to do about my relationship with Anna. I just want to love her, but I think I'm doing it all wrong. She's over there now, sitting next to Joey, and all I want to do is pick her up and sit her on my lap. I want to hold her. Everything's such a mess. I really need your help. What do you think of her? Do you like her? I bet you do. She's lovely. I don't think the feeling is mutual anymore. I don't know. I'm trying. I'm worried that I'm going to lose her. I feel so lost right now. I miss you all so much. Please hear me. I really need you. Give me a sign. Tell me you're with me.

'Wake up, Jake,' said Joey loudly, nudging his arm. 'Nate's talking to you.'

He could feel that his eyes were glossed over. He daren't blink in case he created a tear. 'Hmm?'

Nate shook his head. 'I think you're ready for your bed, mate.'

'I'm okay,' said Jake, clearing his throat.

Joey leaned closer to him. 'Nate was saying one of us should give Freddy a call, just to make sure about the food, otherwise we'll get some chips on the way to the boat.'

'We should call Wes as well,' said Tessie. 'Tell him we'll be heading back to him in a minute.'

Jake nodded. 'Good idea.'

Joey reached for her phone. 'I'll call Freddy.' She huffed at the screen. 'No signal in here.' She stood up. 'I'll try outside. Won't be a sec.'

'Wait, I'll come with you,' said Tessie. 'I can call Wes while you're doing that.'

Nate helped her to stand in his coat. 'I'll give the girls a shout.'

Jake watched them all leave. There was only Anna left, but he didn't want to look her way. Missing his family had deflated him. He suddenly felt alone and empty. The last thing he needed was a rejection look from her.

Anna got up and moved to the seat next to him. She shuffled the chair closer so that her arm was resting against his.

What is she doing?

'Are you cold, Anna?'

'No,' she replied, without looking at him. 'You just look sad, so I want to sit next to you.'

Pity is the last thing I need.

'I'm just tired, that's all.'

'We're going home now.' She stopped pinching at her glove and faced him. 'I mean… well… it's your home.'

He watched her eyes roll over to his. All he wanted to do was kiss her.

'Jake,' she said, almost whispering. 'It's your home. I shouldn't be the one who stays there.'

He tried to keep his breathing steady.

She looked down at her lap. 'I could ask Freddy if he'll take me over to the mainland. I could catch the train to London.'

He felt his heart die.

Please don't leave me, Anna.

'If that's what you want to do.'

Don't say that, you idiot. Ask her not to leave. Tell her you love her. Say something.

'Anna, I…'

Joey leant over the table to have one last gulp of her hot chocolate. 'Come on, we're leaving.'

He watched Anna move away from his arm to walk over to Tessie.

Joey nudged his shoulder. 'Hey, Jake. I just got the weirdest text from Gran. I wouldn't mind, but when we want her to text, she says she doesn't know how to use the stupid thing. Her words. Anyway, she told me to tell you what a difference a day makes.'

What a difference a day makes? What is she on about? What a difference a... Dinah Washington. Bloody hell, that's Gran's favourite song. She said it was played ten times over at Mum and Dad's wedding, thanks to her. It ended up becoming their wedding song. I wish I could remember that day. All I can remember is stroking Mum's baby bump.

Joey's eyes widened at him. 'You and Gran got some secret code going on?'

Jake smiled as his heart came alive with love. 'Yes. I guess we have.'

48

Anna

Starlight Cottage was starting to feel like a lonely place. The silence was making it feel as though the home was completely empty, and the lack of Jake's familiar scent was depressing Anna.

She looked at the Cottages and Lakes calendar stuck on the fridge.

December 2nd.

She sat down at the kitchen table and stared gloomily at her cold slice of toast topped with Josephine's cranberry port jam. She wasn't feeling breakfast. Her mind was occupied with thoughts of Jake the day before. He was so close to her. Just a few steps away at all times. He had spoken to her. Passed the time. He had been courteous, and helped her on the ice, but none of that mattered. Not when she was missing him. She felt as though he had been in her life forever. His absence hurt. She had wanted to talk to him about their issues, but they were kept busy all day with customers, mostly women on Jake's stall, and then with their group of friends at the ice-rink.

I love you, Jake Reynolds, but I'm scared.

Max trotted into the kitchen for a drop of water, waking her from her daydream.

'What do you want for Christmas?' she asked him. 'Saying that, thanks to Jake, you seem to have everything. You'll have your own car next. I've read about that. Rich people buying their dogs their own car.'

Max dripped water on her feet as he passed her by.

'You could do with a bib.'

They both looked towards the front door, as someone was knocking.

Mrs Blake was standing on the pathway, holding a large, thin box.

Anna was surprised to see her standing there. Her frail face was covered in pastel makeup, and her bright pink coat glowed more than her matching lipstick.

'Hello, Betty.'

'Hello, dear.'

Anna opened the door wider. 'Come in.'

Betty walked as far as the inside of the doorway. 'I'm not stopping, Anna. My daughter's in the car. I've just popped here to hand over the keys to the shop. I'm not giving them to *Moneybags*.' She held out her free hand and placed a set of keys into Anna's palm.

Anna glanced down at the small laminated paper attached to the keys.

'That's the alarm code,' said Betty. 'I can never remember it. The alarm box is just beneath the counter. Not that it's needed. No one breaks into anywhere around here. Crime is low in Pepper Bay, you know.'

Anna smiled warmly.

Betty placed the box down on the floor at her feet. 'You can open that when I've gone.' She gave Anna's fingers a gentle squeeze. 'Now, listen. The only reason I gave Edith Marshall's grandson my shop is because of the way I saw your face light up the moment you stepped inside it. I have good strong instincts, me, and I knew straight away that you were the one I had been waiting for.'

Anna could see the tears sitting in the bottom of the old lady's eyes.

Oh, Mrs Blake.

'Anna, you look after my baby, you hear. I'm trusting you.'

Anna leaned forward to give her a hug, but Betty backed off.

'No, dear, I don't go in for all that mushy stuff.'

Anna bit her lip to stop herself from laughing.

'I'm off now. They've finally cleared the road to Sandly this morning. Well, some of it, so I hear. Anyway, you take care, Anna Reynolds.'

Anna felt her heart thump. She waved from the doorway as Betty turned to her before getting into her daughter's car. She caught a glimpse of Dana Blake, then the black sports car pulled away.

Anna Reynolds.

Max was sniffing the box on the floor. She bent down and picked it up and took it over to the kitchen table.

'Let's see what we have here.'

She placed the shop keys down and pulled open the cardboard flaps on the box, and a dark wooden frame came into view. Her hand slid inside and tugged the frame out to come face to face with Mr Blake's painting of Starlight Cottage.

'Oh, wow!'

The beautiful oil painting was now hers.

'Thank you, Betty,' she whispered into the emptiness.

She knew exactly where she wanted it to go. She picked up the shop keys and jiggled them at Max.

'How about we go check out the bookshop?'

* * *

The smell of books hit Anna as soon as she swung open the door of The Book Gallery. Feeling unsure, she stepped inside and straight away stubbed her foot on a plastic, wedge-shaped doorstop. She bent over and forced it into the bottom of the door so that it would stay wide open. The air outside wasn't as cold as it had been the last few days, so she welcomed the salty freshness coming in. Plus, she loved hearing the seagulls.

She noticed that Betty hadn't set the alarm, as no noise bleeped or screamed. She jumped up the counter to peer over the top at the alarm box to see if it was flashing or anything. It was switched off.

Oh, Betty, what are you like.

Pepper Lane was quiet, so she knew she wouldn't have to deal with customers. She glanced at the old copper till taking pride of place on top of the counter.

Not sure I would know how to use that anyway.

Max sniffed the floor around her feet.

'What do you think, Max?'

He wagged his tail and went off for a mooch.

Anna looked around the shop at the dark shelves filled with books, then around at the few pieces of artwork hanging on the walls.

The paintings were all beautiful impressions of Pepper Bay from one angle or another. There was a cluster of pictures in frames leaning against the back wall, and a black bin bag with rolls of vintage wallpaper poking out of its rim alongside the back door.

She walked over to the back door, unlocked it, and peeped outside.

A narrow, cobbled alleyway was all that was out there. The deep snow had been cleared away, leaving behind only remnants of the freak storm behind. The walkway was wide enough for the rubbish collectors to come along to take the bins away by foot.

She looked left and right to see that some of the shops had wheelie bins sitting outside their backdoors. She wondered where the bookshop's one was, or if it had one at all.

She closed the door and turned to another dark-wood door at her side. It wasn't locked, so she pulled it open and walked up the stairs that were lined with a dusty carpet that looked worn through.

The flat upstairs was the same size as Edith's flat. That was the only resemblance. Betty's flat was dull and smelled like decay.

Anna went over to the back window and pulled back the thick curtains. She coughed as dust leapt into her throat, and then she quickly opened the sash window for the room to get some much-needed ventilation. Waving her hand in front of her face, she turned to get a better view of the property.

Betty Blake's home looked as though no one had lived there for a hundred years. Cobwebs hung from every corner of the ceiling, and a thick layer of dust sat upon every surface. Her 1970s style vanilla and beige furniture had been left behind, which made Anna feel sad.

She took a breath. 'Okay, let's look at the potential.'

Max's nose poked into the room. He sniffed and immediately sneezed, making Anna giggle.

'This would make a perfect art gallery, eh, Max?' She pointed towards a bedroom. 'One of the rooms could be an office, and we'll keep the toilet, and…'

Max made a low bark up the stairway.

'Yes, let's see if it has a rooftop like Edith's.'

She left the flat and made her way up the stairs to another unlocked door. Outside was a small square terrace, much like the one above the tea shop, only this one was only filled with a light covering of snow.

'Potential, Max,' she whispered into the cool air.

She peeked over the side to see the cobbles below, and then she looked to her right at the view of the sea.

'Wow, that is some view.'

She let her imagination take her to summertime where the sky was powder blue, the sun shone brightly, and the water looked inviting. She sighed heavily and glanced down at Max.

'If only this really was ours.'

Max looked straight at her.

'I know. But it doesn't feel right. I can't just accept this gift. It's too much. It's bloody perfect, but too much.'

Max lowered his head, whimpered, and placed his right paw over his nose.

Anna arched an eyebrow. 'Really, Max, that's your opinion, is it? Well, I'm in two minds. I want to. Obviously. But… Oh, I don't know. What should we do, Max? Should we accept?'

Max barked.

'Was that a yes or a no? Don't answer. I think we both know where your loyalty lies.'

Max huffed happily and ran down the stairs.

49

Jake

A dog's bark made Jake step forward and turn his head to his left. He felt his heart thump and his body still as he saw Anna standing on the terrace of the bookshop a few shops away. He knew she wouldn't notice him on his own rooftop terrace because she was looking down at, what he presumed was, Max.

Mrs Blake must have given her the keys. She's there weighing up her choices. Make the right choice, Anna. Take the shop. Stay.

He made his way back down to the tearoom and stopped in the doorway that led to the small kitchen.

Joey could obviously sense his presence. She turned to look over at him. 'You all right, Jake?'

'Hmm?'

'Penny for your thoughts.'

An inquisitive look was sitting in his fixed gaze. 'Anna's in the bookshop.'

Joey nodded and smiled. 'That's a good sign.'

Jake was undecided. 'Is it?'

She gave a half-shrug and waved her yellow spatula towards him. 'Go and see if she's made up her mind about owning it yet.'

He took a step forward, then dithered, looking down at his clammy palms.

'Go on,' urged Joey. 'Or I'll flick this buttercream at you.'

Jake failed to find the amusement. Make or break time was causing something inside him to wobble.

Joey breathed out a laugh. 'Jacob Reynolds, never before have I seen you look so nervous. It's quite funny.'

He rolled his serious eyes her way. 'It's not funny.'

'It is,' she mumbled to herself.

Inhaling the fresh aroma of coffee, he glanced at the row of upturned white teacups sitting on a shelf over behind the glass counter out front. 'I suppose I could take her over a cup of tea.'

Joey eyed the shop's counter. 'Go on then, but leave your money on the side.'

His mouth dropped open a touch. He went to say something but stopped. He left her to her cupcakes and went into the shop to pour Anna a tea.

A cool breeze blew in from the opened front door, making him realise that the tea would probably stay warmer if he poured it into a takeaway cup.

There were twenty-three long strides from Edith's Tearoom to The Book Gallery, and each one made his legs feel heavy. He swallowed hard before stepping inside. He couldn't see anyone or hear any movement, so he placed the disposable cup down on the counter and made his way to the back of the shop. He froze as Anna came down from the flat. They locked eyes and, just for a second, Jake's brain went to sleep.

'Jake,' she greeted.

'I brought you a tea,' he managed to say.

Her eyes widened as they glanced over at the cup. 'Thank you.'

An awkward silence lingered between them for a moment.

Jake swallowed hard and adjusted his footing. 'I... I don't want you to leave here, or me, but if you do want to leave me, for good, that is, then, that's fine. Well, I mean, it's not fine. Clearly, for me, it's not fine, that is, but for you, yes, that would be... completely acceptable. I would, though, very much like you to take ownership of this delightful bookshop. Please believe me when I say I am not trying to tell you what to do. I just know that you will give this place the love it deserves. Besides, I'm pretty sure Betty Blake would find a way to haunt me, even though she's alive, if it stayed in my name, or worse, ended up a Café Diths.'

He looked at the floor, embarrassed by his rambling.

What are you going on about?

Anna took a step towards him. She seemed to hesitate. 'Stan told me what Rob did to me. If you hadn't tried to get him to buy me out, I never would have known about it, so thank you for that.'

My pleasure. You're welcome. Shut up, Jake.

He controlled his breathing, then looked over at her. 'Anna, I don't know what to say about that. I can get my solicitor to deal with him, if you want.' He stopped talking as she started to shake her head.

'I'm pleased in a way. Now I have no connection to him anymore. I don't want to invite him into my life by fighting with him or holding on to grudges. I'm free now. I just want to move forward and put that part of my life to bed.'

I understand.

He gave a slight nod. 'But just know that you wouldn't have to face any of the stress. I would do it all for you.'

'No, Jake. I'm happy with my life now. Please, will you let it go?' she asked softly.

'Of course.'

She was twiddling with her fingers. 'I am really happy, you know. I was happy before coming here, but it was only at level six. Now it's level nine and a bit. I do want to stay here. I'm not sure about this shop though.'

Jake looked around. 'What are you not sure about?'

'You giving it to me. No one's ever done anything like this for me before.'

He frowned in amusement at himself. 'I've never done anything like this before for someone, so I guess we're in the same boat, in a way.'

She smiled slightly. 'It has a lot of potential.'

Love was burning in his eyes every time he looked at her. He could feel it rushing through his body, and he didn't care if it was visible.

'Yes, it does,' he said, thinking about their relationship.

She lowered her head a touch. 'I think… I might… It's possible, I would feel more comfortable if we… if we owned it together.'

'If that's what you want.'

She raised her eyes and held a sheepish look. 'Is it what you want?'

Jake tried to fight back the smile that was trying to grow on his face. 'I would prefer to have a different type of partnership with you.'

Her eyes flashed with a moment of confidence. 'In that case, I'm hoping that you won't think that I am strange by telling you that I love you already. I mean, I know it might seem a bit early to say that, but…'

Jake's heart somersaulted to a place he had no idea existed in him. Before he could think about what to say, he propelled himself towards her, cupped her face in his hands, and pressed his mouth down firmly onto her lips, taking his breath away, along with hers.

'I love you too, Anna,' he muttered in between kisses. 'God, I love you so much already.'

Anna slowed him. She gazed dreamily into his piercing eyes. 'You must promise me, that from now on, you don't make decisions for me. We make them together, as a team.'

He nodded. 'I promise.'

She smiled warmly, making his heart melt.

Max nudged his legs, joining in their embrace.

Anna glanced down at him. 'You already had his heart.'

Jake smiled at Max. 'And you both had mine.'

'Nine and a bit just went up to ten,' she announced happily.

He smiled. There was something so comforting about her delicate fingertips tracing his cheekbone. Something welcoming about her faint apple fragrance, and something warm about her soft skin.

She feels like home.

'I really do love you already, Jake Reynolds,' she whispered close to his mouth.

He held her tightly to his heart, never wanting to let go. 'And I love you too, Anna, more than that romance section I'm looking at can ever describe.'

He felt her giggle in his arms, and as he glanced around at the mass of books surrounding them, the paperbacks, the hardbacks, the magazines and comics, he suddenly understood her attraction to love stories. They did exist, and they could start anywhere. Even up on a roof.

* * *

If you enjoyed this story, why not come back for another visit to Pepper Bay with Josh and Joey.

Honeybee Cottage

The last time Joey Walker watched Josh Reynolds leave Pepper Bay was three years ago. She decided there and then that the next time he visited she would never in a million years, even if her life depended on it, sleep with him ever again. She was done with secretly being in love with him. She couldn't keep falling into his arms every time he was around. Josh was never going to see her as anything more than a holiday fling, or a sure thing. She had made her decision and had happily stuck to it, but only because he wasn't around. She soon realises just how hard keeping him at arm's length actually is when he unexpectedly turns up just before Christmas.

Josh had always loved Joey, but he knew she never took him seriously. She had no reason to. Growing up, he only went to his grandmother's family home in Pepper Bay for the summer. As an adult, he knew that the world viewed him as a playboy heir to his grandfather's millions. This year, he was determined to prove just how reliable he could be. He was back, and on a secret mission to get Joey to fall in love with him, because she was all he had ever wanted.

Printed in Great Britain
by Amazon